A DREAM OF EBONY AND WHITE

THE FOUR KINGDOMS AND BEYOND

A DREAM OF EBONY AND WHITE

A RETELLING OF SNOW WHITE

MELANIE CELLIER

LUMINANT PUBLICATIONS

For Katie,
the sort of friend you'd like by your side
for any adventure

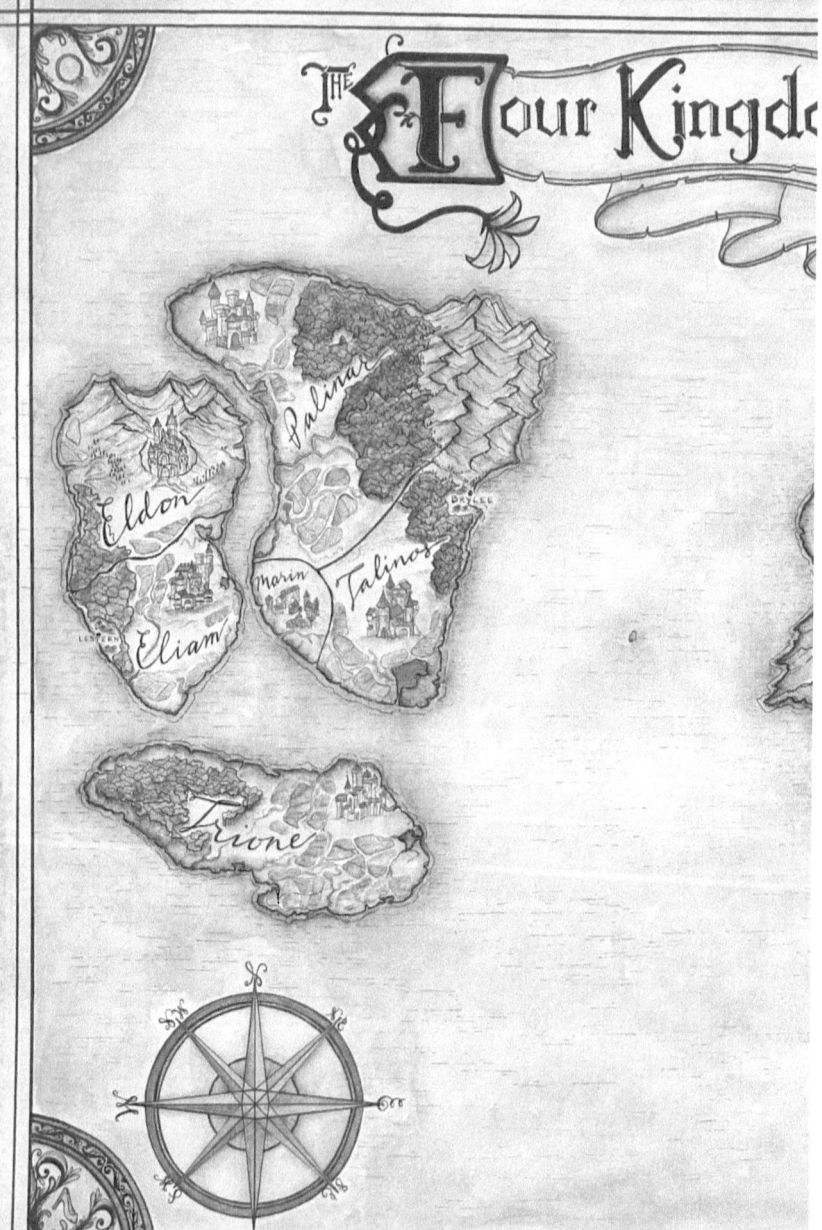

...OMS and Beyond

Northhelm

NORTHGATE

GREENHOME

RANGMEROS

Rangmere

Arcadia

BORDER HAMLET

WESTER CASTLE

The Great Desert

ARCADIE

LAHARE

Lanover

CATALIE

INVERNE

BANISHMENT ISLAND

PART I
THE PRINCESS

CHAPTER 1

*S*kin as white as snow. Lips as red as blood. Hair as black as ebony. I stared at myself in the mirror. It was no wonder my father had given me the name Blanche. Or that my friends called me Snow—and envied the perfect, symmetrical features that I had apparently inherited from my mother. The ones that everyone said made my face so beautiful. Surely a godmother must have blessed me while I was in my mother's womb, they said. Even though no godmother had been in these lands giving out gifts at the time of my birth.

My father had always said I was even more beautiful than my mother. As if no greater compliment could be given. Not that I would know since I had never seen her. Her desperate dream for a child had been her undoing.

A ripple ran across my so-called perfect features.

Ebony was hard and strong. Snow was cold and unforgiving. And blood...well, blood was passion and power. Were those the things my mother had hoped for her daughter when she made her fateful wish?

If so, then she had failed. I was none of those things.

The crash of breaking porcelain made me spin, startled from

my useless reverie. It took a moment to recognize the missing piece from my dressing table. A particularly ugly dust collector that I had always hated.

My eyes flitted back to the mirror for a brief second, my lips twisting. A perfect example of my weakness. I was a princess, and yet I couldn't even bring myself to send away a decoration I disliked. From my own room, no less. Easier to just let things be. To let my life be ordered for me.

The maid had made no move to collect the broken pieces, seemingly frozen in place, her duster in hand, and her eyes wide. I crossed over to her.

"There's no need for concern, Gertie. In truth I've never liked that piece anyway."

None of the horror dropped from her face, and I frowned. Gertie had been one of my maids for years, and I was hardly an object of fear to any of them.

"Truly, Gertie, you don't need to worry. I'm not angry."

"No...no, Your Highness." She made a visible effort to pull herself together. "Only, do you think it was worth a lot of money?" She whispered the last words.

My brows knit together. "I have no idea. But what does it matter? As I said, I never liked it. I won't bother to replace it."

Her eyes flew to mine. "But we got the new orders just this morning, Your Highness. And the steward had them from Her Majesty herself. Any breakages are to come from our wages."

My eyes narrowed. The queen. My stepmother. Issuing new orders for the staff already, although only one night had passed since my father's funeral. Had she no respect?

I sighed. Of course she had not. That was hardly a surprise. And who did I expect her to have respect for? Me? The thought almost made me laugh.

"Well, then," I said, after the awkward pause dragged on too long, "we must clean up the pieces and hide them somewhere. I certainly won't report it broken."

"Oh!" Gertie looked at me, her face transforming. "Are you sure, Your Highness?" I could see a new worry in the back of her eyes. This one was for me—although it was less pressing than the worry on her own behalf had been. I tried to keep my face from twisting. Even my maids knew that I never stood up to my stepmother.

I forced my back to straighten, my tone strengthening. "Of course I am sure."

Gertie didn't quibble further, cleaning up the mess with careful fingers, making sure not a single shard remained behind as evidence. When I tried to assist, she waved me away, so I had nothing to do but watch her wrap it in layer after layer of paper.

"If anyone notices and asks," I said. "I'll tell them I broke it myself."

Gertie gave me a tentative smile. "That's right kind of you, Your Highness. I'm so sorry…" Her words trailed away before she seemed to grasp some courage. "I'm sorry about your father. He was a good king, and a kind man."

"Yes, he was." I turned away, not willing for her to see how easily the tears welled in my eyes.

"And now that he's gone, I suppose you…" This time when her words failed, no courage came to finish the sentence.

I kept my face averted, silent. I didn't need to hear the words to know what she meant to say. And the hope behind the sentiment cut at me.

My father, the king, had died. And I was his only child. So didn't that make me queen? But for all her hope, I noticed she still addressed me as Your Highness while she called my stepmother Her Majesty. And why should a lowly maid have the courage that an entire court lacked? I had barely heard much in the last week, the fog of grief cocooning me from the ordinary sounds of life. But I knew I would have noticed that. Not a single person had called me queen.

A knock, followed immediately by the sound of an opening

door, made me startle again. I silently berated myself. I was a princess in my own chambers. If I couldn't feel secure here, there was no place for me anywhere.

A footman entered, his face impassive. Gertie stepped back, her hands tightening around the parcel she still held. But the man didn't even glance her way, his eyes on me.

"Princess Blanche. Her Majesty requests your presence in the throne room."

He waited, as if expecting an answer, and I wondered how he would react if I refused the 'request'. But I shook off the thought long before the words could rise to my lips. It wasn't really a request, and I knew it.

"Very well," I said at last, inclining my head. "I will be along shortly."

For the first time the footman showed an emotion, brief uncertainty crossing his face. I raised a single eyebrow, and he hastily bowed and left the room.

I squashed the fleeting pleasure that filled me at my small act of defiance. I was no longer a child, and such childish games were beneath me.

"I must wear a state gown," I said to Gertie, and she nodded quickly, carefully depositing her burden before dashing across to my wardrobe. For a moment I considered directing her choice but found I couldn't muster the energy to care. I would dress properly in respect for my father and defiance of my stepmother. But I couldn't bring myself to have an opinion on the dress itself.

In all too short a time, I faced the long corridor to the throne room. Our castle was old, the dark gray stone worn from the passage of so many years. I had always found it comforting, an old friend even if it was less beautiful than the palaces of some of my friends. But in the last week it had turned hard and cold. I felt the weight of it pressing down on me, the stone cold and unrelenting. I shivered.

A flicker of movement to one side caught my attention, and a tall man stepped into the corridor ahead of me. I called a glad welcome and hurried my steps, but he didn't meet my eyes.

Instead, he dropped to one knee, his fist clasped against his heart. "Your Majesty."

My eyes widened, and I looked around to see if anyone else was near. Thankfully we were alone.

"What are you doing, Alex? Get up!" I hissed the words, not wanting to draw further attention if someone should happen upon us.

Alexander looked up and met my eyes for the first time. His own were a darker gray than I remembered, storm clouds brewing in their depths. Slowly he rose to his feet, his tall frame towering over me.

"But I heard that your father..." He shook his head. "I raced home from Eldon as fast as my poor mount could ride."

The ready tears rushed forward, but I willed them away. I didn't have time for crying.

"Yes. Father is dead. His funeral was yesterday. I'm so sorry you missed it, Alex. He would have wanted you there."

Pain passed across his features. "I am sorry for your loss, Your Highness."

I shook my head, exasperated as always at his refusal to use my name. "Both of our loss, you mean. I know you loved him like a father yourself."

He looked down. "It is not my place. I am only a huntsman. *Remember*, Your Highness?"

I sighed and drew closer to him. Anyone else might have supposed his emphasis suggested resentment, but I knew better. He was always trying to remind me of the difference in our stations. But I had just lost the only parent I had ever known, and I wished that for once he would forget I was a princess and embrace me as he used to do when we were both children.

"Yes, only a huntsman." I stood so close now that he would normally have backed away, but he didn't move, and it gave me hope. "The most skilled of all the royal huntsmen. Son of the old head huntsman. Protege of the old king himself."

My voice hitched at the word 'old' in reference to my father, and with a sound half-sigh, half-groan, Alexander folded me into his arms. I rested my head against his chest and felt myself relax for the first time since I had seen my father breathe his last.

Being near Alexander again felt almost like being near my father. My father had spent so much time on the hunt—the woods his favorite escape. And always with the head huntsman by his side. I knew that in their hearts, the two had viewed themselves like brothers, despite the vast difference in their stations. And, of course, always with Alexander and me trailing behind.

How many times had I seen the warm glow of pride in my father's eyes as they rested on Alexander—the son he never had? I might have been jealous if I hadn't known how much my father loved me too. He hated to be parted from me and let me run wild as a child, despite those in court who chided him for it. He had apologized once that I had no close friends among the other noble girls. That I spent my time with an "old man" as he put it, instead of with children my own age. But I had told him that I didn't want to be away from him. And besides, I had Alexander. At that he had laughed and thrown me high into the air until I was laughing as well, so hard I could barely breathe.

My insides tightened at the memory until I once again struggled to breathe, but this time for a different reason. I leaned more heavily into Alexander.

Neither of us spoke because there were no words. But I drew comfort and strength from his presence and his strong arms. I could have stayed wrapped up in them forever. But all too soon, he drew back, putting me firmly away from him.

"I saw many in the court moving toward the throne room." He looked down at me. "Are you to hold court already?"

I shook my head, my eyes darting around once more. I lowered my voice.

"No, of course not! And you must stop saying such things. It is not I who rule in Eliam, as you very well know."

His eyes narrowed, his hands balling into fists. "But your father is dead. *You* are—"

"Shush!" I cut him off. "I have been summoned along with the court, but if you think my stepmother intends to bow me up to the throne you must have run mad in your weeks in Eldon." I glared at him, although I knew he wasn't the one who deserved my ire.

It was my father who had sent him on the mission to our northern neighbor of Eldon, and my stepmother no doubt who had put him up to it. Badgering a dying man until he sent away someone he regarded almost as a son. Queen Alida had never liked anyone who proved themselves more loyal to King George than to herself, and Alexander had never bothered to hide his disdain for her.

A new worry gripped me, overwhelming the relief and joy I had felt at his presence. I looked at him sharply.

"I have no doubt you'll worm your way into the back of the throne room. You must promise me that if she asks for some sign of loyalty you will give it."

"Never." He ground the word out between gritted teeth. "I endured her for the sake of the king, but I will never—"

I cut him off again, leaning forward to grip his jacket in both hands. "You must promise me, Alexander! Who knows what she will do to you if you do not? You cannot leave me alone here."

My final words stilled the protest that had been building in his face. He frowned down at me while the storm in his eyes grew wilder.

"You must promise me," I repeated again.

I could feel his capitulation before he spoke it, his whole body slumping in defeat.

"Very well, Your Majesty. I shall do as you wish." Defiance

glinted in his eyes. "I shall always obey the commands of my queen."

Reluctantly I let him go and stepped around him to continue toward the throne room. "If that were true, you would call me Snow, like you used to when we were children. I'm sure I've asked often enough." I glanced back over my shoulder and caught a glint in his eyes. "Now go, before someone sees you. And, remember—you promised!"

He bowed low before disappearing down a side corridor. I sighed and walked the last few steps with a heart both heavier and lighter than it had been before.

Alexander had returned. I was no longer alone.

Alexander had returned. I had a new fear to add to the weight that already crippled me.

My heart skipped and then sped up when I rounded a corner and approached the small royal reception room that led into the back of the throne room. A forbidding and all-too-familiar figure stood guard. Randolph—now head of my stepmother's personal guard.

His black eyes accused me, and I had to restrain myself from glancing over my shoulder. I knew Alexander was long gone, and there was no way Randolph could have seen us from here.

I had never liked the man—he seemed always to be waiting for me to make a fatal mistake—but I had positively loathed him ever since he tried to intervene in the Princess Tourney over a year ago. He had been trying to cheat to ensure I won.

In a competition where the 'reward' was marriage to a cursed monster. I knew my stepmother had put him up to it, although he denied it later. She would have loved nothing so much as seeing me forced to marry a prince who would take me far from Eliam. It would have solved all her problems to have me safely gone before my father's death. No matter how monstrous my groom might be.

Randolph hadn't succeeded, of course. It had been stupid,

really, for him to think he could circumvent the powerful magic of the Tourney using such clumsy methods. And he had been arrested for it. I had even heard news later that he had succumbed in prison to a deadly illness, the consequence of crossing the magic of the Tourney.

Only then the Tourney had been destroyed. And apparently its magic with it, since he made a miraculous recovery. But still he remained in prison in Marin, and for six beautiful months I had been freed his presence here in my home.

But somehow my stepmother had negotiated his release. I had lacked the courage to question her on how she managed it. And my father's health had become so precarious at that point, that I dared not raise it with him. At least the queen had waited for his death to officially promote her favorite lackey to head of her guard. She must have known my father wouldn't tolerate his presence anywhere near their elaborate shared suite.

Randolph bowed to me as he opened the door, the action at odds with the threat in his eyes.

"Your Highness," he murmured as I sailed past, but I ignored him, keeping my gaze firmly ahead.

I had expected my stepmother to be awaiting me in the reception room, but it stood empty. Reluctantly I glanced back at Randolph, and he gestured toward the closed door that opened onto one side of the dais that held the thrones. So she had already begun without me. Why was I surprised?

Drawing a deep breath, I opened the door and strode through, my heavy skirts rustling around me.

CHAPTER 2

*I*t took only a moment for me to absorb the scene before me. My stepmother held court from her usual place in one of the two great thrones. While my father had lived, she had ruled equally beside him. But now that he had died, she should have taken one of the smaller chairs to either side. One of the seats that usually belonged to me.

But no one in the assembled court appeared to have taken issue with her position. And surveying the crowd, I concluded that the entire court must be in attendance—every noble born family in Eliam represented, and even some of the more influential merchants. Had she ordered them all here? Or had they hurried here of their own volition—eager to show their loyalty? I suppressed a shiver.

A slightly startled count knelt at the bottom of the steps, his eyes now on me. He was clearly one in a long line pledging their support to Queen Alida. My stepmother gave me a single glance that promised I would feel her anger later before turning a smiling face to the crowd.

"Ah, my dear daughter has joined us at last."

Her words set my teeth on edge. And not because of her not-so-subtle rebuke. I hated when she called me her daughter. A ripple blew through the crowd as they bowed or curtsied toward me. But a lifetime of etiquette training told me none of them bowed deeply enough for a reigning monarch.

Except for one tall man in the back. I forced my eyes to skim quickly over the familiar tangle of my friend's dark hair, hoping no one else had noticed the small anomaly.

With a wave of her hand, my stepmother gestured for me to cross over and join her. She indicated the smaller chair set back to one side of her own throne, instead of the smaller one I had previously occupied next to my father's throne.

For a moment I hesitated, indecision sweeping through me as anger almost overpowered my caution. I had expected a show of power from her eventually, a moment of crisis between us when I would have to choose. But I had not been expecting it so soon. And I had not been in this room since my father's death—his empty seat mocking me and lending fresh fuel to my grief.

What would she do if I took his great throne instead of the place she indicated for me?

My eyes turned to the crowd. What would the court do? Rightfully the seat belonged to me.

But the soft sound of an opening door behind me drove all thought of rebellion from my mind. Only one person could be there, and I had no desire to turn and see Randolph's dark eyes on me again. I already had their threats memorized.

Instead I crossed the dais, my steps heavy, and took the seat she had indicated. My father had been ill for a long time, and she had won over too many of the guards in that time. They followed her, and the court clearly had no wish to demur. All I had was one loyal huntsman. My eyes wanted to seek out his in the crowd, but I forced my gaze to stay in my lap.

"I am so glad to have your support beside me, dear child," the queen said. "Together we must soldier on, despite our tragic loss."

The next in line, a junior baron, nodded solemnly and

professed his condolences. Ah. So that was how she had framed this. The court had come to offer their support to a grieving widow—who also just happened to be their queen.

I had no doubt that my stepmother's words had been chosen carefully. They generally were. *Together*, she had said, coming just short of outright rejection of my claim to the throne. But *dear child* she had called me, reminding everyone present that I wasn't yet of age. She clearly had no intention of adding the legally correct Regent to her royal title, and as noble after noble and official after official came forward to offer their 'condolences'— none of them using the address of Queen Regent either—any whisper of hope that someone intended to call her on her over-sight died.

I steadily looked into the eyes of every person who came forward, yet another small and insignificant act of defiance as I forced each of them to face the one they had betrayed. I took careful note of those whose gazes skittered over mine, unease or guilt lurking beneath the surface of their gaze. I was glad for their discomfort, however uncharitable that might be. At least that meant they felt some sense of their own treason. Better than those who showed no qualms at all.

And I took even more note of the few who directed their condolences toward both queen and princess. They made no protest to my stepmother's place, but their gazes on me carried not guilt but grief. Would they have acted if their number had not been so few?

One in particular gave only the shallowest of courtesies to my stepmother, his eyes instead lingering on me. A tall man with graying hair, his years gave him dignity rather than weakness. And unlike most of the others, I didn't recognize him. Yet something about the line of his nose and the sweep of his brow looked familiar.

He was already retreating back into the crowd when a shock

of recognition swept through me. They were familiar because I had been looking at them in the mirror only today.

The crowd parted respectfully before him, cementing my certainty that I had just faced the duke of Lestern for the first time. My grandfather.

As a child, when I asked about him, my father would say only that the duke never came to court. It was one of my maids—an older woman long since retired from service—who had whispered more of an explanation, the words meant for another maid not for my curious ears.

The duke was heartbroken at the death of his only daughter. And his grief turned to anger when the king chose to marry again so soon. He refused from that day forward to attend a court that had so quickly forgotten my mother. A court ruled over by her replacement.

Even at my young age, I hadn't needed her to speak the rest of it to understand. Why would he want to see a granddaughter who had been the means of killing his beloved daughter—however unwitting an object of death I had been?

And yet now here he stood. I struggled to understand it. Unless it was indeed evidence that the entire nobility were here under royal command? Or perhaps death had been enough to win his forgiveness, and he had come to attend my father's funeral. I would certainly not have noted him in the crowd during the event. I had barely been able to see the ground beneath my feet through my constant tears.

It took some effort to train my attention on the next in line rather than following his retreating back. Would he approach me later, in private? Did I want him to?

Finally the whole court had presented themselves before us. The steward stepped forward then, the small collection of servants and local citizens who were present mirroring his movement, although they lingered toward the back of the hall. He offered his condolences on behalf of the servants and the people, and as one the small crowd behind him bowed or curtsied low, each of their murmured words lost in the mass of voices.

This time I could not prevent my gaze searching out a certain face. Relieved, I saw that Alexander was lost among them, his bow sufficiently reverential. Only, when he finally looked up, it was at me he looked, not the queen. I quickly jerked my eyes away, hoping again that no one was taking note of the individual servants.

Glancing across at the queen, I saw that she looked satisfied. The black of her mourning gown suited her fair coloring, and even I had to admit she looked beautiful. Not as beautiful as my mother, the whispers said. But beautiful enough to catch a grieving king in matrimony.

When she looked toward me, I quickly looked away. I had never felt so drained, and I had no desire to challenge her in the moment.

Graciously she thanked the court and the people and dismissed them. As the room began to empty, she turned toward me. The smile remained in place, but it didn't reach her eyes which flashed furiously at me. What had so enraged her? My formal court dress which made me look older than my sixteen years? My delay in answering her summons? Or my hesitation after she directed me where to sit?

But apparently I would have to wait to find out.

"I am most disappointed in you." Her words were spoken too low to be heard by anyone else. "You dishonor the memory of your late father."

I straightened, sucking in a breath at her words, but she didn't give me a chance to deliver the hot retort on my lips.

"Attend me in my chambers after the evening meal." She swept to her feet before pausing to look over her shoulder, her eyes narrowed. "And this time, don't be late."

I didn't reply, holding myself stiff until she had disappeared through the side door, her loyal guard at her back. And then I waited until the whole room had emptied before letting myself slump back into my seat. So it had been my tardiness that had enraged her.

I rubbed at my head, nearly dislodging the tiara I had forgotten I was wearing. No doubt another cause of the queen's ire. Placing it in my lap, I massaged my temples.

I knew all too well what to expect in her rooms. She had always loved to call me in for a "little chat," although never with my father present, of course. I had never known anyone who could harangue and rail as she did without actually raising her voice. Or even saying anything strongly enough that someone—like me—might report it to my father.

But every compliment came with a barb. Every suggestion for my improvement carried with it an expectation—an expectation that I would fail. Because if there was one thing I knew for certain, it was that I had always been a disappointment to my stepmother. Every look and every word she directed at me carried the weight of it.

With my father gone, how could I bear this life?

Hazel, the middle Marinese princess, was a good friend. My closest excluding Alexander—for all he tried to decry the title. Perhaps I could make an extended visit to Marin?

Running away? So quickly? asked a snide voice in my head. But why shouldn't I run? What was left to hold me here?

But even as I thought it, unbidden, an image rose in front of my eyes. Gertie's face from only a few hours before. If I turned and ran, what would Alida do to my father's kingdom? To my kingdom.

My hands balled uselessly into fists among my skirts. If only I weren't so weak. If only I could make myself stand up to my stepmother. I hadn't even spoken up when she had announced that my mourning necessitated my staying away from the upcoming wedding of Celine and Prince Oliver of Eldon.

We had no such custom, and I had thought at the time she wished to keep me away from Alexander who had still been in the northern kingdom. But now I suspected she wished to keep me from spreading tales of her actions here and perhaps gathering foreign support for my own reign and a different regent. One who would actually acknowledge the title and my upcoming claim.

I thought of the bride-to-be and sighed. Now there was a princess with backbone. Celine would never have rolled over and let someone treat her the way I let my stepmother treat me. If only I could borrow some of her determination and strength.

But whenever Alida looked at me with that hatred and disdain in her eyes, Randolph's lurking presence behind her, the defiance froze inside me. I had told myself that it wasn't worth causing trouble that might hasten my father's decline. Only now that he was gone, it seemed I couldn't throw off the habit of years.

I bowed my head. My people deserved a better princess than me. A better queen than me. If Alida had ever shown herself worthy of ruling, I would have gladly put aside my own claim. But she had never shown interest in anything but wealth and power. And even when it came to wealth, she lacked wisdom, showing only a short-term interest in her own gain. I knew our economy faltered, and that the other kingdoms attributed it to my father's failing health. But I knew better. I knew whose orders had led us into trouble, and they hadn't been his.

I stood wearily to my feet. I should have told him what was happening. But the sight of his graying face, aged too quickly by pain and illness, filled my mind. How could I have brought such news to him? And to what efforts might it have roused him? He would only have killed himself in his attempts to set things right, and then we would all have been no better off.

And you would have had less time with him, murmured a selfish voice which I tried to ignore.

I had thought the betrayal of the court hurt, but it was

nothing to the sad, wounded look in the eyes of the servants I passed on my way back to my room. Gertie had stopped just short of voicing their hope earlier, and clearly the news had already spread that I had proven myself a disappointment.

A vague thought of the library had been filling my mind, but I directed my steps instead toward my room where I could ensure my solitude.

Running away again. Too cowardly to face your own servants. The disdainful voice didn't even make me pause. I was too used to its presence.

The evening meal had been served late for some years, so that those of us who spent our days at the king's bedside could eat after he had retired for the night. It meant it would be dark before I had to present myself to my stepmother.

I ordered my meal delivered to my room, unable to face company of any kind, before shedding my court dress in favor of a comfortable dressing gown and giving myself one last afternoon to wallow in my grief. But when my meal eventually arrived, and I finished off the last mouthful, I knew I would have to change. I couldn't face Alida in such attire.

I was standing in front of my bed, surveying several choices of dresses laid out on it, when the door to my small dressing room swung open. I spun, biting off a gasp. My dressing room had no external access, and no one had entered my room since I had returned. Had someone been hiding there for all these hours?

But when my eyes landed on the intruder, I understood. The dressing room did have a window, and a determined climber could make it up the vines which snaked down the three stories beneath. But it had been many years since Alexander had used that method of access to the castle.

One look at his face made me fall back a step, the smile of greeting dropping from my face.

"Alex?" I whispered.

His eyes swept over me, and he flushed, falling back a step

himself. I looked down, following his gaze, and rolled my eyes. I had forgotten I still wore my dressing gown, but it enveloped me from neck to toe, the thick material keeping my curves well-covered. He had seen far more in the years before my father's illness when we would follow our fathers through the forest, my skirts tied up around my thighs, doing our best to keep up until we were eventually discovered and—after some token protest—I was put up in front of my father on his great mount, and he was permitted to join the hunt.

"Alex?" I asked again, and my voice seemed to jerk him back to his purpose.

Striding over to my main door, he turned the key that always sat in the lock. The one I never used. I frowned, hugging myself.

I didn't feel even the slightest whisper of concern to find myself locked in a room with Alex. I could no more imagine him hurting me than I could remember the face of my mother. But fear filled me all the same. I couldn't imagine what might have driven him to such behavior.

When he turned back toward me, the look on his face confirmed my feelings, deepening them into terror.

"What is it?" I managed to gasp out.

"Get dressed," was all he said, gesturing toward the gowns on my bed. "Your most practical clothes."

I didn't hesitate, reaching to slide the dressing gown from my shoulders, and he flushed again, spinning to put his back toward me.

"I'm not naked under this," I muttered, pulling the garment off.

The back of his neck turned red to match his face.

Would he respond like that to any girl? I wondered as I ignored the dresses already laid out and instead crossed over to pull out my most practical gown. Or did his face betray what his voice would not? I held onto the small hope that Alexander might see me as more than a little sister or a princess owed loyalty.

But the familiar question couldn't occupy my mind for long. Something had happened since I had seen him in the corridor. Something drastic or he would never have climbed into my room in such a way.

"Tell me what's going on," I demanded. "You can consider that a royal command, if necessary. Oh, and you can turn around now."

He spun, the unusual color gone from his face as he assessed my choice of dress. Reluctantly he nodded, and I only shrugged. I didn't know what he had been expecting. I only had the wardrobe of a princess to choose from, so I had no hope of matching the practicality of his own clothes.

"You can pack a few things but be quick. And keep them light."

"Pack?" I gaped at him. "What do you mean?"

His brows drew together and then cleared as if he had forgotten he had yet to explain himself. "We have to leave. Right now."

CHAPTER 3

" *L* eave?" I stared at him stupidly. Surely he could not mean...

He nodded once. "We need to be gone from the castle as soon as we can."

"Gone?" I wished I could do something other than repeat his words like an idiot. But I couldn't seem to make sense of what he was saying.

My eyes traveled to the door he had just locked, but he shook his head without my having to say anything. "Not that way."

When his eyes moved significantly toward my dressing room, I shook my head fast, my hands coming up defensively in front of me. It had been far too many years since I had clambered down the vines. And I used to wear shorter skirts in those days.

"It's the only way, Snow," he said.

My eyes snapped back to his, my nickname on his lips telling me more than any of his other words. He was serious, and he was scared.

"There's no time for explanations," he added. "Do you trust me?"

I looked at his face, so strong for someone so young—the opposite of mine—and didn't have to think about my answer.

"Of course I do."

"Then pack anything you absolutely need. But hurry."

His final words broke the spell holding my feet in place, and I flew through my rooms. My mind wanted to speculate on what could be driving him, but I forced myself to think about what essentials to pack instead. All too soon I had filled the small leather satchel he thrust into my hands. I closed it with a longing gaze at the pile of books beside my bed. I knew well enough what he would say if I tried to claim them as essential packing.

I had barely fastened it when he lifted the bag from my hands, slinging it over his own shoulder. I made no protest. Not if we were really going down the vines.

We both squeezed into the dressing room, Alexander closing the door behind us despite it having no lock. I peered out the window. I was sure it hadn't been so far down last time I did this.

Someone—presumably Alexander—had left a lantern on the ground just below my window. It simultaneously cast enough light to illuminate a terrifying drop, and too little light to high-light any sure footholds. I looked back at him and licked my lips, hoping he would relent and tell me there was another way.

"I'm sorry, Snow." The words were quiet but sincere. "I daren't..." He took a breath. "Have faith in yourself. You've done this before, you can do it again."

I peered out again. "That was a long time ago."

"It works just the same," he said, gently edging me to the side and swinging one leg over the stone sill. "I'll go first. If you slip, I'll catch you."

I appreciated his words, although I doubted the vines would allow him a strong enough purchase for such a thing. But I thrust the doubt from my mind. It wouldn't help with what apparently had to be done.

As soon as he disappeared from view, I hoisted up my skirts, tying them well up my legs as I used to do so long ago. At least my boots were sturdy, the most practical item I owned.

I swung one leg over and adjusted my grip, looking quickly down to check Alexander had descended low enough to allow me to clamber all the way out. He had paused, his disapproving eyes on my leg.

"Oh, please," I hissed at him. "You try doing this in skirts."

A brief smile crossed his face, although it didn't quite reach his eyes, and he made no protest. Reluctantly, I swung the other leg out and draped my waist across the sill, my feet seeking a foothold among the vines.

I found one quickly, the thick growth reassuringly solid beneath my toes. Letting myself slide down, I found purchases among the greenery for my hands. Once I had a solid grip, I pulled one foot free, questing lower for another foothold. Slowly, step by step, I descended.

And as I went I became more confident, even moving a little more quickly. For all it had been years, my body still remembered how to do this, checking each hold before committing my weight. I remembered that you didn't find new hand and footholds with your eyes—the reason why a single lantern was enough.

I smiled, almost exhilarated by the old feeling of freedom that rushed through me. Twisting, I looked over my shoulder and down, seeking Alexander. He had kept pace just below me, but my eyes swept over him, instinctively seeking the ground below.

I had expected it to be closer, and the expanse of open air made me gasp and wobble. I instinctively clutched for the vines, but the movement only dislodged me further. I felt my feet slip and managed to gasp Alex's name before my weight jerked against my hands, ripping the vines free from my grasp.

I fell, scrabbling at the greenery, seeking a new purchase—any purchase—but they slid by too quickly.

Until another, harder jerk, stopped my fall, wrenching my

shoulder so hard that tears sprang to my eyes. Alexander's firm grip encircled my wrist, his other hand tangled among the vines. But even as I looked up at him, I saw them begin to separate from the wall, unable to hold our combined weight.

Seeing my fear reflected in the gray of his eyes galvanized me to action, and I swung myself against the wall, seeking for a safe hold with both feet and my free hand. One foot found grip first, followed by my fingers as they curled around a particularly gnarled root.

I felt the instant easing of pressure in my shoulder, and Alexander must have felt it, too.

"Are you—?"

I nodded up at him, and he slowly released his grip, pulling off one finger at a time as if reluctant to let go. I clung to the vine, drawing shaky breaths as the rush of panic subsided somewhat. I couldn't stay here, though. I needed to make it the rest of the way down. And I was beneath Alexander now. He couldn't catch me again.

I closed my eyes and willed myself to move. Nothing happened.

"Snow?" Alexander's soft voice above me unlocked my limbs. He wouldn't leave me here, but he couldn't carry me down, either. Which meant I had to get us down this wall.

Slowly one foot pulled loose and slid down. Only when it was firmly in a new place did the other foot follow. The rest of the descent was accomplished at a snail's pace, and I could feel tension radiating off Alexander. But he said nothing to rush me, matching each of his movements to mine.

I didn't look down again, so when my reaching foot felt solid earth, it caught me by surprise. I let go, collapsing down to sprawl in the dirt. I had never been so grateful to feel firm ground beneath me.

Alexander leaped down from above me, landing elegantly on his feet. He looked around, his eyes scanning the nearby trees.

Obviously whatever he saw satisfied him, because he doused the lantern before turning to offer me a hand. I took it, relief making me smile up at him with almost giddy abandon despite our strange situation.

After he'd pulled me to my feet, he didn't let go, dragging me behind him as he started off into the trees. I stumbled as I tried to keep pace, and he slowed slightly but didn't stop. I abandoned any hope that he might explain now that we were out of the castle. Clearly he wanted to get further away.

We ran, ducking between trees in the darkness. But how did he intend us to get past the wall? Unlike the front of the castle, where only a courtyard stood between the building and the castle wall, my rooms faced onto the back where previous generations of my ancestors had allowed a small wood to grow up in the large space between the back of the castle and the wall.

When we were young, we had crawled through a small drain, splashing through the tiny creek that it had been built for. A loose grate had made it the perfect means of escape. But while I might have some hope of squeezing through that way still, one glance at Alexander's broad shoulders ruled out the possibility. And if he tried to send me through on my own, without explanation, he would soon discover my limits.

But he didn't lead us toward the grate, a route that to my surprise remained familiar, even in the dark and after so many years. Instead he led us to a small wooden door, grandly named the south gate. I blinked in the low light of the torch at the gate, bright after the darkness of the trees. But I could see no sign of any guards.

I frowned, looking around again as Alexander tugged me closer. He didn't slow, clearly not fearing anyone would be there to raise an alarm. When we stepped out into the open, I saw why. Two figures slumped against the wall, their weapons sprawled uselessly beside their still fingers.

I wrenched my hand from Alexander's, stepping toward them, but his words stopped me.

"They're alive. Leave them."

One gave a loud snore, as if to corroborate his words, and I stopped. Biting my lip, I looked between Alexander and the guards. He had been here before, then, clearing our path somehow.

Even I knew better than to try to stop for explanations at this point. Alexander pulled open the gate, and I followed, stepping aside as he closed and locked it behind us, placing the key in his pocket. The woods appeared to continue south unbroken, thickening to a true forest, but I knew the sight was deceptive. Only a thin band of forest reached around the southern side of the castle. The true depths of it lay to the west.

And, sure enough, Alexander took only a few strides before turning sharply right and heading due west. We were heading away from the city—which lay on the other side of the castle, stretching out from the main gates and away to the north and east—and into the trees.

I stumbled along behind him, too focused on not losing my footing in the darkness to pant out any questions. We would have to stop eventually, and once we did I was refusing to start again until I understood exactly what was going on.

Only we kept going and going and going. All too soon my aching legs reminded me that it had been far too long since my old days of running after my father and Alex. Endless hours beside a sick bed had done little to prepare me for this nighttime flight through the woods.

Roots appeared from nowhere, sending me stumbling again and again. Alexander—sure in his own strides as he led the way—always seemed to be there, though, his arm ready to steady me before I actually toppled over. But as I grew more and more tired, I faltered more and more often. The hoot of an owl, or the flash of the moon through a sudden hole in the canopy, were enough to unbalance me, even without the unsteady footing.

Our pace slowed even more, and finally Alexander seemed to realize I could go no further. With a whispered word, and a firm hand under my elbow, he directed me through a gap in the trees and into a small clearing where a shallow cave—little more than a crevice in the rock—gave us somewhere to rest.

The summer air was warm enough even at night to mean a shelter wasn't necessary, but I was grateful to have solid stone at my back and somewhere to lean my exhausted head. I let my eyes flutter shut, but the unfamiliar sounds of the forest soon drove them open again, my heart beating an uncomfortable rhythm.

I found Alexander watching me. I expected him to look away when I met his gaze, as he so often did these days, but he held steady. Something in the grave concern I saw reflected in his face unnerved me as much as his open fear had done earlier.

I realized it had been more than exhaustion which prevented me asking questions sooner. A deep reluctance for the answers had held me back. More cowardice in the face of my new father-less reality. I had longed to flee—even considering running to the Marinese princesses—and then my childhood friend had let me do it without feeling the sting of responsibility for my actions. Something deep inside me had wanted to hold onto the idea that we were simply on an adventure, as we might have done so many years ago.

But I was no longer a child. And I could not flee my responsibilities, however much I longed to be free from the place where every stone reminded me of my father. It was time for some answers, however unpleasant.

"You asked me to trust you, and I have," I said. "Now you need to tell me what in the kingdoms is going on."

He looked away at last, his hands rising and then falling uselessly beside him. His mouth opened and then closed, his jaw tightening.

What was so hard for him to say? I tried to think of a way to help him tell the story he so clearly didn't want to speak aloud.

"Where are we going?"

Alexander had always been practical and so capable. Focusing on the plan might settle him now. But instead his head shot up, his eyes once more flashing to mine, and he let out a quickly stifled bark of laughter. One without humor.

"I don't know. Away, I suppose."

I shivered, trying to hide the involuntary movement from him. No plan? I didn't know what to do with that information. After several moments of my heart thumping against my chest, I tried again.

"Away from what?"

"That woman." He spat the words, his whole face darkening.

"My stepmother?" I longed to be away from her every day, but that wasn't a reason for a sudden flight through my window. "What do you mean?"

He took a deep breath, his eyes on the forest around us, alert and watchful.

"I wanted to return as soon as I heard, and Princess Celine could tell, I think..."

I frowned. What did Prince Oliver of Eldon's betrothed have to do with this? I tried to puzzle it through.

"Did you discover something in Eldon? Some threat?" He hadn't mentioned it when we spoke earlier in the day.

"No. Well...yes. But that's not..." He sighed and looked at me, an apology in his eyes. "I'm not doing well at this."

"Just start at the beginning."

He looked away again, angling his face so that I couldn't see it.

"I was in Eldon, as you know, and due to remain there until the royal wedding, although I longed to be back here." He swallowed. "When we received word of your father's passing, I knew I couldn't stay there. I had to get back to..." His eyes flashed to me and then away again too quickly for me to read their expression.

"Princess Celine saw my desire to return, I think. And she has a kind heart."

A stab of jealousy shot through me, but I pushed it away and tried to focus on his words.

"We had just learned of the escape of a prisoner. One involved in the enchantment that has gripped Eldon until recently. They believe he may have escaped into Eliam, so she sent me back with an urgent message of warning."

He still wouldn't meet my eyes as he continued. "After that performance in the throne room, it seemed obvious that the Eldonian royals would expect me to deliver the message to Queen Alida. So earlier this evening I went to the royal suite to deliver it to her. And I overheard her talking."

My eyes narrowed as I watched the little bit of his profile I could see. An unlikely sounding story. Especially the part where he just happened to be there to hear an important conversation.

"You mean you found some way to eavesdrop on my step-mother with the message as an excuse for your presence if you got caught. And now you don't want to admit that because you know I'll be angry at you for putting yourself in danger."

"I don't know what you mean," he said, but a smug look crossed his face that told me all I needed to know. The expression quickly fell away, however, as he continued his story.

"She was expecting you to arrive shortly. And she was giving orders to that blackguard henchman of hers."

I didn't have to ask who he meant. Alexander hated Randolph nearly as much as I did.

"What sort of orders?" I had to work to keep my voice from trembling, even now with so much distance separating me from the castle.

"Orders of the worst kind. I knew then that I had to get to you and run. As far and fast as we could. And so, here we are—without a plan."

I sat up straight, indignation driving away my lingering fear.

"Oh no, you don't, Alexander Huntsman! I know that you're only trying to protect me, but those orders clearly had to do with me, and I have a right to know what they are."

When he looked over at me, reluctance clear in every line of his face, I fixed him with my sternest glare. "I deserve to know the truth. I need to know the truth."

He seemed to deflate, and I could see that it hurt him even to say the words, but I held firm.

"She was giving orders to Randolph to kill you. Tonight."

CHAPTER 4

I gasped, my hand flying to my throat. "Kill me? Are you sure?" It seemed a stupid question, but I couldn't help it spilling from my mouth. I knew she disliked me and wanted to see me married off, but I hadn't suspected her of assassination.

A look of something—horror, perhaps, or disgust—filled his eyes. "There was no mistaking it."

I bit my lip, my voice dropping but not wavering. "You have to tell me everything."

His jaw tightened again, his whole posture going rigid. "She said too many at court remained sympathetic toward you."

I snorted—she had apparently seen a different court today from what I saw—but he ignored me.

"She said that it was one thing now while you were underage, but she didn't trust them not to make a fuss in the future. And then she said that if she was to get rid of you, it needed to be now, when it seemed most plausible."

"Plausible?" I cried in outrage. "I don't believe even the court would find killing her own stepdaughter plausible!"

"No, of course not." He shook his head. "Which is why she

needed some way to make it look like an accident. Something entirely beyond her control."

I frowned. "In her own chambers? Plausible is still not the word that comes to mind."

He sighed. "No, it wasn't to happen in her chambers." He bit his lip and gestured around at the surrounding forest. "It was to happen out here."

For one wild, unthinking moment my mind—still reeling from his revelation—became unhinged, and I had to force myself not to scramble away from him. My stepmother had ordered me brought into the forest and murdered, and I had followed without question.

But another second, another heartbeat, brought clarity. Alexander would never hurt me. He had brought me out here to save me, not to kill me. I swallowed, waiting until I felt sure my voice wouldn't tremble.

"So Randolph was to drag me out here and kill me. And she would make it look like…what?"

He swallowed, his hands fisting so tightly the tendons stood out along his arms. "He was to make it look like you had been attacked and killed by wild animals. Partially eaten—although she warned him to ensure you were still recognizable. He was to…he was to bring her your lungs and your liver before sunrise. Proof he had completed the task."

I shuddered, my sight going black. She didn't just want me dead—she wanted me ripped apart and desecrated. I felt myself rocking back and forth, my breath coming faster and faster, and then strong arms gripped me.

Alexander pulled me against his chest, one hand making rhythmic circles on my back as he murmured into my hair.

"He won't hurt you. I will never let him hurt you. Breathe, Snow. Steady now."

I let myself sink against him, my frantically racing heart

slowing to match the rhythm of his as my breaths slowed to match the rise and fall of his chest.

"And how did she mean to explain such a thing?" I managed to ask at last.

He gave a long sigh, his arms slowly loosening at the calm in my voice.

"She intended to make it look as if you had run away. Stricken by grief for your father, of course. That's why it had to be now."

I swallowed. Hadn't I contemplated something all too similar? Perhaps the court would even have believed it. Or at least, pretended to do so, the story just plausible enough. Plausible—just as she had said. I shuddered again, and Alexander's arms briefly tightened.

But a new thought made me sit up straight, jerking away from him.

"But wait. Isn't that exactly what I've now done?"

"Run away?" Alexander frowned. "Yes, I suppose you have." He shook his head. "But with one very important distinction—you're not going to be attacked by anyone—human or wild animal. I won't—"

He broke off abruptly, his head turning as he scanned the trees around us. When I took a breath to speak, he held up a hand to silence me. I froze, every muscle tense, every sense alert. What had he heard?

But my ears could hear nothing, and my wildly darting eyes could detect no sign of danger.

Silently, Alexander stood, gesturing for me to remain in place. With long strides, he crossed the tiny clearing and melted into the trees. I sat, still frozen, struggling to make my breaths as silent as his steps. I counted them even, in an effort to remain calm.

Seventy-four. Seventy-five. Seventy-six. Was that movement in the trees just there or merely the wind shaking a branch?

One hundred twelve. One hundred thirteen. One hundred fourteen. Was that Alexander returning? Or a fox in the bushes? Or…

One hundred fifty-five. One hundred fifty-six. One hundred fifty-seven. A cloud crossed the moon, and I flinched.

Two hundred. Two hundred one. Two hundred two. What if the queen had sent the guard after us? What if they had caught Alexander? What if Randolph decided to rip him apart instead? But no. Alexander was born and raised a huntsman. He knew these woods better than any guard.

Two hundred eighty-eight. Two hundred eighty-nine. Two hundred ninety. What if it was me Randolph found? Alone here and defenseless. What if he slipped around Alexander in the dark? Again I reminded myself of Alexander's skill. He had promised me. He would not let anyone find me here.

I swallowed a scream as a figure appeared from between the trees. Alexander returned as silently as he had left, his expression worried. He didn't speak until he stood directly above me, and then his words were the faintest whisper.

"They're here in the forest. We're being tracked."

I bit my lip, my eyes darting around him as I strained yet again to see anything other than trees in the dim light of the moon. He quickly shook his head.

"They're not here. Not yet. But they're getting close. We need to move."

He hauled me to my feet, and I stumbled against him. I had been so frozen I hadn't even noticed my foot go numb.

He looked down at me in silent concern, but I just shook my head, pulling away, my face flushed with embarrassment. He could track people through the forest as easily as he tracked wild animals, and I couldn't even manage to sit in one place without incapacitating myself.

My foot tingled and throbbed as feeling returned, but I ignored it, determined not to disgrace myself again. One glance at the fear in his eyes reminded me that my life might depend on it.

He led us on through the trees, but not in the headlong rush I had imagined. We moved more slowly now, more carefully. I tried to follow his footsteps exactly, but I still couldn't manage to move silently as he did. Every crack and rustle sounded deafening in my ears, and I winced with each one, my ears straining to hear shouts of discovery or the sound of pursuit.

But I could still make out nothing but the night sounds that had surrounded us before. The wind in the trees. The hoot and screech of distant owls. The rustle of small animals in the underbrush.

The tension began to wear on my already tired muscles, and I felt my legs trembling with every step. I tried to step more carefully, not less, but the noise I made increased despite all my efforts. Not once did Alexander shush me, his patience and forbearance as steady as the arm which constantly reached back to brace me.

At one point, we veered sharply to one side, moving onto a long stretch of rock bordering a small creek. Loose gravel made walking silently even more difficult, and I gritted my teeth against the scraping sounds, focusing my attention on not twisting an ankle.

Alexander led me parallel to the creek for what felt like a long way before he stepped straight into the shallow water. But instead of crossing directly, he turned and began to slosh through the water, moving upstream against the light current.

I followed, glad I had never pulled my skirts loose. My boots should keep out the water from such a tiny stream. Keeping my footing here was even harder, however, and I abandoned all pride and clung to the back of Alexander's jacket for balance. If the pursuers were far enough away to make disguising our tracks in such a way worthwhile, then the small noises we made must not be a danger.

The creek twisted and turned, and we followed it for what seemed an interminable time. The moon had dipped lower in the sky, or perhaps been covered by a thick bank of clouds, and only my grip on my companion kept me from falling and soaking myself through. Once my eyes actually drifted closed, jerking back up a brief second before I lost my grip on the soft leather.

At last, Alexander paused. He remained still for a moment, surveying our surroundings, before abruptly turning and scooping me into his arms.

I squeaked, too shocked to actually protest. He looked down at me, his eyes warning me not to speak, and I subsided. In truth, though I wished I didn't need his assistance, I wasn't sure how much longer my legs could hold me up. And his arms were so very strong and sure around me. His chest so warm and inviting. I snuggled against it, his arms tightening in response.

Admit it, Snow, said my irritating internal voice. *You're not going to complain because you're exactly where you want to be.*

But what was so wrong with that? If I had ever needed comfort, surely tonight was the night.

Alexander strode through the forest, his new load not slowing him down at all. If anything, I suspected he was moving faster and more freely now. I looked up at him, admiring the soft light on the angles of his face. He looked down and met my gaze.

"One set of footprints. And not like mine, either. Heavier."

I blinked, trying to get my brain—which was half asleep—to process his words. What was he talking about?

Sudden comprehension dawned. I didn't know whether to be disappointed or relieved. Relieved to discover he hadn't picked me up because I was too useless even to walk on my own two feet, disappointed because it hadn't been any desire of his that had prompted the action.

No, the expert huntsman had ensured the tracks which left the creek—far, far from where our tracks had entered it—looked nothing like our tracks at all. Instead they would appear to belong to a single man, one larger and heavier than Alexander. It was no wonder he was so good at his job.

The brief conversation—if it could even be called that—did little to hold off my exhaustion. The rocking movement of his walk, and the warmth of his body soon made it almost impossible to keep my eyes open. After a while I gave up trying and let myself drift into a half-sleep. A delicious state in which I could briefly forget my fear and anger, conscious only of the safety and comfort of my best friend's arms.

I might have fallen deeper asleep than I realized, because my body jerked when we finally stopped. I would have fallen if Alexander hadn't been gripping me so firmly.

I flushed, wiping surreptitiously at my mouth and hoping I hadn't embarrassed myself. But Alexander was placing me gently down on a surprisingly soft clump of ferns, his soft voice telling me not to stir.

"We'll be safe here. You can sleep."

My traitorous arms tried to reach for him as he pulled away from me, but I forced them back down, tucking them under my body to keep them from going rogue. And then my lids were dragging down and true sleep was rushing up, and I was gone.

Hours must have passed before a sound woke me. Although I couldn't have said what sound. For a disorienting moment I couldn't imagine where I was, and then memory returned, rushing back all too clearly.

I pushed myself up, blinking in the sunlight, my arms sinking slightly into my bed of ferns. The warmth of the sun had driven out any lingering cold from the night, but everything still ached. When I struggled to my feet, my legs wobbled beneath me, cramping in painful bursts.

I closed my eyes and resisted the pain, forcing myself to take a couple of steps. I rolled my shoulders and my neck as I did so, trying to shake out every part of me that was protesting the exertion of the previous day followed by my sleep on the forest floor.

I put a determined smile on my face before I opened my eyes again, remembering my humiliating performance of the night before. I wouldn't let Alexander know how much I hurt this morning.

But when I opened my eyes, I discovered the effort had been for nothing. Alexander was nowhere in sight. I spun around, looking in every direction. I was alone.

I called his name softly, too wary to call loudly. No reply came. I tried to calm my racing heart. No doubt he had stepped briefly away and would be back any moment. To relieve himself most likely. Perhaps it had been his departure that woke me. I should take the same opportunity.

It was fine. Everything was fine. I would wait, and he would soon be back.

And so I waited. And waited. And waited. The sun climbed high above me and still I waited.

Until at last I was forced to accept the truth. Alexander was gone. I was alone.

CHAPTER 5

*T*he most obvious answer—that he had abandoned me while I slept—I rejected without thought. Alexander would never betray me in such a fashion. In him alone of the whole court—the whole capital—I was certain.

The remaining possibilities terrified me. But they were almost as quickly rejected. If Randolph had found us, he wouldn't have left me sleeping peacefully. And no wild animal could have carried Alexander off without waking me in the process.

Equally impossible was the option that he had stepped away as I had first supposed and lost his way or fallen afoul of the forest. Not when I had seen his skill firsthand the night before.

But what did that leave? He couldn't have simply vanished into thin air.

But as the hours wore on, the question of what had happened to Alexander was overtaken by a more urgent one. What should I do now?

Even if I had dared return to the castle, I had no idea how to find the way. And I had too much trust in Alexander to doubt his story. Nothing but death awaited me anywhere within reach of the queen.

But already my stomach rumbled uncomfortably, and my mouth and throat felt dry in a way I had never felt before. How many hours had it been since I ate or drank? I tried not to tally them, knowing it would only make the hunger and thirst worse.

I wanted to stay here, to keep hoping for Alexander's return, but I had more to concern me than the empty state of my belly. We had been tracked last night, for some distance at least. And now that I had truly fled, my stepmother would have reason to call out the entire guard and set them to combing the forest. She might even pretend fear that I had been abducted.

No doubt she intended to keep searching until I was found. Alive or dead with a definite preference on dead. I shivered.

If I stayed here indefinitely was I only sealing my own fate? I had no hope of protecting myself against Randolph or a troop of guards. Not alone.

Where are you, Alexander?!

But the forest made no answer to my silent cry. A nearby rustle made me jump, and I knew in that moment that I couldn't remain here. It would drive me mad if nothing else.

With no way to gain information, I could do nothing to puzzle out Alexander's disappearance. Instead I needed to focus on my own survival. I needed water, I needed food, and—eventually—I would need shelter. Preferably shelter far from the questing eyes of my stepmother.

I only wished our kingdoms hadn't been cut off from the godmothers until so very recently. If only I had been given a godmother at my Christening. Now would have been just the moment to call on her. I didn't know if such a being would find me deserving enough, but surely she wouldn't have questioned my dire need, at least.

But those thoughts were as foolish and useless as wishing my father back alive. I didn't have a godmother, and I had no reason to suppose one would come for me now. Alexander had saved me last night. Now it was time for me to save myself.

Except when I stood up, full of determination, I found myself staring blankly at the forest. I didn't have the slightest idea which direction I should take. I could barely even remember arriving in this spot, and I was just as likely to walk back toward the castle as away.

After long moments of painful indecision, another rustle made me start and jerk forward, my feet moving of their own volition to carry me away from the sound. My steps quickly slowed as I silently berated myself for my skittishness, but I didn't stop altogether. With no idea which way to go, this direction was as good as any other.

At least the bright sunlight made the forest easier to navigate, and I managed to move without stumbling or tripping. It helped that I was alone and could tie my skirts up even higher than I had done previously. After some minutes of forward progress, my ears caught a faint sound, distinct from the previous noises of the forest.

I froze, straining to hear it more clearly. Was I rushing straight toward capture?

But the sound continued on, too even and continuous to be the sound of other people. And my eager body recognized it before my mind could catch up. Water. Beautiful, wonderful water.

I adjusted my direction, my steps picking up speed as I rushed toward it. My dry mouth propelled me forward, no thought of caution or listening for pursuit in my head. I barely maintained the attention to avoid tripping on roots and branches.

The sound grew stronger and stronger, and I knew before I burst out of the trees almost on its banks that I was moving toward a larger stream than the one we had waded through the night before. Sure enough, this one was almost big enough to qualify as a river. It burbled and rushed, flowing along the mossy grass of its bank.

I sank onto my knees and stopped just short of thrusting my

whole face into the sweet, cool liquid. Instead I used my hands to cup mouthful after mouthful of relief down my parched throat. Only when I thought my stomach might burst did I let my hands drop, rocking back on my heels.

I groaned at the sloshing feeling that now filled me, doing little to alleviate my hunger. Perhaps I shouldn't have drunk so much. And yet, eyeing the water flowing past me, its clear depths revealing rocks beneath, I almost wanted to down another gulp.

I edged back, eventually collapsing into a proper sitting position. My eyes lingered thoughtfully on the almost-river, my mind working more clearly now that my most immediate need had been met.

There could be no question that this was a different waterway from the one last night. Or, if it was the same one, it was a very different section of it. And I was equally certain we hadn't passed this one in the dark, even as I slept. Alexander wouldn't have risked carrying me across the slippery stones of the bottom. Not given the depth and the swiftly moving current.

Which alleviated the second of my most pressing concerns. I wasn't backtracking our earlier progress. But a new decision faced me. Did I ford this stream and continue through the forest? Or adjust my course and follow its banks?

I didn't have to think long to make a decision. Despite the water dripping from my face now, I could clearly remember the dry feeling that had plagued me since I woke. If I left this stream behind, who knew how long before I found another? My bag had rested in the ferns beside me when I awoke, but I had only been able to pack things from my room. And I had no water skin or anything able to hold water in there. Alexander had been carrying our only water skin.

As I forced myself to my feet and began to traipse beside the stream, I told myself my decision had nothing to do with not wanting to half-splash, half-swim across the treacherous bed of the stream. I needed water and here it was. It would be foolish to turn away from it.

And as I walked further, another thought buoyed my confidence. I didn't have the skills required to survive alone in the forest for any length of time. One way or another, I must find shelter with other people. And people needed a constant source of water. If I followed the stream long enough, I would either find another human or a way out of the forest. Eventually.

But my spirits fell as the afternoon began to draw toward evening. I had seen a few berries, bright red against the green foliage, but I hadn't dared eat them. I could no longer remember the tips my father had given me as I rode in front of him as a child. The tips that would let me distinguish an edible berry from a poisonous one.

I had done far less than a full day of walking, but my legs still ached from the day before, and weakness crept over me, growing along with the pain in my empty middle. I knew I would have to stop soon, but I kept hoping just a little more walking would bring me to someone who might at the very least be willing to give me some food. Perhaps they would trade for something in my pack, although I hated to part with any of my now-meager belongings.

Only when the sun actually set directly in front of me, spectacular streaks of red and orange reflecting on the forest as if autumn had come early, did it burst upon me that I was traveling almost due west. A wave of relief was almost overtaken by an equally strong feeling of foolishness. If I was traveling west, it meant I could be sure I continued to move away from the castle. But how had it not occurred to me to use the sun as a marker of my direction? I hadn't thought myself so inept as to miss something so obvious.

When the sun disappeared completely, I knew I could go on no longer. After a long drink, I ventured a little way from the water, finding a patch of undergrowth that looked softer than most. It was the best I could do in the circumstances, and I knew I should be grateful it was summer. Except I couldn't seem to muster anything resembling gratitude as sleep slowly claimed me.

By the time the sun rose the next morning, I was longingly remembering my exhausted stupor of the first night. I had thought I would sleep equally deeply after my day of fear and exertion, but my aching body didn't appreciate the ground—which seemed to grow harder as the night wore on. And the knowledge that I was truly on my own—ill-prepared and ill-equipped—made me jerk awake with every sound.

And my concern for Alexander—which I had been trying to suppress—only made it harder to sleep, my mind turning to him every time I startled into wakefulness.

When at the end of one of these sessions of fear and anxiety, I remembered that the morning light would bring only the promise of further effort, with no breakfast in sight, I shed silent tears into the cloak I had rolled into a pillow. It was the only time I was glad to be alone.

The water tasted a great deal less sweet that second day, the dissatisfying liquid making my jaw ache for something to chew. I swallowed it down, however, and resumed my chosen path. At least the stream still led me westward.

As the day continued on, even the bright sunlight wasn't enough to prevent my stumbles, hunger and fatigue draining the strength from my muscles. The fear of Randolph—or even real wild animals, which I had yet to encounter—had faded before a more pressing terror. How long would it take to starve to death alone in the forest? Perhaps a quick death at someone—or something—else's hands might even be preferable to the protracted pain and fear of such an end.

I tried to recall maps of our lands. Eliam was the smallest of the kingdoms—excluding Marin, which was only a duchy. But it was still large enough that one foolish girl could stumble for days on end through its forests without reaching the other side. Eventually, of course, if I could keep going, I would hit the western coast and the fishing villages there. Or even the city of Lestern. But I suspected at my current pace I would easily succumb before then. And I would only get slower as I got weaker.

Now when I started at some unfamiliar sound, I felt almost as much hope as fear. Had I found the first signs of a village? Or the even more appealing, but also more foolish, hope—had Alexander found me?

And yet, despite my straining ears, no sound warned me before I stumbled into a small and obviously inhabited clearing. The briefest of glances told me this was no village. But I had long since ceased caring what form my salvation took.

The small cottage was set some way back from the stream but still in clear view. Its thatched roof showed care and good tending, although its paint looked faded and worn, and in some places had started to peel. A small vegetable plot to one side held neat green rows, and if it had been later in the season, I would have fallen on it with desperation.

As it was, I could see no fully-formed vegetables, and a short moment of consideration returned enough sense to send me to the door of the cottage before I began outright stealing. My steps took me past a large chicken coop, where several hens pecked quietly at the ground.

A thin, lazy stream of smoke curled up from the single chimney, and the sight gave me hope. Straightening my back, I knocked on the front door, one hand going uselessly to my black curls. It was best not to think about the state of my hair.

But as the seconds dragged by with no response to my repeated knock, the tension inside me drained away. I stepped back to peer up again at the smoke. Surely someone must be home. But another second's thought made me realize the thin stream could merely be the result of a banked fire.

Slowly, feeling awkward, I circled the house, peering into the windows. Several were covered with brightly colored curtains, but I found one, made of eight small panes, that gave me a view inside. I pressed my face against it, poised to leap back if I saw anyone inside. But the large, dim interior appeared empty.

Well, not empty. Just empty of people. And the contents were enough to override both good sense and basic courtesy. Rushing back to the front door, I opened the latch and thrust open the door. The relief at finding it unlocked brought tears springing to my eyes. Apparently the remote inhabitants had no fear of burglars.

The thought that I had been reduced to burglary produced only a dim and passing sting. Because something far more pressing had consumed my mind. A low, well-worn wooden table stood to one side of the room, and plates covered it. Many of which still held food. Food whose scent filled the air and drew me like a siren call.

I ignored the chairs, which seemed strangely small, and dropped to my knees. Using my fingers, I shoveled two huge mouthfuls of scrambled eggs into my mouth. A piece of meat of unknown origin, the congealed fat clinging to it, followed it down.

But as soon as it hit my stomach, my body rebelled, and I dropped my head to the floor, inhaling deep breaths as I fought to keep my stomach from expelling its new contents. When the heaving subsided, I sat up, moving much more slowly and cautiously.

This time I took small bites and forced myself to chew slowly. I avoided the meat, moving from plate to plate to take the left-over piles of egg. When I found an untouched half of toast on one and a quarter of an early harvest tomato on another, I decided they should be safe as well. Or at least my desperate desire over-rode everything else, and they joined the eggs in my stomach. Thankfully they stayed down.

Far sooner than seemed possible, I felt my stomach stretch

uncomfortably tight. I eyed the remaining plates but, remembering my earlier close call, decided to stop.

With my most immediate need met, I surveyed the rest of the cottage. Although the building wasn't large, it was large enough that it surprised me to find it a single, open room. A hearth—which, sure enough, contained a banked fire—and various cooking implements occupied one corner, and the table took up a large portion of the open space. Beds lined one wall, although cushions of various sizes seemed strewn at random around the rest of the room.

The largest of the beds looked almost improbably large, while the three single beds beside it looked equally small. My conclusion that the cottage must belong to a family with three children didn't seem borne out by the mass of untidy plates on the table.

The puzzle could do little to occupy my mind, however, when my eyes kept being drawn back to the row of beds. None of them were made, but the large pillows looked impossibly soft, and the mattresses deep and springy. Now that my stomach had been filled, my aching muscles and drooping eyes made me forget all about the impropriety of my presence here.

Surely the owners would be gone for a little while longer, and it would do no harm to their bed if I lay down on it...I would wake soon enough and prepare my speech for their return. It would probably be best if I awaited them outside, as well. But just a little sleep first wouldn't hurt anything...

CHAPTER 6

"*Y*ou didn't clean up breakfast. Again!" The complainer sounded young.

"Of course not." The response came from someone even younger. A child, for sure. "If I'd cleaned it up, I couldn't eat my leftovers as soon as I...hey! Where's the rest of my toast? I left it right here."

"Oh, please! I'm sure Louis swiped it as soon as your back was turned. That's the stupidest excuse you've used yet to try to get out of chores." The original speaker didn't sound impressed.

"No, he didn't. He left before I'd finished. I was the last one out. I'm sure of it." The child ignored the repeated rebuke, too focused on their grievance.

Two more voices, each loudly proclaiming their innocence, joined in the chorus, while my confused mind struggled to make sense of any of it. What were these children doing in my bedchamber? And why did every part of me hurt?

"Ahhhh, Jack...I think I know who ate your toast," said a new voice.

"What? Who?"

"There's someone in your bed." The words made me jolt upright, my eyes flinging open.

I wasn't in my bedchamber. And I also knew who had eaten the child's toast. Me.

The dancing shadows and mass of confused movement made me blink. Was this the same place that I had fallen asleep in? But when I glanced at the open window, I realized that my short sleep had lengthened into something else entirely. Dark was already falling.

"I..." But words failed me as I faced five astonished faces, all turned toward me, all rendered speechless with apparent shock.

But the silence didn't last long. And as soon as one began to speak, the other four all joined in.

"Who are you?"

"You're in my bed!"

"Did you eat my toast?" That one sounded even more accusatory than the question about the bed.

"Wow, you're so beautiful!" That one was said by the smallest of the faces, a young girl who couldn't have been more than five and who would have looked cherubic with her blond curls and blue eyes if not for the giant streak of dirt that ran up one cheek, across her nose and into her hairline.

"Um..." I had never gotten around to preparing that speech, and I wasn't sure I could have delivered it to five astonished and enraged children anyway.

"Who are you?" asked the oldest, the one who had previously accused me of occupying her bed. Her darker skin suggested she had originated further south, and her glossy black hair had been carefully combed and plaited into two straight braids before being pinned to her head. She was also the first speaker, the one who had complained that the toast boy hadn't cleaned up breakfast.

I opened my mouth to ask after their parents, when the door opened, banging against the wall as two more figures strode in.

"There you are," said the oldest girl. "You'd better lock the door for once. We've started getting intruders."

"Intruders?" One of the newcomers scoffed as he kicked off his boots and flung his jacket onto a pile next to the door. "What's that supposed to mean?"

He swung around before the question was fully out of his mouth, and his eyes fell on me, still sitting bolt upright in the small bed. His mouth fell open, and apparently no one felt the need to reply.

The other new arrival was the tallest of the lot, but his gangly frame made it obvious he was still in the awkward phase of a growth spurt. I looked behind them, but the door didn't open again, and the last of the light was well and truly fading now.

"But...but you're all children." The words escaped my mouth before I could think them through.

The younger of the two newcomers scoffed again. "What were you expecting? Dwarves?"

I looked at the small chairs, haphazardly surrounding the low table, and felt foolish. But how could I have anticipated a lone house in the middle of the forest to be full of unsupervised children? A quick headcount told me there were seven. The same number as plates of breakfast, if you discounted the ones that appeared to have been used for serving. Obviously four of them must share the big bed. It was certainly large enough.

But who were they?

"Who are you?" The question—asked by the children for the third time—mirrored my own thoughts. But with a pang I realized they had more right to wonder than I.

I scrambled out of the bed, straightening the blanket neatly behind me, the effort looking foolish next to the chaos of the rest of the house.

"Umm...I'm Snow."

"Snow? That's a funny name." It was the cherubic girl again.

I started to tell her it was only a nickname but cut myself off before I could get any words out. If these children didn't recognize me, it was far better for all of us that I kept my identity to myself. So I merely shrugged.

"What are you doing in our house?" The older boy's manner was less belligerent than his companion, but the serious look in his eyes lent his words more weight.

"I'm so sorry," I said, the words tumbling over each other. "I got lost in the woods. I've been walking and walking, and I hadn't eaten in days. I knocked, but no one came, and I saw the food. It looked like you were done with it, so..." I looked from face to face, my own heating up. "And then I saw the beds, and...I truly didn't mean any harm."

"She ate my toast." The younger boy directed the comment at the two newcomers since everyone else could hardly help already being aware. "I was going to eat it when I got home."

The scoffer just rolled his eyes. "Weren't you on clean up this morning?" He eyed the cluttered table disparagingly.

The toast boy launched into a long and involved defense of his lack of cleaning, and all of the children joined in on one side or the other except for the oldest boy who continued to eye me speculatively.

"You said you got lost," he said, his voice cutting over the argument and pulling my attention away from the squabble. When I looked over at him, he had something familiar in his hands. My bag. I didn't even remember dropping it near the entrance. My heart sank.

"Because this is a strange thing to take with you for a walk in the woods," he said. "Are you sure you weren't running away?"

Sudden silence fell. Now he had the undivided attention of everyone in the room. Until one by one the children turned wide eyes back to me. They looked concerned, scared, or curious, depending on the set of eyes, but for once they all remained silent.

I worried at my lower lip. "I suppose you could say that."

One of the middle ones turned to the older girl. "She looks pretty young. Not much older than us, really."

The girl eyed me with a look that seemed far too old for her years. "No, not much older. And she's very beautiful." She bit her own lip before glancing at the tallest boy, who met her eyes across the heads of the youngsters.

The toast boy sighed heavily. "I suppose it's all right she ate my toast, then." He gave me a stern look. "Just this once. Since you were so hungry. But don't do it again. We don't eat each other's food."

I didn't need to look to tell who the subsequent scoff came from. "Don't we? Tell that to Louis."

"Hey!" One of the other boys spun around to glare at him while I tried to process their words.

"She can share the bed with me," said the dirty cherub, smiling at me in a friendly manner.

"Don't be ridiculous," said another girl. "There are already four of us sharing it, and she's bigger than any of us." She cast a quick look at the gangly boy. "Well, she's the oldest, anyway."

The young girl grimaced. "But I don't want Anthony sharing with us. He kicks!"

"Ummm…" I knew I hadn't been winning any points for eloquence so far, but I couldn't seem to think of anything to say. Did I understand what these children were implying? Were they inviting me to stay here?

The oldest girl sidled up to me and put a gentle hand on my arm. "You don't have to tell us what you're running from. There's no one who's likely to find you out here. It's safe. That's why we stay."

Her earnest eyes told me she had spent enough time outside this forest hideaway to have observed how a young and beautiful girl might find herself feeling harassed enough to want to flee, and I almost burst into tears at her insinuation. I only wished my situation were so simple.

Could I really take shelter with a bunch of children? The situation seemed ridiculous. And yet, I had to take shelter somewhere. And who else would not only not recognize me but ask me no questions either…

"Thank you," I said at last, acting the coward yet again. I knew I should walk out right now before I brought trouble to their door, but the vast forest scared me too much to face it alone. At least not yet. Not tonight. Perhaps tomorrow when it was light again…

"Woohoo! That makes us even!" crowed the middle girl who thought I shouldn't share the youngsters' bed. She stuck her tongue out at the toast boy who promptly began to chase her around the room.

The older boy, who still looked a shade uncertain, called them to order and commanded them to line up for introductions. They formed into a line in apparent age order, as if waiting for a royal inspection. With a shake of my head I reminded myself that these children had no idea I was a princess. And it needed to stay that way.

As I had guessed, the late arrival was the oldest, introducing himself as Ben. By his cracking voice, I guessed him to be thirteen, and surely not much older than the oldest girl who turned out to be called Daria. Despite their youth it was easy to see they took on an almost parental role over the younger children, although there was no hint of the couple between the two of them.

Next was Anthony, the scoffer. Followed by Louis, the apparent food thief. The middle girl, Danni, came next, and then the toast boy, Jack. Youngest of all was the cherub girl, Poppy.

How many times would I forget their names before I got them all straight in my head? The food and sleep had somewhat revived me, but I still felt heavy-headed and slow. I ran up and down the line with my eyes, repeating the names in my head like a litany.

Ben, Daria, Anthony, Louis, Danni, Jack, Poppy. Poppy, Jack, Danni, Louis, Anthony, Daria, Ben.

Then I reminded myself that I couldn't stay here long enough for it to matter. Just long enough for me to regain some strength…And maybe get some tips on foraging in the forest.

Anthony—the scoffer, and the third oldest—had started glaring at me, and when his gaze flicked to one of the small beds next to the one I had appropriated, I could guess why.

"I don't move much in my sleep," I said. "I'm sure I wouldn't take up much room in the big bed." My eyes fell on the still-messy table. "And why don't I help you clean up breakfast, Jack? It must be time for the evening meal soon." I hoped my words didn't sound too hopeful.

Jack just stared at me with wide eyes. "Wow, she's actually nice!"

What about my appearance made that a surprise? My age? My looks? Or just the fact that I had earlier stolen his toast? Danni rolled her eyes and shoved him with one shoulder.

"None of us are going to offer to help with *your* chore, so you shouldn't stand there like an idiot. She might change her mind."

That effectively galvanized him into action, and he rushed forward to take one of my hands, tugging me toward the table. How old was he? Six? His grip felt nothing like Alexander's, and yet the feel of his hand in mine reminded me of my missing friend. His had been the last touch I felt, and it already seemed distant enough to have been a dream.

I remembered the sensation of being cradled safely against his chest and had to fight back tears. What had happened to him? Where could he be?

Thankfully Jack didn't notice my distress, keeping up a running stream of words as he instructed me on their usual practice for disposing of leftovers and washing the plates. I worked as quickly as I could, despite the unfamiliar tasks, conscious that the eyes of all the children dwelt on me as they busied themselves with their own evening activities.

Somewhat to my surprise, it was Anthony who took the lead in preparing what appeared to be a stew, although both Poppy and Louis assisted him in a somewhat haphazard fashion. Listening to their chatter, I realized that most of the chores were shared on some sort of rotating basis.

With a flush of embarrassment, I realized how ill-equipped I was to be added to such a roster. I had no idea how to scramble eggs or cook a stew. Or even gather the eggs in the first place—beyond the general assumption that it must involve going into the coop and then looking around. How would I explain my ineptitude?

But thankfully, for the evening at least, they stayed true to their promise not to ask questions. And the smell of the stew soon made other thought difficult. I still restricted myself to small bites and slow chewing, but I let myself eat until my stomach felt uncomfortably full. My bowl still held food when this happened, so it hadn't been my imagination earlier. My stomach had shrunk.

When I noticed Louis eyeing my leftovers, I pushed them over to him with a smile. His eyes lit up, and he dug in without a word. Anthony shook his head, his face scornful, but Ben looked at me approvingly. I managed a smile for him as well, although my muscles seemed to have grown more sore from the rest than they had done from the previous exertion, and even sitting felt almost unbearably painful.

I forced myself to leap up and help with clearing the table after the meal, anyway, earning a head nod from Danni whose turn it seemed to be. I had no great experience with children, but I had expected a house without adult presence to be chaos in the evening, with no one interested in bed. But to my surprise, all of the younger children drifted quickly toward their various beds, Louis, Danni, Jack, and Poppy all piling into the big bed, while

Anthony took the smaller one on the end. His face defied me to go back on my earlier words, so I carefully avoided any indication of dismay or disapproval.

Only Ben and Daria remained sitting at the faded fire, having pulled over two chairs from the table. My back ached almost unbearably, and I longed for one of the comfortable sofas from my personal sitting room back home. But I tried to remember instead the discomfort of the previous night, and to remind myself that the aches and pains from my headlong flight and two nights sleeping on the ground would pass soon enough.

And if that was the worst I suffered, I could count myself fortunate. Memory of my stepmother's orders to Randolph flashed through my mind, and I shivered. Daria watched me, her eyes concerned, so I made myself smile and gathered several cushions in front of the fire to sprawl on. At least they were softer than the too-small wooden chairs.

For a long time, silence reigned, the murmurs and grunts and sighs of the younger children giving way to the rhythmic breathing of sleep. Daria, who had been occupied in knitting something that looked like a sock, put her work aside and gave Ben a significant look. He murmured something about checking on the donkey and slipped from the cottage.

Daria grabbed a cushion of her own and lowered herself to sit beside me. My eyes had begun to droop, but I stiffened at her presence, my mind racing again.

For the second time this evening, the younger girl placed a gentle hand on my arm.

"I said you didn't have to tell us anything, and you don't. But sometimes it helps to talk about it. And if you want to talk…"

I stared at her face, so full of concern and sympathy. What would happen if I opened my mouth and spilled out the truth?

CHAPTER 7

*B*ut for all her air of weary responsibility, this girl was years younger than me. And she had no experience of the world of royalty and privilege and duty and intrigue and disguised hatred from which I had fled. How could I, who felt so insufficient myself, place such a weight and a burden on her?

And what would she do if she knew what danger followed you? asked the unpleasant voice in my head. *What would happen to you if she decided you were too much of a danger for her sanctuary?*

I pushed the thought away. I had neither seen nor heard any sign of pursuit since I had awoken without Alexander in the forest. And he had gone to great lengths to hide our tracks before that. No one was following hot on my heels. I could afford one night of rest.

Still, I felt guilty that she clearly thought I had fled unwanted attentions. And I felt I should say something to prepare her for how little I knew of this life.

"Thank you for your shelter," I said. "I appreciate it more than I can say. I won't stay long—"

She quickly shook her head. "I don't mean to chase you away. We all have stories we prefer not to remember." She glanced back at the sleeping figures, her face darkening. "But this is truly a safe haven. You are the first person to ever stumble upon us. And I've been living here for years. And Ben's been here longer than that."

I frowned at the fire. "But how did you all end up here, then?"

She shrugged. "Ben and I were the first. And we were brought here by the old lady who originally owned this cottage. Her husband built it, apparently, although she never told us why they wished to live so remotely. And he had died before even Ben arrived. I guess she took us in because she was lonely."

I examined her face since her own gaze had latched onto the fire. There was sadness there when she spoke of the lady, but not deep grief. What had she been like? My own thoughts wanted to turn to my father, but I forced them to stay on Daria's words. I had allowed myself to be swallowed by grief for far too long and look where it had led me. I had been completely unprepared for my stepmother's plans.

"There's a small town two days' ride from here," she continued.

I stiffened, unsure whether I felt more fear or hope.

Daria quickly laid a reassuring hand on my arm. "Don't worry, no one from there knows where we live. And we always take care to wind through the trees in a different pattern, so we don't make any sort of permanent track."

I threw her a questioning look, and she explained that they had a small cart and a single donkey. "He's old but serviceable, and we usually use him for hauling rocks. But several times a year some of us make the trek into the town to trade for things we can't make ourselves. Once we even went further, all the way to Lestern."

"It's a small city on the coast," she explained, presumably because of the spasm that crossed my face at the mention of the center of my grandfather's holdings.

"Yes, I've...I've heard of it," I managed.

"And on some of our trips we've found someone new to join

us," she said when I didn't elaborate. "Children like us who had nowhere else to go. Or who needed a refuge—somewhere far away and safe. The villagers are used to us now, they don't question our presence. And we don't have anything valuable enough to tempt anyone to try to find where we come from."

I regarded her with wonder. She said the words so simply, as if they were nothing. As if she hadn't come from nothing herself and yet found a way to do such good in the lives of others, despite her few years.

"And so, you see, you're perfectly safe here," she told me earnestly, taking my hesitation for uncertainty and fear.

"Yes, yes, I see," I said slowly. "I just..." I bit my lip, trying to think of the best way to frame my words. "I'm afraid I won't be much use to you all. I know I'm the oldest here, but I'm not used to a life like this. I don't..." I looked down at my hands as my words trailed away.

Daria placed her own hands over my clasped ones. "Yes, I noticed."

I looked quickly up at her, and she smiled. "Your hands, I mean. You don't have the hands of someone used to a life like ours."

I flushed, but she just shrugged.

"And yet, whatever the life you're used to looks like, something happened to send you flying from it. That's all I need to know. The rest you'll learn soon enough. I'm sure you'll be of more use than Poppy was when she first arrived. She was little more than a baby when we found her." She chuckled softly, and I shook my head in fresh wonder.

I still felt a tug to reassure her somehow that I had not fled from what she feared for me. But then I remembered what I had fled from. A dead father. A stepmother who hated me enough to order her loyal henchman to take me out into the forest and rip me apart as if I had been set upon by a pack of wild animals.

A shudder ran through me despite the almost unpleasant heat

of the fire. What I had run from was bad enough. Perhaps nothing needed to be said, after all.

The quiet sound of the door opening made us both jump, but it was just Ben. His presence dispelled any further chance of confidences, and we all began to move toward bed.

When I eyed the enormous bed, full of sleeping children, Daria appeared beside me again.

"If you'd like, I could—"

But I cut off her offer before she could finish. "I've already stolen your bed once today. I won't do it again. I'll be fine in this one. Truly."

And despite my earlier nap, I now felt so tired I believed my own words. Poppy had snuggled against Danni in her sleep, so I slipped in on her other side, curving myself around her small sleeping shape. I took care not to actually touch her, but I needed to use all the space I could wrangle if I wanted to avoid falling straight back out again.

I had done nothing to exert myself, but my heart raced, and I took deep, careful breaths in an effort to slow it down. Was all of this just a dream? Would I wake to find myself still on the ferns with Alexander keeping watch beside me? But the aches in my legs and back told me his absence was no dream. And the soft pillow beneath my head told me my new haven was no dream either. And yet, when I thought of my life only three short days ago, it was hard to believe any of it could be real.

What would my father say if he could see me now?

When I swam back up to consciousness, roused by a variety of unfamiliar sounds, I found that my efforts to remain separate from my bedfellows had been thwarted by sleep. I lay some distance from the edge of the bed, Poppy sprawled across my legs, and both of Danni's arms clinging to one of mine.

Danni must have woken at the same time as me, though, because she hastily pushed my arm away, sitting up and clambering out of bed over the protesting form of Jack. Louis had already left; in fact I couldn't see him anywhere in the large room.

Poppy was harder to dislodge, reminding me of a contented cat who had found a comfortable stretch of sunshine. But Danni, who had sped out of the cottage only to quickly return with a clean but dripping face, soon pulled her protesting from the bed and sent her outside to "help Louis."

The two children soon returned together, bickering over something and both carrying a small basket with fresh eggs. Some of them even still had small, wispy feathers clinging to them. I tried to disguise my interest in such a trivial thing, but Danni gave me a curious glance and Daria a knowing one.

Over breakfast I could make little sense of the general chatter and ended up having to beg for an explanation. It turned out that as well as tending to the chickens and the garden and chopping wood and laying small traps in the surrounding forest, the children had discovered a shaft from a long-abandoned mine.

"All the main veins were well and truly tapped a long time ago," Ben explained. "But we can find small slivers that were trapped in too much rock to be worth collecting by the miners. And if we're careful and slow we can work them free."

"Gemstones!" said Jack, his eyes shining.

I admired his enthusiasm for something that sounded like exhausting and back-breaking work for little reward.

"We trade them in the village for the supplies we need," Daria added. "Many of the villagers are the children of the old miners, and they think we're crazy to work so hard for slivers that are worth so little. But we don't really have any other choice—we don't grow or collect enough of anything else that we could use to trade."

"What about hunting, and skins, and such?" I asked, thinking of Alexander.

Anthony shot me a hard look, a harsh laugh in his tone. "Poaching you mean? Doesn't strike us as a good idea. Not when we don't want anyone nosing around our business."

"Oh." I flushed, once again feeling foolish. I had forgotten that the forest was largely owned by the crown, except for the portions owned by large estates such as my grandfather's. That's why the castle was able to employ a whole team of huntsmen. No one else was permitted to hunt anything but the smallest game. "I didn't think...No, of course not."

Anthony narrowed his eyes. "Obviously not."

Daria shot him a glance before speaking to me in a much kinder tone. "Even a small village like the one near us has royal officials who would report the appearance of any stolen hunt. And a good thing for us, too, or we wouldn't find ourselves so alone out here. But the royal hunters don't venture so far, and no one else dares risk it. Not when they can't sell or trade their catch."

Anthony gave a small snort, and she rolled her eyes at him. "You know what I mean."

I looked back and forth between them, and she took pity on me again. "Lots of the forest-dwellers poach for their own tables if they think they can get away with it, of course. But no one lives this far in but us. And it's not worth it for others to trek so far merely for their own table. Not when they can't gather a full catch and trade what they don't need."

"Oh, I see."

I wanted to tell them all that I actually knew a great many things. But somehow I didn't think they'd be very impressed by my knowledge of exactly what depth of curtsy was required for foreign dignitaries of different ranks. And it would certainly raise some unfortunate questions. So I swallowed my pride and took the pitying and condescending looks thrown my way with what grace I could muster.

It was a lesson I had to repeat many times throughout the day. Even Poppy and Jack at times became my instructors. I didn't find even a single chore that I could do unaided except for the sweeping, which I rushed to do before someone else could claim the broom, desperate to be able to do at least something. And even then I could see Daria itching to show me a better way. But thankfully for my sense of self-worth, she refrained, and let me complete the job in my own, inefficient style.

Ben, Anthony, Louis, and Danni had all taken the donkey and cart to the abandoned mine while Daria stayed behind to supervise Jack and Poppy—and me. She explained that one of the older ones always stayed behind to keep an eye on the younger two, but I suspected she had taken the task today in order to help me.

Apparently, the day before, Louis had taken Jack and Poppy out berry-picking, hence the reason why I had found an empty house. The others had only collected them on their way back home.

Their efforts had been fruitful, and Jack and Poppy bounced around all morning in high spirits while Daria prepared dough for several pies. I watched her work with interest, but she refrained from requesting my assistance for any but the simplest baking task.

Instead I helped feed the chickens, weed the vegetable patch, and collect bucket after bucket of water. Daria thanked me profusely each time I popped back inside, explaining that Poppy and Jack were no use for fetching water, but her gratitude only made me uncomfortable. The smell of the baking pies filling the cottage only reminded me who exactly it was that owed the most gratitude in this situation.

The others returned earlier than they had the day before, drawn by the promise of pie, I suspected, and Danni carefully showed me several tiny slivers of winking light which she tipped onto her palm from a small leather pouch.

"Diamonds," Jack breathed, peering over my arm.

I heaped praise on them, hoping my face didn't show how small and few they seemed for so many hours of work. Daria met my eyes over the heads of the others, and I suspected she must have guessed something of my thoughts. But her expression reminded me of her earlier words. They had reason to be grateful for the meagerness of their haul. If enough of value remained to be truly worth the effort, then others would have come chasing it.

When I leaned back in my chair after the meal, my belly warm and full of sweet pie, I remembered with a start that I had been going to leave during the daylight. I bit my lip. Tomorrow would do just as well, no doubt.

Except that when the next day came, the children explained that they were to take a day off from the mine in order to check their collection of traps. Naturally they expected me to accompany them, and it seemed too good an opportunity to pass up. While we walked through the forest, I could ask which plants and berries were safe to eat. Perhaps I might even be able to learn how to set up a small trap and skin any catch.

But at the end of the day, it was clear I needed more than a single day's lessons in such craft. And so I told myself that another day could do no harm. We had seen and heard no sign of anyone.

And so another day passed. And then another. And then another. I needed help with fewer and fewer chores now. And it became increasingly hard to imagine anyone intruding on our small bubble of forest. The children assured me that no one ever came here, and every indication supported their assertions.

The exuberant energy of the younger ones, and the simple routines of their life, made it hard at times to remember there even was a world outside this stretch of forest. Except at night. I had grown accustomed to sleeping with two small girls tucked up beside me, or sprawled over me, but I could not keep away the dark thoughts that night allowed in. Grief for my father. Fear for Alexander.

But I had learned to shed my tears silently. And eventually sleep always overtook me.

Finally a momentous day came. Daria announced that I was to be the one to remain behind to supervise Jack and Poppy. The younger four all regarded me with wide eyes, even Danni and Louis seeming to think I should be honored by being found worthy of the responsibility. Perhaps they remembered the first day they themselves had been deemed up to the task. Anthony, still wary of me, hid a smile at their expressions, and made no protest to the arrangement.

And for all my advanced years—at least in comparison to this bunch—I actually found myself nervous as I waved the rest of them off. There had been no sign of the dreaded wild animals, but I kept imagining a wolf or a bear appearing from the trees to snatch one of the children. I couldn't even guess what I would do in such a situation.

So preoccupied was I with this unlikely possibility that I reacted instinctively to the faint crack of a twig behind me. As a tall shadow swept over the ground, I snatched up a sturdy branch —one I had previously taken note of for just such a purpose—and swung around to face the intruder with a beating heart and a scream of warning on my lips.

But it wasn't a bear I faced. It was a man.

CHAPTER 8

For an unthinking second, I stood frozen. And then madness overtook me, and I charged toward him, screaming a challenge, my branch swinging in front of me.

All I could think of was Jack's mischief and Poppy's trusting face, and the dark intentions of those who pursued me. I could not let this man take back news of my location to Randolph.

My panic clouded my vision, and I could barely make out his hooded form as I swung the branch toward the lump of his head. He neatly side-stepped my attack, gripping the branch and ripping it from my grasp. Stepping forward, he interrupted my forward momentum, swinging me easily around until he had me trapped in his arms, my back against his chest.

I screamed again and tried to kick backward but was unable to gain any purchase. His voice finally made its way through to my consciousness.

"Snow! Snow! Stop!" A familiar voice.

I went limp in his arms, my eyes fluttering closed as relief robbed my limbs of the surging energy the fear had provided.

"Jack!" Poppy's high voice sounded as soon as she rounded the corner of the cottage, no doubt drawn by the screams which I had intended to send her running. "Come look! There's a man hugging Snow."

At her words, Alexander's arms dropped instantly away from me, and he stepped backward just as I stepped quickly forward. I glanced back at him in time to see the same flush I felt on my cheeks reflected on his.

Jack careened around the corner, nearly sending Poppy flying.

"A man! What man? Oh…" He slid to a stop and gaped at Alexander.

"That man," said Poppy, pointing at him unnecessarily.

I cleared my throat, my mind still reeling from all the rapid changes of emotion. "His name is Alexander."

Both children turned to look at me.

"Is he a friend of yours?" Jack seemed unafraid of the unknown adult intruding on his domain, and I wondered if either of these two even remembered the circumstances that had forced them to flee into the forest. I found myself hoping they didn't remember enough to make them afraid, even as I hated how vulnerable their fearlessness made them.

If it had been someone other than Alexander who had so easily disarmed me…

"Yes." I tried to make my voice sound confident and sure although my limbs still trembled. "He's my oldest friend. You don't have to be afraid of him."

The words seemed pointless since they clearly weren't, but I couldn't help uttering them. Perhaps I was the one who still needed reassurance.

Jack's eyes had stuck on the large bow and quiver slung across Alexander's shoulder. "Are you a poacher?"

Poppy followed his gaze, her eyes equally wide. "Have you ever shot a bear?"

"Uh…" Alexander looked between them and then toward me.

I shrugged helplessly.

"No and no," he said after a brief pause. He focused his gaze on Poppy, perhaps deciding hers was the safer question. "Bears are a little large for a bow and arrow. It would likely take many shots to bring one down, and in the meantime you would be facing a large and enraged animal. In desperate circumstances, or with a team of hunters..." He shrugged and then smiled. "But I prefer to just avoid them. There aren't actually that many in the forest, you know."

"Ooohhhh." Poppy's face suggested she had fallen just as hard for Alexander's sincerity and capable air as I had done so long ago. I hid a smile, but it quickly turned wistful as my eyes strayed back to him.

I couldn't help visually checking over him, looking for signs of injury or illness or harm of any kind. Because I had spent a lot of nights worrying about what had happened to him. And now that he was standing in front of me, strong and whole, my relief mingled with faint traces of resentment. Where had he been? Why had he left me, and why had it taken so long for him to find me?

When he looked over and met my eyes, such a weight of grief and fear and relief met me, that I revised my first impression. Perhaps something terrible had happened to him after all. Something whose scars were hidden beneath his clothes. And his face held as many questions as mine, but he was as unable to ask them as I was, equally restrained by the presence of two curious sets of ears.

The thought of the children reminded me of the most urgent thing.

"Is there anyone coming? Are we in danger?"

He shook his head before I had even finished speaking, and a fresh wave of tension leached from my body. I had done little in the way of chores this morning, but I already felt weak and tired.

"Well, in that case, I suppose you can make yourself useful until the others return."

"Others?" He looked curiously from the cottage to Jack and Poppy.

I nodded. "There are five more." He glanced at the small cottage again, and I smiled. "All children."

"All children?"

"Yes. So are you going to stand there all day repeating me, or are you going to make yourself useful?" I put my hands on my hips, putting on a show for the sake of the younger children.

He grinned at me easily, some of the fear falling from his gaze as he watched me, his eyes making the same assessment of me I had previously made of him.

"Yes, Your Majesty."

The title made me stiffen, but I forced my body to relax. "Oh, haha, very funny." I exaggerated my words, rolling my eyes before shooting him a glare that the children couldn't see.

Sorry! he mouthed at me, and I just rolled my eyes again.

I surveyed the clearing thoughtfully. We couldn't talk with the children here, and we couldn't leave them alone. So I might as well make him useful. My eyes fell on the dwindling pile of wood just peeking from the back of the cottage.

"There's an ax around the back. In the top of the wood pile. Can you cut us some more wood?"

Alexander rocked back on his heels once, his eyes darting around the clearing before he shrugged. "Certainly."

I almost suggested he put his bow and arrow inside, but I knew better than to expect him to be parted from it while he was still in the forest. Instead I waved him around the house and tried to chase the children back to their assigned tasks.

It didn't take long to realize this effort was doomed to failure. The allure of Alexander was simply too strong. So when the others returned, it was to find the three of us lined up on the ground, watching with rapt interest as Alexander chopped up a large branch he had dragged out from the surrounding forest. Naturally I was supervising the children and making sure they didn't venture too close to the swinging ax. My presence had nothing whatsoever to do with the fact that at some point during the afternoon Alexander had removed his shirt and jacket, the muscles of his broad chest and shoulders bunching and rippling with each swing of the ax.

Despite my unimpeachable motives, I jumped guiltily at the first startled exclamation behind us. It was followed by another and another until the tumult of confused noise joined with Jack and Poppy's excited explanations, rendering the whole lot of it impossible to understand.

I scrambled to my feet—casting one sympathetic glance at Alexander, who stood frozen, ax still in hand and sweat on his brow—and shouted for silence. Amazingly they all actually obeyed, their eyes swinging between me and Alexander.

"This is Alexander," I said. "He's an old friend of mine." I carefully met both Ben and Daria's eyes. "An old, trusted friend. He came looking for me, and I thought I'd put him to work while we waited for you all to return."

"I thought the wood pile looked bigger." Ben's eyes measured Alexander without the antagonism that lingered in Anthony's gaze.

Alexander wiped his shirt across his face before slipping it back on. "I'm just following orders." He gave Ben an easy smile while I glared at him, willing him not to start calling me Your Majesty again.

"Will you be...staying for dinner?" Daria sounded wary.

Alexander glanced between her and me, his eyes asking me a question.

"Yes," I answered quickly for him. "We'll help, of course. We can gather water for you right now." My eyes pleaded with her, and she seemed to understand, giving me a small nod.

"Very well. Louis and Anthony, you can bring in that wood he's just chopped for the fire. Danni, Jack, Poppy, you can help me with the dinner."

"But I—" Jack took two steps toward Alexander before Daria cut him off.

"I think there was a pie left from our baking yesterday. Unless Louis ate it while I wasn't looking."

"Hey!" Louis turned indignantly, a chunk of wood already in his hand.

Jack gasped and ran for the house, Danni and Poppy trailing behind. I smiled gratefully at Daria. I didn't deserve her endless consideration. But neither was I going to waste it.

I ran for the house after them, almost tripping in my haste, and returned with two wooden buckets. Alexander tried to take them both, but I only handed over one, leading him down to the water.

Only Ben remained outside, but after watching us silently for a moment, he sighed and joined the others inside. I didn't know how long Daria would manage to keep the younger ones contained, so my words spilled over each other, almost too fast to be decipherable.

"What happened? Where have you been? Are you all right? How did you find me?"

Any hope of his understanding me was thwarted by his own stream of simultaneous questions. We both stopped, and he quirked an eyebrow at me while I shook my head.

"I'm the princess, I get to go first."

Now it was his turn to shake his head at the familiar words from our childhood. I had always needed every possible advantage just to keep pace with the huntsman's son.

"Very well then, *Your Majesty.*"

"Stop that!" I said, knowing he was only trying to rile me but glancing uncomfortably back at the cottage anyway. A small face, Jack's I suspected, peered at us from one of the front windows. But for now, we were still alone.

I took a deep breath, trying to decide which question to begin with.

"What happened? Why did you leave?" I decided on as he knelt to fill his bucket.

He looked up quickly, regret filling his face. "I only meant to be gone for a short time. You were sleeping so peacefully..."

"Well?" I prompted, too impatient for him to tell the story at his own pace. "What happened?"

"I went to do some scouting, to see if they had picked up on our trail." He scowled. "They hadn't, but your stepmother must have had at least half the guard combing the forest. And some had managed to get disconcertingly close. I had to detour to lay decoy tracks. I was going to circle back around, but..."

"They caught you." The blood rushed from my head, and I checked his body again for signs of injury.

His hands balled into fists as he dropped his gaze toward the water. "Randolph got the drop on me. I'm sorry, Snow." He shook his head, still not looking at me. "I failed you."

Just the mention of Randolph had me shaking. "What did he do?"

Alexander busied himself filling up my bucket which I must have dropped at some point after we arrived at the stream.

"He was suspicious to see me, of course. I had no choice but to pretend I'd been out hunting since the day before and had no idea what was going on. And when he ordered me to use my tracking skills to join the search..."

He stood up abruptly, his face showing how keenly he had felt my abandonment. He was usually more reserved in his display of emotions. Did he want to make them clear to me now? Or was just the memory of it too much for him to hide?

A small feeling of betrayal—one that had lodged itself deep in my heart without my awareness—broke loose and dissolved. I had been right in refusing to doubt Alexander. He would never willingly abandon me.

"At least I was able to lead them far away from you," he continued. "But still I feared. Had Randolph seen through me?

Had he sent guards to search the places I carefully had him avoid?" He took a step closer, the water sloshing in the buckets. His earnest eyes pleaded with me to believe him. "I tried to convince him I could track better on my own, but he would have none of it. No doubt he knew that if I found you, I would never turn you over to them. I had to aid in the search for days and—when they finally abandoned it—I had to return with them to the capital."

"Abandoned it?" My fear melted into delight. "They've ceased searching for me?"

He frowned, his lips twisting slightly. "They cease to scour the forest, certainly. But do you really believe your stepmother will ever stop searching for you?"

My mood deflated, reality crashing quickly back in. "No, I suppose not," I mumbled. Now it was my turn to twist away, hiding my face and my constant foolishness from him.

"Snow." His voice was gentle. Too gentle. "At least the immediate danger has lessened. And enough days passed that I was able to leave for one of my usual hunting trips. The location where I had left you was burned in my memory, but your trail from there had gone cold. And I had to ensure that their letting me leave wasn't just a ruse. It took me a full day to be sure no one was tracking me." He grimaced. "I would have got here sooner if I could."

I placed a hand on his arm. I wanted to tell him that I knew, that I trusted him. But I also knew I didn't need to say the words. My touch was enough. Alexander and I had always trusted each other.

His breathing slowed slightly, deepened. He looked back up toward the cottage. Three faces watched us from the windows now.

"I feared the worst." His voice was soft, almost inaudible. "I certainly never imagined this."

I chuckled, shaking my head. "Who could have? I certainly did not."

"But who are they? And how did you end up here?"

"I followed the stream. It was heading west, and it provided me with water. I thought it would lead me to people eventually."

He looked impressed, and a flush of guilt made me look briefly away. When summarized like that it sounded far more canny than I had actually been. But I didn't want to tell him what it had really been like. Not when he clearly already carried his own load of guilt.

And not when the truth would make you look so very incompetent and helpless. I shifted, thrusting the internal voice away. My truth was already too heavy, I didn't need more in this moment.

Instead I rushed to explain the situation to him, describing the children and the haven they had built. "I only meant to stay a day or maybe two, but…"

I trailed away, the guilt flaring again. It was hard to defend myself, to explain how isolated it had felt. Not now that he had arrived, proving we were still moored to the rest of the kingdom after all.

"I'm glad you stayed," he said. "I could have been chasing you forever."

He was being kind. Even with all the factors slowing him, I would never have been able to outrun him on my own. Not at the pace I had been traveling before I found the cottage.

I glanced again at the watching faces. "I suppose we should go in." I looked down at the buckets in his hands. "We have the water now."

He nodded and stepped toward the door. The faces disappeared.

When we came in, everyone pretended to be busy about their various tasks. The younger children's efforts were lackluster at best, but we had taken long enough that the meal was almost ready anyway.

After a single lingering glance around the inside of the cottage, Alexander crossed to the table and lowered himself to the ground beside it. The low table was too high for him like that, but it would be workable. Less ridiculous than him attempting to fold his long body into one of the small chairs. And more diplomatic, as well. We had only eight chairs.

With Alexander safely at the table, the space in the cottage seemed to grow, a slight tension draining from the air. His adult frame had filled the space in a way that even seven children didn't.

Jack abandoned even the pretense of activity, edging closer and closer to Alexander, until at last he found the courage to take one of the chairs beside him. And once he had done so, the others rushed to follow. I hid a smile. No one wanted to be shown up by a six-year-old.

Once the food had been served there was a lull, as if no one quite knew how to start the conversation.

"So what do you do, Alexander?" Anthony's eyes lingered on the bow and quiver that Alexander had finally relinquished, leaving by the door. I suspected that, like Jack, he thought Alexander a poacher.

Alexander paused, considering his answer. "I'm a huntsman."

"A royal huntsman?" Ben sat straighter, exchanging a look with Daria. Alexander just shrugged.

"He was helping me," I rushed to say, my eyes on Daria. "And we got separated. That's how I came to be lost."

"Oh." Her face softened.

"But he doesn't hunt bears. They're too big." Poppy spoke the words gravely, as if the insight were her own.

"Thank you, Poppy, that's so helpful." Danni rolled her eyes.

"But he could shoot a bear. If he needed to." Jack seemed to feel the need to defend his new hero.

"If I needed to." Alexander's grave manner suggested he took the children seriously. And I could see it was making a favorable impression with them. "I just wanted to be sure Snow was safe," he added.

And with that I knew he had fully won over Daria. Ben still looked unsure. I was betting he hadn't forgotten the royal huntsman part. And no doubt he had noted our failure to provide any explanation.

"Must be nice to work for a king," said Anthony. Obviously he hadn't forgotten either.

"A queen, you mean," said Alexander.

I shot him a look, but he didn't meet my eyes. His words were true regardless, I supposed.

"Has the king died at last, then?" asked Louis.

His casual question sent a dart of pain through me, and the weight of Alexander's eyes told me he knew. I hoped none of the others noticed.

"We haven't been into the village in a while." Daria seemed to feel the need to defend their ignorance.

"We'll need to go soon," said Ben.

"And I suppose we'll find the taxes have been raised yet again." Anthony sounded sour, his eyes suggesting he placed the blame for this likelihood on Alexander.

Sadly it seemed all too likely a prospect with my stepmother now in charge of the kingdom. But my mind had snagged on one word.

"Again? What do you mean again?"

The older children all regarded me with surprised eyes. Even Alexander looked away, his posture uncomfortable.

"How long were you wandering around the forest?" Anthony snorted. "The taxes have only been raised four times in the last year already."

Four times? I opened my mouth to protest only to close it again. Why would he lie to me? And I hadn't really been paying attention to such things.

I bit my lip. So my stepmother hadn't even waited for my

father to die before beginning to change his policies. Had he known? But I instantly rejected that thought. He would not have stood for such a thing.

"Taxes?" Poppy wrinkled her nose. "Aren't those the things you were complaining about, Louis?"

The other boy sighed sadly. "We used to have pies like we made yesterday all the time. And other desserts and yummy things. But now we can't afford much sugar. That's what Daria says, anyway." He glared at the older girl as if it was her fault.

She reached over to pat Poppy's hand. "We have to buy essentials first. And pay the taxes. You all know that. If there's any coin left over, then…"

I quickly looked away, shame rushing through me that the children should be denied such a simple pleasure just to fill the palace coffers. Alexander reached out as if to place a comforting hand on my arm but let it drop before making contact. Clearly he had known. Why hadn't he told me?

Why didn't you ask? This time I didn't push the voice away. I had cocooned myself in my grief. Let it consume me. And my friend had respected that. The fault was mine.

A vision of the few winking slivers in Danni's hand filled my mind. How hard these children worked for the little they possessed. And Alida wished to strip even that away from them. For what? She already had enough diamonds for any one person.

But your father. What would knowing the truth have done to him?

The selfish thought stung me as I sat here among children who had taken me in, no questions asked. They had shared their food and their home—even their bed—although I had little to offer in return. Whatever it would have cost my father, our people deserved it. That was the burden of leadership.

I had been his shadow, keeping vigil at his bedside. But I should have been his eyes and ears. I knew Alida was not to be trusted. Which meant I was far more to blame than him.

And what about now? The needling thought made me grip my

fork so tightly I thought it would bend. *If you hid away then, what are you doing now?*

I took a deep breath and looked around the table. This cottage had been a haven when I needed one most, but I could not stay here. My kingdom needed me to return. To be a queen.

I just needed to work out how.

CHAPTER 9

*A*lexander made no offer to help with clearing up after the meal. No doubt he sensed how out of place he was within the cottage. Instead he gathered his bow and quiver and departed with a murmured thank you for the meal. At the door he paused, looking back at me as I trailed close to his heels.

"I'll sleep in the forest nearby. I'll be back in the morning."

I nodded, trying not to let him see the relief that filled me at his words.

"We'll talk properly then." He didn't wait for an answer before striding from the cottage. I swallowed, watching the door close behind him. A promise, or a threat?

I forced my spine to stiffen. No doubt he would disapprove of my plan to challenge Alida, but I had no hope of success if I bowed at the first hint of opposition. And from the most friendly of sources, as well.

I had told him earlier that I was a princess, and he must defer to me, although the words had been humorously meant. If I truly intended to pursue this path, however, I would have to make the words real. If I wished to take my place on the throne, I would have to become accustomed to command. It felt like a heavy burden, and one I did not wish to bear.

But if not me, who?

I wished, uselessly, that my mother had lived to give me brothers and sisters. Perhaps I could have abdicated safely to one of them. But my birth had destroyed that possibility. And I could only be glad Alida had borne no children. No doubt she would have long since arranged an unfortunate accident for me if she had a child of her own blood to inherit in my place. Perhaps she would even have willingly taken the title regent in such a circumstance.

But it was as empty a thought as the dreams of my mother. I alone had the right to the crown. I alone could challenge Alida without splintering the kingdom irreparably.

Was that why I had so dreaded my father's death? Because I shrunk from the responsibility it thrust on me? But that thought I squashed. I had loved my father with my whole heart. I would not doubt my feelings now. I would have mourned his death no less if ten older siblings stood between me and the throne.

I let myself dwell on my grief in the darkness of the night, shedding silent tears into the pillow. But when the sun rose, I put the tears away. Since my father had first taken ill, I had shed enough tears to fill a river. The time had come for action.

Carrying a bowl of porridge outside, I found Alexander lingering near the edge of the trees. He came forward and took it with a quiet thanks, making quick work of the hot food. Jack appeared just as he was finishing, his eyes full of excitement, but I thrust the bowl at him and told him to take it back inside.

I could see he wanted to protest, but a quick glance at Alexander made him change his mind and go scampering back toward the cottage. Eager, no doubt, to be of service. I took the opportunity of his absence to speak as quickly as I could.

"I'm going back to the capital. I have to challenge Alida and take the throne. She's going to destroy this kingdom otherwise."

He opened his mouth to respond, but I cut off his protest before he could utter it.

"The throne is rightfully mine. You said so yourself."

He tried again, but I once again jumped in too quickly for him.

"It doesn't matter what you say, Alex. I'm determined. I'm going back."

He opened his mouth for the third time, and I knew I should let him speak. He would say his piece eventually, no doubt. But in truth I still felt afraid. Afraid that I would weaken and give in to his arguments in favor of my safety. And so I once again went to cut him off.

"Snow!" He spoke loudly, overriding my flow of words. I stopped, startled, and he shook his head at me.

"I agree. You are the true queen, and Alida shouldn't be allowed to just steal the throne from you."

"Wait...what?"

I stared at him, my mouth hanging open, and he shook his head again.

"Haven't I been telling you from the start? I support the true queen."

I looked around quickly, but Jack had yet to reemerge. I lowered my voice to a whisper.

"So, you'll help me go back." I pulled a face. "I'm not actually sure I could find the way on my own."

"I'll help you. Of course. But not to go racing straight back to your death."

Ah. I deflated. I knew the protests would be coming.

"You're not ready to take her on, Snow."

I wished I could protest, but his words were so obviously true it felt pointless. If I returned, I would no doubt be dead long before I managed to face the court. It was the thought I had been trying not to think about ever since my new resolution to take back my throne.

He took a quick step forward at my defeated expression, gripping one of my elbows. "That doesn't mean we can't do it. Just that we need to be smart about it. To prepare the way."

I frowned, biting my lip, my mind racing.

"You're right. You need to train me." I gestured around us at the clearing. "And here we have the perfect opportunity."

"Ahh…" His brow crinkled, and he stepped away from me. "That wasn't exactly what I had in mind." He blinked a couple of times. "Train you…?"

"Yes." I nodded my head with decision, buoyed up by my new certainty. "I'm sick of feeling useless. I want to be able to move through the forest silently, like you do. And track. And find my own food. And defend myself. And climb walls without almost falling to my death. And just generally be able to sneak around."

I grinned at him triumphantly, and he laughed reluctantly.

"Just those, huh?"

I grimaced. "Well, maybe we can refine the list a little. Prioritize."

"Maybe that would be a good idea," he said gravely. "If you want to take back your throne this decade."

I punched him lightly in the arm. "Thanks for the vote of confidence, Alex."

But a slow grin was spreading across his face. "No, no. You have all my confidence. In fact, I think it's a great idea."

"You do?" I looked up at him suspiciously. "Really?"

"Really." He nodded once.

"Great." I rubbed my hands together, looking around us. "What should we start with?"

I half-expected him to protest an immediate start, but instead he seemed to take my question seriously. His eyes flicked several times to the cottage behind me, and I spun, expecting to find we'd finally gained an audience. But we were still alone, Daria somehow managing to keep them all inside.

"These children must know what they're doing," Alexander

said at last. "If they've survived out here on their own all this time."

I nodded. "I've been watching them and learning what I can. I certainly know more than I did before I arrived."

He looked pleased as he drummed his fingers against his leg, muttering to himself too quietly for me to hear.

"You want to learn to defend yourself," he finally said. "And I think that's an excellent idea. Do you think some of the older children might want to learn as well?"

I blinked at him, my thoughts racing to Daria's solemn expression when she had reassured me that she understood the dangers out there in the wider world. She had fled to a life in the forest because she never wanted those dangers to find her. But perhaps if she knew how to defend herself, she might feel differently about venturing out one day.

"They just might. Shall I ask them?"

Alexander nodded. "I'll wait out here. Either way we need to get started this morning." He shifted slightly and glanced up at the sun.

I ran for the house, musing over his words. I had expected him to think I was in too great a rush, but he seemed to be the one in a hurry.

I pulled Daria and Ben aside, glad to see that no one had left for the day while I was distracted talking to Alexander. My eyes locked on Daria, although my words were directed at them both.

"You saw how useless I was when I arrived here. I've been learning a lot from all of you, but I want to learn more. I want to learn how to defend myself. And my friend has agreed to teach me. We're wondering if you'd like to learn, too."

Daria looked startled, but Ben's eyes immediately flew to the window, as if he was hoping to get a glimpse of Alexander outside. His expression seemed pleased—and almost relieved. A pang shot through me. Ben had such a calm demeanor generally.

Unflappable. But how greatly did the care of all these younger children weigh on him?

"I suppose..." Daria glanced at Ben. Whatever she read in his eyes made her straighten her spine. "Yes, I suppose we would. I'm sure Anthony would like to learn as well. Perhaps we can cancel the trip to the mine for today."

Of course as soon as the plan was explained, the younger four clamored to be included. Alexander took this easily in stride, setting them to simple tumbling and running exercises with a gravity that made them accept their basic assignments with determination.

The older four of us he set up in pairs. I had thought he would put the girls and boys together, but instead he paired me with Ben. When he caught my glance, he shrugged.

"It's rare to need to defend yourself against someone smaller than you. Once I've shown you the basics, you'll all have a chance to practice against me."

He proceeded to walk us through a series of moves that would allow us to escape a captor's grip. He also showed us the best ways to temporarily unbalance or disable a potential captor.

"The aim is always to give yourself a chance to run," he explained, as we slowly mirrored the moves, making sure we had the technique right before trying them for real. "You would need far more training than I can provide to enable you to hold your own in a fight. But getting free and giving yourself a moment's head start—that's achievable. And could make the difference as far as survival."

When we actually started testing the moves on each other, the younger children all came over to watch. But when they realized that Alexander intended to drill us on the same moves over and over—and over—they quickly lost interest.

"You need do them so many times that your muscles remember even when your mind isn't thinking clearly," he explained. "And there's no way to do that except to practice. A lot."

I had wondered if Anthony might lose interest when it became monotonous, but he approached every exercise with grim persistence, never flagging or becoming distracted. The other two also kept pace without complaint, and I was reminded once again of what all of these children had already achieved. For years now they had maintained their refuge without adult assistance. And they had no one to turn to for training of any sort. Now that someone had unexpectedly arrived, they obviously didn't intend to waste the opportunity. Their determination inspired me.

With all the opportunities available to me, I had never even considered learning anything like this before. If I'd asked my father, he would no doubt have told me it was unnecessary, given I would always have guards to protect me. But he wouldn't have refused if I'd insisted. And I could always have asked Alexander to do it without going through my father at all. I had wasted so much time.

By the afternoon my muscles ached almost as much as on my first arrival at the cottage. But I also felt a swelling of pride. I could break Ben's hold from several different positions.

Then Alexander had us each attempt it with him as our partner. All pride immediately died. His muscles seemed to be made of iron, his arms so much longer and his grip so much stronger than Ben's. I couldn't escape from him.

Alexander himself had only praises for us all, however.

"You've made excellent progress for one day. The key is to just keep practicing. Keep building your strength and your technique, and soon you'll be able to break free from anyone."

I tried to hold onto his words through dinner, but my eyes kept drooping, my body and mind both exhausted by the new activity. It was hard to believe any of it could ever feel natural.

But, contrarily, as soon as I rolled into bed, my mind refused to drop into sleep. The even breathing of the younger ones soon told me I was the only one awake in the huge bed, but now that I was lying down, my sleepiness had fled. The underlying fatigue remained, but my mind was too active to give in.

And I found my thoughts circling my early morning conversation with Alexander. He had said that any attempt at re-taking the throne would require preparation. But he had then seemed surprised at my suggestion of training, so that obviously hadn't been the preparation he meant.

The answer, of course, was obvious. I should have seen it immediately. And once my mind started down that track, sleep became even more difficult. Eventually I slipped back out of bed and rummaged through my bag until I located a small piece of parchment and pen.

I wrote furiously for several minutes—with occasional pauses to stare into space. When I finished, I looked at the list I had made and wondered whether to be encouraged or discouraged at its length. But now that I had committed my thoughts to paper, my body was calling me toward sleep. I sighed and shoved the paper back into my bag. There was nothing more I could do tonight at any rate. I would discuss it with Alexander in the morning.

CHAPTER 10

*M*y late night meant I was one of the last to wake the next morning, scrambling out of bed to the smell of cooking breakfast. When I hurried toward the stream for a quick wash, I nearly stumbled, my gaze caught on an unexpected sight.

Daria and Alexander stood just inside the clearing, clearly in deep conversation. The girl sent me a contemplative look as soon as I appeared, and a flush raced across my face. What was Alexander telling her? I nearly changed direction and veered toward them, but neither gestured me over or called a greeting, so I kept to my original course. I would ask Alexander about it on my way back. Assuming they had finished by then.

But when I returned from the water, both of them had disappeared. I was the last to the breakfast table, so I refrained from questioning Daria in front of the others. Alexander hadn't joined us—in fact he hadn't entered the cottage since that first meal. Had someone already taken him food? Perhaps that had been what Daria was doing.

"Louis, you'll be staying back with Jack and Poppy," said Ben, interrupting my thoughts. "The rest of us will be back at the mine as usual. But we'll make a late start and take an hour to train before we go."

"I can watch the children," I said quickly. Did they mistrust me at the task since Alexander had shown up on my first day alone?

Daria shook her head. "Alexander has offered to check our traps for us. You're to go with him."

Ah. Another phase of my training then. And Alexander had already sorted it out with the children. I wasn't sure whether to be grateful or annoyed at being cut out of the process.

But after an hour of training—working muscles already sore from the day before—I didn't have the energy to be either. I tried to hide my exhaustion from Alexander as he led me into the forest, but I could see from the mix of compassion and amusement in his face that I had failed.

"It will hurt less over time, I promise," he said.

I made a face and didn't reply. Silence stretched between us as we walked, but it was the comfortable silence of old friends, used to each other's presence.

It had been a long time since we had spent a day in the forest together that didn't involve running for our lives. But it used to be a common occurrence. Of course I had been more interested in flower gathering in those days than in trapping or tracking, my only concerns being how to keep up with my long-legged friend and how to convince him to carry my flowers back for me when I gathered too many. He always protested, and then he always obliged in the end.

Of course, then he tried to get me to reciprocate by helping him carry any small game he managed to catch, but I'm afraid I was always far less amenable. I tried to make up for it whenever we got back, though, by sneaking into the kitchens and making off with sweet buns for us both. The pastry chef had a soft spot for me and always turned a blind eye.

The memories brought moisture to my eyes. Those had been

good days, before my father's long illness began. Alida had been the only shadow on our lives then. Neither my father nor I had ever said it aloud, but there was a reason we both escaped to the woods whenever we could, preferring the company of huntsmen to the court where we could not avoid my stepmother.

"How do you know where to find the traps?" I asked at last.

He glanced at me. "Ben told me the general direction and showed me the markers they use. I'll find them."

So he'd talked to Ben as well as Daria. I bit my lip. "I suppose you'd better tell me how to do it, too. What are you looking for?"

But he shook his head swiftly. "You're not here to help me with the traps."

"I'm not?"

"No, you're here so we could have a chance to talk in private. And so I could give you some more training."

"But this would be training. I want to know how to feed myself if I ever end up alone in the forest again."

"I know." He gave a little sigh, a shadow of his earlier guilt crossing his face. "But you don't need me to do that. These children can teach you how to recognize edible plants and how to set traps."

My eyes flew to his face. "You're leaving." It wasn't a question.

He grimaced. "I have to. I take extended hunting trips, sometimes, but there's a limit to how long I can be gone. I don't want to arouse any suspicions."

A pang shot through me as I tried to calm my suddenly racing heart. I hadn't forgotten the danger which lurked in the capital even though I had decided to return there myself as soon as I was ready. I hated the thought of Alexander far away from me, facing that danger on his own.

Because you'd be such a help? I pushed away the unwelcome thought. That's why I was training, after all.

I guess I'd hoped he could stay until I was ready. But the more I thought about it, the more obvious it became that such an idea had been foolish. Especially given the piece of parchment currently tucked into my dress.

I forced myself to straighten, trying to look as if I'd always known this was the plan.

"How long do you have?"

"I can stay for training tomorrow morning. But I need to be on my way back well before nightfall."

"So soon." I sighed. "That doesn't leave me much time. I'll have to work fast this evening."

He shot me a questioning look, and I managed a smile.

"I'm going to write some notes for you to deliver."

His eyebrows raised, so I rushed to add. "Anonymously, of course. I don't want anyone knowing you're involved in this."

His eyes narrowed, a shadow passing across his face as he regarded me silently. I waited for him to protest, but he didn't.

"Notes?" he asked instead.

"I was thinking about what you said. About being prepared. And I realized you didn't mean training."

"It's a good idea," he said, cutting in.

I smiled at him gratefully but continued. "You mean we need allies. Back in the capital. We need to make sure we have support, and that when the time comes we'll actually be able to rouse the court." I pulled out the parchment and handed it to him. "I made a list last night. Of all the nobles who I suspect are sympathetic to my claim."

He frowned as he took it from me. "Who are loyal to the crown, you mean. Who respect the law." Anger rumbled beneath his words.

I sighed and rubbed a hand across my face. "How can I blame them? When I'm terrified of Alida myself."

His eyes suggested he didn't forgive them so easily, but he made no further protest, instead running his gaze quickly down the list.

"It's short, I know." I twisted my hands together. "Shorter than I'd like, anyway. But I think it might be long enough."

I watched him anxiously, trying to read his thoughts on his face. He gave nothing away.

"Writing notes is a good idea." He glanced at me quickly for permission before folding the parchment and tucking it away. I didn't need it, I had the names memorized.

I worried at my lip as we continued to walk. "There's one thing I haven't figured out, though."

He glanced at me questioningly.

"How can they get a reply back to you? I might be wrong about some of them. And if I am, I don't want them being able to trace the note back to you."

"Leave that to me."

I stopped, reaching out to grab his arm. He halted and swung around to face me, his expression impassive.

"Alex, you have to promise me you'll deliver those notes anonymously. That you won't do anything to let any of them know who you are."

He didn't say anything, so I shook his arm.

"Promise me or I won't write them at all."

He sighed. "You should have more trust in me, Your Majesty."

I narrowed my eyes and raised my chin, and he actually chuckled.

"You look very regal, Snow."

I released his arm and put my hands on my hips. Was he teasing me?

"You haven't promised."

"Very well, I promise not to reveal myself to any of these people. I will think of a way for them to contact me and include it in a second note enclosed with yours."

I eyed him skeptically. "Perhaps I should include the instructions in my own note."

He shook his head. "I might need to change the arrangement

or use different ones for different nobles. I'll need to assess the situation once I'm back in the capital."

I considered his words before giving a reluctant nod. I didn't like it, but neither did I want to lock him in to something that might prove to be a dangerous course of action.

He paused for a brief moment before speaking again. "You know there's still going to be a danger that one or more of them can't be trusted?"

I resumed walking. "I know. I'll have to meet them in person eventually, too. But this is a start. The rest we can work out once we have a chance to read their replies." I looked down at the ground. "There's no path forward from here that doesn't contain at least some danger."

A short, uncharacteristic hitch in Alexander's stride was his only response. But I didn't need to look at his face to know that he was aware. And that he didn't like it. But what could we do? We were only two people against a queen. A usurping queen, perhaps, but currently a queen all the same. We had to start somewhere.

Neither of us spoke of it any further, and I was soon hard pressed to speak at all. It turned out that while Alexander assisted the children by checking and resetting their traps—making up for the day they lost to training yesterday—he had a series of endurance and strength exercises for me.

When we stopped in a clearing, he made me dash back and forth between two trees on either side of the small space, not letting me stop until I almost lost the contents of my stomach. When we stopped among trees, he made me climb one of the sturdier looking trunks. He called up soft advice on foot placement and ways to improve my grip, and by the end of the day he was selecting trees with more complicated branch placement.

When my arms began to shake from exhaustion and strain even when I wasn't climbing, he had me run again. By the time we returned to the children, I was wishing fervently I had never suggested training in the first place. In truth I might have abandoned the effort half way through the day except that Alexander never gave even the smallest hint he thought I might not be able to follow his instructions. And I wanted to prove him right.

But that wasn't the only thing, I realized as I dragged my tired feet back toward the cottage. I also wanted to prove something to myself. To prove that I had strength buried somewhere inside me. That I could be the sort of queen that subjects like my new friends deserved.

I wasn't convinced yet, though. Not when I could barely place one foot in front of the other. Not when I needed Alexander's presence to stop me from sinking into the first patch of fern I found and never moving again.

Only when we got back to the cottage and I collapsed into a chair, did I remember that I still needed to write all those notes. I put my head down onto my arms and groaned.

"Tough day?" Ben sounded a little too amused, and I lifted my head to glare at him. He actually chuckled.

"Poor thing," said Daria, as if she hadn't spent the day pounding at solid rock for little reward. "You just sit there, and we'll have food sorted in just a moment."

I opened my mouth to make a weak offer to assist but shut it when I remembered the notes. If she was giving me the reprieve, I needed to take it.

With murmured thanks, I drew out a clean piece of parchment and positioned myself in the most private corner of the cottage. Several of the children eyed me curiously, but thankfully no one asked outright what I was doing.

It took several attempts, but I finally had a note that I felt hit the right tone. And thankfully I could merely copy the wording for all the others with only slight adjustments. I soon had several written out neatly and tucked safely away in my bag unsealed. I would seal them last thing in the morning with the royal signet I kept hidden on a chain around my neck. I didn't know if any of my new house-mates would recognize my seal, but I didn't want to take the risk.

I barely spoke at dinner, and by the sympathetic glances of the older children, they attributed my silence to exhaustion. But, in truth, it was motivated by guilt. Penning the messages to my potentially loyal nobles had reminded me all too forcibly of the danger that surrounded my existence. Danger that I had brought into the home of these children. Danger that I still hid from them.

I reminded myself that Alida's guards had ceased to search the forest for me. At least for now. None of us were in imminent danger, and I would be gone soon enough. But still the guilt lingered.

The next morning I woke early, slipping out of bed to heat some wax before anyone else awoke. I sealed all of the now-completed notes and hurried outside. Despite the early hour, Alexander already awaited me, seated calmly just inside the trees. He leaped to his feet at my approach and took the missives without comment. A look of understanding and resolve passed between us, and gratitude overwhelmed me. Where would I be without him?

Dead. The answer came quickly, and I couldn't help throwing my arms around his neck and resting my cheek against his chest. He froze beneath my touch, making no move to embrace me back.

"Thank you," I whispered. "For everything. I don't deserve a friend like you."

His body relaxed slightly, and one hand came up to pat my back. "Of course you do, Snow. Despite everything, you care about people. Unlike your stepmother. You want to do the right thing—to make a difference. You are your father's daughter, and he was a good and kind king."

The mention of my father made the breath hitch in my throat

as I swallowed back tears. What would my father think if he could see me now?

Alexander's hand stilled, and then he grabbed my shoulders, pushing me away from him and gazing down into my face.

"He would be proud of you, Snow." Could he read my mind? "You're doing the right thing." He hesitated. "*I'm* proud of you."

Warmth crept up my neck and across my cheeks, and I looked away. I instantly resolved to train just as hard in his absence as I had done under his watchful eye. I knew he would return as soon as he could, and I wanted him to be proud of my progress.

Neither of us said any more until we all began morning training. Alexander stayed long enough to oversee our efforts, instructing us on where our technique had gone wrong, and to give us each a chance to practice against him. I still couldn't break any of his holds, but his smile was warm after my attempts.

"Keep up those strength and endurance exercises, and you'll be escaping from me no problem when I return," he promised.

I smiled back, my mind clinging to the assured way he spoke of his return. Alexander was smart and capable. He could navigate the capital and return safely. I had to believe that. I had to.

He farewelled the children without emotion, and I walked with him a short way down the stream.

"They've agreed to train you on foraging and trapping," he said into my silence. "And some basic tracking." He shook his head. "And none of them asked me any questions about who we are. It's remarkable really."

I nodded. "They are remarkable. And I would have died already without them. I'm sure of it."

A hiss of indrawn breath beside me made me wince. I hadn't meant the words as an accusation. "And without you, of course. I don't know why I have so many people looking out for me."

Alexander shook his head. "Only you would see your horrible situation in such a light. You are the true queen, remember, so really there are far too few people looking out for you. But the

High King and his godmothers are on your side, at least, so maybe it isn't such a surprise that your steps would be guided in the right direction, after all."

I tried to smile, but I knew the attempt was weak. The godmothers might have returned to some of the other kingdoms, but we'd seen no sign of them in Eliam. And weren't they known for favoring those who were deserving rather than those with a blood right to rule? Perhaps they had avoided our kingdom so far because they saw no one who fit that description.

"You should get back," he said, startling me from my uncomfortable thoughts. His eyes twinkled down at me. "Your training awaits."

I grimaced and gave him a playful shrug. "Ugh, don't remind me."

His expression turned serious. "You can do this, Snow. I just wish I'd thought to suggest something like this earlier."

I shook my head. Only Alexander could consider that to be somehow his fault.

"I'm the one who should have asked. I'm the princess, remember?" I threw our usual joke back at him, reminding him where the responsibility—and, therefore, fault—lay.

An expression crossed his face that I couldn't read. "You were the princess, you mean. Now you're a queen."

"Not yet I'm not, whatever you insist on calling me." I tried to stand tall and look confident. "But I will be. And you'll be my Chief Adviser."

He looked like he wanted to laugh, so I grinned at him.

"Or Head Huntsman, or…any position you want. You can take your pick."

"And if I want to be a duke?" The laugh sounded in his voice as well as his eyes.

"Done!" I said instantly. "Just pick which one you want me to behead. Or strip of his title, or whatever."

He snorted, and I giggled.

"Maybe not the best way to start my reign?"

"Maybe not." He shook his head, and his expression fell. He didn't need to speak for me to know his mind had turned to all the obstacles still to be overcome before I had any hope of a coronation.

I knew because my thoughts had flown to the same place. The barriers seemed insurmountable, but I thrust the thought away. I couldn't hide out here forever; my kingdom deserved better than that. Which meant I had to try. Even if it meant I ended up dead. My eyes roamed over my companion's face, and I swallowed.

Even if it meant Alexander ended up dead? That possibility was less easy to stomach. But I knew perfectly well he would never agree to step aside out of danger. And, in truth, I also knew I would have no hope of success without him.

Old words of my father's echoed in my ears. This was the hardest part of ruling: making decisions that others had to bear the consequences of. *It's supposed to hurt*, he would tell me if he was here. *If it didn't hurt, you wouldn't be worthy to rule.*

I tried to take courage from his memory, but fear for Alexander overwhelmed me. Yet another sign that I wasn't worthy.

Alexander clasped my hand, squeezing it in his strong, capable one. How much of my inner conflict could he read in my face? I wanted to open my mouth and tell him I'd changed my mind. Tell him not to go. Tell him we could run away together. But the words had lodged themselves in my throat, and apparently he couldn't read the message in my eyes.

He bowed over my hand, pressing his lips to it so quickly I didn't feel their burning warmth until he had already pulled away. And then he was gone, too fast for me to speak even if I had been capable of doing so.

My hand hung in the air for several moments, even that brief touch of his lips against my skin scorching through me. I had lost my chance. He had left toward danger, and I could do nothing now to help him.

A tear ran down my cheek, and I wiped it angrily away. I couldn't let myself forget that we were both acting with purpose. Doing the only thing we could. And I had a part to play, too. There would be danger enough for both of us, soon enough. For now, I needed to train.

CHAPTER 11

$\mathcal{A}$pparently Alexander had also discussed my further training with Daria and Ben. Together we continued self-defense practice each morning, and they assigned me only light duties outside of that so I would have time for my other exercises. When I expressed guilt to Daria, she just waved it away.

"From what Alexander said, it's important that you get time to do the exercises he left you."

I gave her a sharp look. What had he told her? I thought he said they hadn't asked any questions.

"Don't worry," she said, apparently reading the concern on my face. "He didn't tell any of your secrets—whatever they are. But I'm not stupid." She paused. "None of the rest of us had someone to come after us. Someone who cared. But you do. You don't have to stay here." She shrugged. "So if this is what you need to be able to have a normal life..."

I swallowed, overwhelmed by her words.

Her face softened, and she leaned in close. "Don't tell Ben, but I also think it's terribly romantic. He's very handsome. I can see why you ran away." She winked at me, and I tried to keep the shock from my face.

Romantic? I chewed on the inside of my cheek while I wondered if I should correct her. Did she think I was some noble or upper-class girl who had run away from whatever match my parents had arranged because I was in love with a huntsman? And now he wanted to make sure I had the skills I needed for us to make a life together?

It actually did sound romantic. I only wished my life were half so simple.

Or that Alexander actually felt that way about you, said my unwelcome inner voice.

"Don't worry, Snow." Daria patted my arm, obviously reading the discomfort on my face if nothing else. "I won't say anything to the others. Boys don't understand these things."

She winked at me, and I reluctantly smiled back. Any attempt to correct her misapprehension would only leave me in a muddle since I couldn't tell her the truth. But I promised myself that one day, when I had defeated Alida, I would return and tell them everything. And repay them in any way they wanted. It was the least I could do.

For an entire week, one of the older three stayed home to watch the younger two, and they used the opportunity to teach the three of us something of tracking and trapping and foraging. I didn't even have the chance to protest to Daria because she explained straight away that it was time Jack and Poppy were learning anyway.

"Normally we like to get through the whole circuit of traps in one day, so we're only missing one day at the mines. But that pace doesn't leave enough time to teach the youngsters properly," she said. "So this is as good an opportunity as any to get them started on what they'll need to know."

Unsurprisingly, Jack and Poppy were not the best of students, so I tried to make up for it with unwavering attention. Even when gutting a rabbit made me nearly lose my breakfast. Anthony was our instructor on that day, and I got the distinct impression he found my disgust amusing and was drawing out the process longer than necessary. I didn't complain, though. I knew I would eat the rabbit stew as heartily as the rest of them that evening, so I had no right to turn up my nose at this stage of the process. And I wanted to prove to Anthony that I was willing to do my bit since he seemed the least impressed with my new training regime.

After a week, I took a walk through the forest, taking in so much more of my environment than I had before. I felt like a child who had just learned to read and was now discovering the secrets of stories that had previously been locked to me. The forest was full of messages that I hadn't been able to read the last time I journeyed through it alone.

I took note of animal burrows and edible plants, picking up on the signs of where the children had recently passed, and the indications that water flowed nearby. And all of this although I was still a beginner. How much Alexander must be able to read.

I turned back toward the clearing, following my own tracks and trying to move quietly. I had spent two hours training that morning—one with the older three and one on my own alternating between running and climbing trees—and I marveled to discover that I felt no particular ache in my muscles. I still wanted to lose my breakfast after each session of sprints, but I recovered so much more quickly now, the effect not lingering to weaken me for hours afterward.

To my chagrin, the younger children had all taken great delight in my tree-climbing efforts and often joined me, challenging me to race or to compete on who could go higher. At first I had attempted to demur and call them down, but Ben just shook his head at me.

"They've been climbing almost since they could walk," he said. "There's not much else out here for a child to do."

I tried to hide my wince at his matter-of-fact words—a

reminder that while this cottage was a haven, for them it was also a prison of sorts.

I had told myself that I shouldn't expect to see Alexander until some weeks had passed, but I couldn't stop myself looking hopefully for him each time I heard a step behind me, or a rustle in the forest. I should have known better, though. When he did eventually reappear, it was soundlessly, just like he always moved.

I was carrying two heavy buckets of water toward the cottage, and his sudden appearance made me squeak in shock. But I didn't drop the buckets. I didn't even spill a drop, and I grinned at him, proud of my steady hands and nerves. The forest no longer terrified me as it once had, when every surprise overturned my calm.

"Snow." He paused and something in his expression made me flush and look away. He cleared his throat. "You look well."

My eyes flew back to him, quickly tracing his form. "You also." Could he hear the oceans of relief in my voice? I had fought every day against images of the worst befalling him. And every night when he hadn't returned, I had reminded myself that it was still too early to expect him back.

"How did…" I cleared my throat. "How did it go?"

He opened his mouth to reply, but a small form catapulted into him from behind, followed quickly by another.

"Alexander! Alexander!" Jack and Poppy swarmed around him, followed by Danni and Louis in only a slightly more sedate manner.

Alexander shrugged helplessly at me above their heads, and I smiled, resuming my progress toward the cottage. He was alive and, from every indication, unharmed. That was enough for now.

Ben insisted he join us in the cottage for the evening meal as he had done on his first night weeks ago, and the children filled the air with chatter, updating him on the simple happenings of our forest life as if he were one of them who had merely been gone on a brief absence.

He listened with attention, showing admiration and concern when necessary. I spoke little, taking the opportunity to watch him instead. I drank in the sight of him, mesmerized by the muscles in his broad shoulders and arms as he passed around food, his strength somehow not at odds with the softness in his face as he interacted with the children. It was a softness that reflected not weakness but kindness and consideration.

When he glanced over at me, I was so caught up in my admiration for him that I forgot to be embarrassed. Instead of flushing or looking away, I smiled at him with all the warmth that filled my heart. The first time he smiled back, but the second time he was the one to color and drop his eyes from mine. He went quiet after that, and I missed the sound of his sure voice.

I didn't create an excuse to leave the cottage with him that evening. He seemed to be anxious to get away, avoiding my eyes, and I knew we would have the chance to talk in the morning. But when I later lay sleepless in bed, I regretted my forbearance.

I couldn't stop wondering what had happened with my missives. Had anyone responded? Had he been in danger? Now that the answers were so close, I couldn't settle down for the night without them.

Eventually I gave up on sleep and slipped out of bed and into my cloak. Pulling on my boots, I left the cottage, the moonlight transforming the clearing around it and the trees beyond. I suppressed a shiver. Perhaps I should extend my training to night exercises if the darkness still unnerved me so much.

I took a moment to breathe deeply, steadying my nerves and observing my surroundings. I looked for all the familiar elements, noting how they looked different in the semi-darkness. I stepped out of the clearing and looked for the signs I had come to recognize during the day. They were harder to spot beneath the trees, where the leaves blocked some of the moonlight, but they were still there.

A rustle behind me didn't even make me jump, and I turned

with a proud smile to watch an owl swoop past. I couldn't wait to show Alexander how much progress I'd made. Except when I looked around for him, I realized I didn't actually know where he went each night to sleep.

For a brief moment I considered tracking him despite the darkness but ended up shaking my head at my own foolishness. I had made excellent progress, but I wasn't that good. I would probably never be that good. Not where someone as skilled as Alexander was concerned.

I stepped back into the clearing with an audible sigh. I should have taken the opportunity when I had it, earlier. Now I would have to return to bed unsatisfied.

But I had only made it a few feet toward the cottage when a soft sound from behind made me spin back around. Alexander stood there, one step back into the trees. I rushed over to him, almost tripping in my haste. He stepped forward, as if to catch me, but stepped quickly back again when I righted myself.

"I was looking for you," I said when I came to a stop in front of him.

"I know."

He said nothing more, and I considered asking him where he slept. And whether he slept at all since he had apparently been as alert to my exit from the cottage in the middle of the night as he would have been during the day. But I decided to focus on more important questions.

"What happened in the capital? Did anyone reply to my notes? Did anyone suspect you?"

"I got several replies, but I've burned them."

"Burned them?" I stared at him blankly, trying to make sense of his words. I wanted to shake him and tell him to stop being so taciturn and tell me everything.

He ran a hand through his hair. "I thought...That is, I..." His face twisted. "The truth is that I couldn't be sure, but I began to wonder if someone might be following me. Observing me. I didn't want to risk having anything in writing."

I gasped, the indrawn breath loud in the darkness, and looked wildly around us.

"They didn't follow me here," he said quickly. "In the forest, at least, I'm confident I can lose a tracker. And it may have all just been paranoia, anyway. But the last thing we need is for all your supporters to be arrested."

I forced a deep breath. "No, you're right, of course. I'm glad you did. But..."

"Don't worry," he cut me off. "I memorized them before I burned them."

My shoulders slumped a little, relief coursing through me. I glared up at him.

"Next time, lead with that information."

He gave a low laugh. "Sorry, Your Majesty. I just wish it hadn't been necessary."

"You're safe, and that's the most important thing." I took a step closer to him. "Maybe you shouldn't go back. You've delivered my messages, you could stay here with us..."

He shook his head, the gesture silencing me. "You know that wouldn't work. This was just a preliminary contact. We still need to arrange to actually meet with them. And gather more supporters, if we can. I have to return."

"But..." I bit my lip, trying to read his eyes in the low moonlight that filtered through the leaves. "If someone was following you..."

"*If* they were following me. We don't even know for sure they were. I'll just have to be extra careful—make sure there's nothing for them to find."

It was so like him. Always there to support me. Never hesitating to do what he felt was right. I tried to imagine what I would have done if he had been arrested instead of put under surveillance. My throat closed, and my breath hitched. Before I knew what I was doing, I took another step forward and placed both hands flat against his chest.

"But I can't lose you, Alexander. I just can't."

He stilled instantly beneath my touch. A slight twitch made me think he meant to pull away, but he didn't move.

"It's not me who's important, Your Majesty. I'm not the one who can save Eliam."

I shook my head angrily, moisture filling my eyes. "You're important to me." I leaned in, rising onto tiptoes, and lifted my face until my lips hovered a breath away from his. If he even swayed forward, they would meet. Fire raced through me at our nearness, and I trembled, fisting my hands into his shirt to give me balance. Every part of me was tuned to his nearness, his height, his broad shoulders, and the strength in his muscles. Silently I willed him to take me into his arms. But still he didn't move, neither closing that final breath between us nor pulling away.

"You're important to me," I said again, my voice the faintest whisper.

The moment stretched out, tension rising in me until I thought I might snap. And then his warmth and strength were gone, ripped from my hands as he stepped hurriedly back. We stared at each other, his harsh breaths and my gasping ones filling the cold space between us.

"You're a queen, Blanche," he said, and my full name felt like a slap across the face. My trembling resumed.

"And I am only a royal huntsman. I know it may seem like you're alone right now, but you can't forget who you are."

My hands balled into fists, my trembling swept away by my anger. "How dare you, Alex! After everything we've been through. After all our years together. Do you really believe my feelings are the result of a moment of loneliness?"

"No." A flash of the moon across his eyes reflected on something that almost looked like moisture. His voice dropped so low I could barely hear it. "Not a moment of loneliness. A lifetime."

I gasped, stepping back. His words cut through me like a blade. I shook my head, and his face softened further. Was that pity in his eyes? I stepped back again.

"I haven't forgotten who I am, Alex. How could I when everything I suffer is because of it? When just my presence puts anyone I care for in danger. I'm not allowed to forget who I am."

He opened his mouth, and I waited to hear what he would say. But nothing came out.

Dashing one hand across my eyes, I turned and fled back across the clearing toward the cottage. I was not free to forget who I was, and apparently I was not free to have feelings either. If I could even trust the ones I thought I felt. What was it he had said? *Not a moment of loneliness. A lifetime.* The poor foolish princess who had no one but her father to love her, clinging obstinately to the boy who was forced by duty to serve her.

At the last moment I swerved away from the cottage door, sure I was going to be sick. But when I reached the safety of the trees behind the woodpile, my stomach remained in place. I sank down onto a pile of leaves instead and placed my head on my arms. For once my eyes remained dry, and eventually sleep claimed me.

CHAPTER 12

*T*he sun woke me, although Danni followed not far behind.

"I found her! She's back here," she called over her shoulder as soon as she caught sight of me.

I grimaced and picked leaves out of my hair, stretching my aching back. Why hadn't I returned to my nice, soft bed? But as soon as I thought it, Alexander's words washed over me again, and the sting of them nearly sent me tumbling back into the leaves. Instead I made myself stand up.

"I'm sorry," I said to Danni, "were you looking for me?"

She shrugged. "You're not normally up before any of the rest of us wake. And you weren't in the clearing." She regarded me with narrowed eyes. "Did you sleep in those leaves?"

I grimaced again and pulled out another one. "Help me?"

She raised her eyebrows in an excellent imitation of Daria but came over and began to pick foliage from my tangled curls. "You should come in, or Louis will eat your breakfast. Mine too, probably."

Despite myself I smiled. Poor Louis. He didn't really eat that much more than everyone else. But the smile quickly dropped away as the memory of Alexander's face filled my mind.

I cleared my throat. "I'm actually not hungry. But you should go."

Danni eyed me skeptically, but when I shooed her away with my hands, she shrugged and left. I trudged down to the stream for a wash, pretending I wasn't intensely aware of the clearing, tensed for any sign of Alexander.

I didn't hear anything, but I must have sensed something anyway because I suddenly felt his presence behind me and spun to find him holding out a bowl of porridge.

"You need to eat."

I crossed my arms over my chest and said nothing.

"We're going to be training. You need to keep up your strength."

"So nice to know you care."

He winced. "You know I care, Snow." His voice was low. "Of course I care. You're my oldest friend. And my queen. But we can't…" His jaw clenched. "We can't care like that."

His obvious pain stabbed at me. I was being unfair, lashing out in my rejection, and I knew it. Of course Alexander cared for me. He had never done anything else. Could I really hold it against him that he didn't love me? That he insisted on being the most loyal and protective of my subjects? He didn't owe me anything—the scales were tipped far the other way.

Slowly I took the bowl and forced myself to eat a bite. I gave him a small smile although his eyes told me he knew it was false.

"Very well, then," I said. "I'll see you at training."

"Snow, I…" He reached out a hand toward me before quickly dropping it again.

"I'll see you at training," I repeated, and wound around him to head toward the cottage. He deserved the same loyalty and care from me that he so freely gave. But my heart hurt too much to face him now. I needed space.

As he oversaw our morning training, giving praise where it was due and correction where it was needed, I discovered I was to have as much space as I needed.

"I have to leave immediately," he told us all. "I was only able to get away for a short hunt." His eyes found mine as he spoke, carrying a wealth of unspoken meaning. Eyes of suspicion were on him, and he couldn't risk giving them reason to doubt.

"I just wanted to check on you all. And let you know I was safe." Again his eyes dwelt on me, although he spoke the word *all*. He had wanted to check on me. Of course he had. Because while I was thinking about my heart, and admiring his muscles, he was focused on my future and my throne.

I sighed. It was hardly any wonder he didn't love me. The only surprise was that he found me a worthy queen to follow. I squeezed my eyes shut briefly. Was he blinded by a lifetime of friendship? Who was I fooling when I thought I could rouse the court to follow me?

A breath against my ear made my eyes whip open again.

"Farewell, Snow. I'll return within two weeks to report on my progress." His voice, already a whisper, dropped even lower. "If I can."

His final three words robbed me of speech, my limbs already paralyzed by his nearness and the warmth of his breath on my face. When he stepped back, the cold air that rushed in made me sway, and it took all of my poor strength to lock my limbs in place.

By the time I had schooled myself enough to risk speaking, he had disappeared. I looked around frantically, but I couldn't even see the place where he had entered the trees.

"Wait. Is he gone? Already?"

Daria hurried over to give me an awkward hug. "Don't worry, Snow. He said he'll be back soon."

Her sympathetic eyes made me want to cry. She thought she was consoling me on the absence of my lover. But Alexander didn't love me. Not like that, at least. And I had once again failed as a queen. Somehow he had been and gone, and I had been so preoccupied with myself, I had failed to even get the names of the nobles who had replied. Let alone the replies themselves. How could he have left without giving me a proper report?

Did he think I had nothing to contribute? And, if so, why did he think I would be a good ruler? Was it merely loyalty to my father that made him seek to put me on the throne? Or hatred for Alida, who didn't even have my mostly good intentions?

The thought of my stepmother made me grit my teeth. For all my failings, I couldn't be a worse queen than her. Could I?

None of the children commented when I threw myself into my training with a new ferocity. I could run for longer and climb noticeably higher now. And I could easily break the hold of all three of the older children. But still I pushed myself harder.

I volunteered each week to do the circuit of traps on my own, pushing myself to run between them, slowing only when I needed to read the forest signs we had used to mark their locations. And I always tried to come back with some extra greenery I had foraged on the way.

Several times Daria attempted to bring up Alexander, but I turned her away with a look and a word and—true to form—she didn't pry. Her eyes seemed sad when they rested on me now, though. And I often had to stop myself from defiantly declaring that I was fine. Just fine.

But when two weeks turned into three weeks, I had to admit —at least to myself—that I wasn't fine. And, far more importantly, it was possible Alexander wasn't fine either. His final three words continued to haunt me. He had promised to return by now —if he could. So what did it mean that he obviously could not?

Except I knew what it meant, of course. It meant nothing good.

As the fourth week began, I abandoned my training one day and walked through the forest. It had scared me once, this place —I hoped it would soothe me now. But the solitude only reminded me that I had stayed safe and hidden here while Alexander strode into danger. I forced my mind to stop endlessly playing through the possible calamities that might have befallen him, and to consider instead something far more practical. What did I intend to do about it?

I could sense that a crucial moment had come. I had—to all appearances—lost my only ally. Without him, I didn't even know which nobles I might safely approach. If ever there was a time to abandon this foolhardy attempt to take my throne, now was the moment.

Yet that option I discarded without further consideration. I had made a promise to my hosts—even if they didn't know it— and I would not abandon them or the rest of my people with so little effort. But even without all that, I knew with every part of me that I could never abandon Alexander. Just as he had never abandoned me.

Without conscious thought, I turned my steps back toward the clearing, following the trail I had left as I wandered in the other direction. A small animal skittered through the underbrush behind me, but I didn't flinch or turn. As I continued on my way, I shook my head at the thought of the fear and desperation that had consumed me the first time I stumbled into the clearing.

As the last of the trees fell away, I paused to survey the cottage. It looked friendly now, familiar. My eyes traveled down to my own arms, hanging beside me. They, on the other hand, looked new and different. The line of new muscle reshaped them, and the calluses on my fingers gave them a new feel.

I was not the same person who had nearly died as I fled blindly from danger. I had worked hard to grow strong, and while the changes might only be skin deep, they still counted for something. I would pretend. Pretend my insides were as strong as my new outside. I would travel to the capital, and I would find Alexander. And together, we would find a way. I was done with hiding.

~

Jack and Poppy protested my departure loudly and long, which touched me more than I cared to admit. Louis and Danni clearly didn't think it was a good idea but didn't want to align themselves with the younger two, while Anthony looked almost relieved. I'd never quite managed to win him over.

Ben made no attempt to prevent me leaving, but his eyes looked worried, and I wanted to hug him for his concern. I carefully refrained, however, for the sake of his dignity.

I had expected Daria to be the most against the idea, but to my surprise she made no demur. Instead she merely embraced me tightly, whispering in my ear, "Don't worry, you'll find him." She pulled back to look into my eyes. "And if you don't, well, you know where to find us."

"Thank you, Daria," I said, wishing I had better words. "For everything." Why did it feel as if I were the thirteen-year-old and she the mother seeing me off into the world?

I left the cottage with many backward glances and waves, taking with me the same satchel I had arrived with. Only this time it held a number of practical items I had been missing before, the most important of which was a large water skin. But I knew that this skin wasn't the most valuable of my new acquisitions. As I walked steadily and swiftly beside the stream, I knew that my new strength and skills were far more valuable.

I had spent some time with Ben while he described everything they knew of the surrounding area, especially the path they had taken on their single trip to Lestern on the coast. I had studied enough maps of the kingdom to bring them to mind now with relative ease, and Lestern was the only point on those maps the children knew relative to their own home. Given their position in comparison to the small city, along with the stream, I was fairly confident I had worked out roughly where the cottage lay within the forest.

And so I had plotted a course back to the capital. I couldn't be sure how long it would take me, although I suspected it would be several days of walking. As long as my path led me beside the stream, I would make better progress than I had coming into the forest. Then I had been weakened by hunger and fear, my muscles not trained as they were now. But once I was forced to leave the stream, I would move much more slowly than I had done in my wild flight with Alexander. Then I had only needed to follow—or even be carried. Now I would be responsible for finding the way.

In the end, the two balanced each other out, and it took me nearly three full days of travel to retrace the steps that had taken me a night and two days. And despite my training, my muscles ached from the nights on the hard ground and the endless repetition of the walking. Nothing to the pain I had felt in the other direction, however.

And my full stomach and knowledge of the forest had given me confidence, chasing away any skittishness at being on my own. Except that by the afternoon on the third day, my old fear had returned, an all-too-familiar friend. Even with my training, I couldn't walk silently through the forest as Alexander could. And every crack of a twig or rustle of leaves made me wince. Because this patch of forest was familiar and far too near the capital.

In the end I gave up and found a dense bush to crawl into to await nightfall. I couldn't risk running into someone who would recognize me, and I didn't trust that I had the ability to avoid anyone else in the area. I was glad for the decision when a huntsman passed my hiding place not long after, heading toward

115

the city with a string of game. And two guards passed not long after that.

Their presence—even though they had shown no sign of detecting me—left my heart racing for long minutes after they had disappeared. What were they doing so far out here? Had the search for me resumed? Or for Alexander, perhaps? Was he on the run and hadn't wanted to risk leading someone to the cottage?

The wait for the last of the light to fade seemed endless.

CHAPTER 13

When darkness finally fell, I crept back out and resumed my progress toward the castle. I knew it better than the city, and Alexander had a room there, as all the huntsmen did. If it seemed safe, I would check his room for signs of him first.

I had made it perhaps half of the remaining distance when flickering light through the trees ahead sent me scrambling for cover. When I peered out from inside yet another patch of bush, I saw a second pair of guards pass by. At least the lanterns they carried had made them easy to avoid. Still I waited until long after the light had disappeared to reemerge.

Twice more I had to duck for cover before I reached the castle wall. By the last time, it had become apparent the guards were on patrol through the sections of forest nearest the castle. I chewed my lip as I made the final approach to the wall. They had never done so during my father's reign. Was Alida afraid? Did she have reason to expect an attack? Or was this somehow part of her search for me?

I kept a careful eye out for further guards as I followed the wall, looking for the drain Alexander and I had used as children. I had mused on our way out that I might still fit through it. I could only hope I was right. And that no one had fixed the loose grate.

When I finally found the tiny creek that had necessitated the drain, I took a moment to steady myself before getting down on my hands and knees and crawling through the water. My eyes strained against the darkness, and it took all my willpower not to imagine the sorts of crawling creatures that might be lurking in such a place.

A brush of something soft against my face made me gasp, a scream only just stifled in time. When my questing hands at last felt the grate, I sagged in relief to feel it give way beneath my hands. No doubt it had been many, many years since anyone had checked on it.

Setting it to one side, I drew in a breath, sucking myself in as small as I could as I squeezed through. For a heart-stopping moment I thought I might get stuck, but with a scrape and a tearing sound, I pushed through.

When I popped out into the castle grounds, I looked quickly around, but no one was in sight. Closing my eyes, I allowed myself a brief moment of relief before turning and thrusting my arms and head back into the drain to replace the grate.

As I crept through the trees, I wished they were as thick as out in the forest. If I had been twitchy out there, it was nothing to my constant state of alert now. Memories of my initial flight so many weeks ago kept racing through my mind. I had been afraid then, but it had been a vague, nebulous fear. And one alleviated by Alexander's solid presence. Now that I walked the same path alone—knowing that not only my safety, but Alexander's as well, might rely solely on me—everything looked different.

By the time I reached the actual castle, I knew that my thought of visiting Alexander's room had been nothing but foolishness. He slept in a busy wing, his room a single one among many occupied by various huntsmen and servants. And all of them would recognize me. Perhaps I shouldn't have come into the castle grounds at all.

But even as I was thinking it, my feet led me to a familiar stretch of wall. I looked up at the distant window. Did I dare? Surely no one else had taken my rooms in my absence. My stepmother must at least be feigning grief at my disappearance... Mustn't she?

I was sure my own servants wouldn't turn on me, if I could just find one of them. I needed information, and I didn't know where else to turn.

I gripped the satchel, tugging at the strap to check it sat securely across my shoulder and chest. I didn't want it swinging free and unbalancing me on the climb.

Stop procrastinating, said my bothersome internal voice. *Get on with it!*

I drew a deep breath and reached up to grip a sturdy handful of vine. I could do this.

And by the time I had ascended to the height of the first floor, a warmth filled my chest. I *could* do this. It wasn't so different from climbing a tree, really. In some ways it was even easier, since the vines grew more thickly than most branches. I began to move more quickly, the memory of my last nearly disastrous descent overtaken by older ones. Memories of clambering up and down these vines as a child. When had I stopped being adventurous and become so afraid?

But I didn't have to think long for the answer to that. When my father became ill and fear had started to consume my life. I pushed the thought of him away. Being back here at the castle brought him all too forcefully to mind, but I couldn't afford the distraction. Not now.

When I reached the window, I let go with one hand and dug a stray hair clip from my tangled curls. Sliding it through the gap between the window panes, I moved it upward, popping the catch up and open. Another technique that had once been familiar to me.

When I swung myself over the sill and into the room, I allowed myself only a single moment of triumph. Creeping to the dressing room door, I pressed my ear against it. Silence. I eyed the gap by the floor, but no light shone through.

My hand trembling slightly against the handle, I slowly opened the door a crack before pausing again to listen. Still nothing. And more than nothing. A heavy stillness—almost a mustiness—overwhelmed me. I pushed the door the rest of the way open with more confidence. No one had been using this room.

The curtains remained open, and the moon provided enough light for me to survey the empty room. Nothing looked out of place, although someone had tidied the mess I had made before my departure. I ran a hand along my desk. It came away dust free. So my maids must still be at work here, although their mistress had disappeared.

I looked a little longingly at my comfortable bed—one I would have all to myself—before turning resolutely away. It had turned out well the last time I had been startled awake in a bed where I didn't belong, but I couldn't risk it here in the castle.

I let my hand run across the book that still rested on my bedside table and then crossed to the door that led to the corridor. But I hesitated in front of it. The late hour meant the passageways should be empty, but where would I be going? I knew where the servants' quarters were located, of course, but I didn't know each of their individual sleeping places. And I could hardly go bumbling through them at this time of night. No doubt some of the servants were loyal to my stepmother, just as the guards seemed to be.

I bit my lip and stepped back from the door. Better to stay here and wait to see who came. Clearly someone still cleaned here, and I could only hope it was my own maids. I glanced again at the bed and decided I could safely remove one of the pillows. I would settle myself in the dressing room. There I would be out of sight but able to hear anyone who entered my main room. And if it turned out to be someone who was less than friendly, then my exit would be close at hand.

I settled down on the single pillow, trying not to think about how often the cleaning was done. What if it was only every second day? Or even every third day? I couldn't wait in this tiny room for days.

The thoughts so consumed me that the soft sound of a door made me sit bolt upright, my indrawn breath quickly stifled. What was someone doing here in the middle of the night?

I scrambled upright as silently as I could and hurried over to the door. I pressed my ear against it but could hear no further sounds. After chewing my lip anxiously for a full minute, I decided to risk easing the door slightly open.

I held my breath as I did so, resisting the urge to squeeze my eyes shut as well. Much better to keep them open and alert. No startled exclamation greeted the small movement, so I risked opening it slightly further. Still no response.

With the door ajar, I could hear faint sounds of indiscernible movement. Someone was definitely in the room, but what were they doing? They didn't appear to have brought a light with them, or to have lit any of the candles that littered the surfaces. Slowly, inch by inch, I leaned my head through the narrow space and peered quickly around the room.

This time I didn't manage to swallow my gasp quickly enough. The maid, duster in hand, looked up and met my eyes. For a long, silent moment, we both remained frozen, me with only my head in the room, and her with her hand still raised.

"Your...Your Highness!" Gertie found her voice first.

I whisked the rest of myself into the room and pressed a finger against my lips. "Shhh!"

She closed her mouth and blinked at me while I stood there

awkwardly and tried to think of something to say. Nothing brilliant came to mind.

"You're back!" She whispered the words this time, and I stepped closer to hear her more clearly.

"Not officially. But I need some information."

"Information?" Gertie lowered her duster at last and hurried over toward me. "We thought you were...well, we didn't know what to think!"

I shrugged. She looked truly concerned, and I hated to think that the servants might have been worrying for me. But I was hardly going to apologize for running, given the circumstances. Circumstances I hardly intended to explain now.

"My stepmother can't know I'm here," I settled on in the end, watching her closely to see her reaction to this announcement.

She nodded vigorously, her eyes wide. "No, indeed, Your Highness. She's been in a towering bad mood ever since you disappeared. We hoped that must mean..."

Interesting. So the servants, at least, seemed to know that Alida wished me harm. And they seemed to care, too. Some of them, anyway. I had always got on well enough with my own maids, so I was fairly sure they would not wish to see me dead. The others, though—did they still hold out hope that I might claim the throne and free the kingdom from its current queen?

I eyed Gertie more closely. She looked pale and tired, although how much of that was the low moonlight I couldn't be sure.

"What are you doing dusting in the middle of the night, Gertie?"

She jumped slightly and flushed. "Well...to be honest, Your Highness, this isn't exactly one of my official duties. But it was my turn."

"Your turn?" I frowned in confusion.

She nodded. "We all got assigned to different duties after you left, but we take turns to come and keep your room in order. In case you return..." She trailed off and eyed me uncomfortably, as if she'd just realized that I had indeed returned but didn't have much use for a clean room.

I softened, touched by her words. "I hope you're not risking getting into some sort of trouble by being here." I gestured at the clean room. "Is that why you're here in the middle of the night?"

"What? Oh. No. I mean, we haven't exactly been announcing our efforts to anyone, but then no one else comes here to see us." She grimaced. "I just couldn't get away sooner."

I stared at her. "But it's so late! You can't possibly have been working until now."

"Her Majesty has seen fit to increase our workload. Seeing as how she dismissed a number of the staff and hasn't been bothered to replace them."

"Dismissed staff? Whatever for?"

Her brows drew together, and a shadow crossed her eyes. "Failure to adequately perform their duties, I believe was the official reason. It's most of the older ones who are gone." She looked at me significantly. "The ones most loyal to your father."

My hands balled into fists as I thought of all the familiar faces that must be missing. "And let me guess. She sent them away without their pensions."

Gertie nodded, and I swung around, striding over to the window before quickly striding back again. How convenient for the queen to save herself all that money.

Gertie watched me, a worried crease between her eyes. "We've all been keeping our heads down, Your Highness. As I'm sure you can understand."

I nodded, my eyes racing around my clean room. And yet they had continued to come here in a silent vigil for me.

"I'm surprised more of the servants haven't chosen to leave if you're being worked so hard," I said. Although the prospect of losing the pension owed to them would keep the older ones tied to their positions, I imagined.

Gertie gripped both hands around the stem of her duster. "We aren't permitted to leave, Your Highness. Not unless we're sent away with a black mark against our name and little chance for other work."

"Not permitted to leave?" I stared at her. "You aren't slaves!"

"Well, no, we still get our wages, I suppose." Her words made anger explode inside me. "But Her Majesty has declared that to leave her service is to show disloyalty to the crown. And we all have families. We can't risk having them branded as traitorous, or the whole family would be out of work. No one would dare employ us."

I shook my head. How had things devolved so drastically in the few short weeks I had been gone? My insides writhed uncomfortably as I wondered if it was my escape that had prompted Alida's harsh actions. If her plan for me had succeeded, she would have had no need to cull those most loyal to my family —and then threaten the others so they couldn't leave now that their workload had increased.

I took a deep breath and pushed my inner turmoil aside. Alida had left me with no other choice—I couldn't have remained and allowed her to kill me. But it was very clear I couldn't risk staying in the castle any longer than absolutely necessary. Not with all of my father's old servants gone and the rest in a state of tension and overwork. Who knew how they would react if they saw me?

"I'm looking for Alexander. Have you seen him? Do you know where he is?"

"Alexander?" Gertie frowned. "I don't think I've seen him in weeks. But then the maids' quarters are nowhere near those of the huntsmen. And none of us have time to be sociable in the evenings these days. All the common rooms are deserted outside of meal times."

I sighed and ran a hand through my tangled hair. I had hoped she might have heard a rumor of him at least. Did that mean nothing had happened to him after all? Had I overreacted by rushing back here?

But no. He had said he would be back in two weeks, and it was closer to four now. I tried to think of who else I might seek out for information. I didn't like to ask Gertie to go searching given everything she'd told me.

She must have seen the concern on my face because she opened her mouth, only to close it quickly again.

"What is it?" I asked.

"Well, I just thought...that is, I wondered..." She twirled her duster nervously.

"Yes?" I tried to make my voice as gentle as I could.

"You should ask your grandfather," she said in a sudden rush.

CHAPTER 14

"My grandfather?" I stared at her blankly. Of course she couldn't mean my father's father, the old king, who had been dead for many years. But then she must mean...

"The duke is still here? In the capital?"

She nodded eagerly. "Yes, indeed, Your Highness. And if it's information you need, he's well-connected in the city despite having been gone for so long. He visits the castle sometimes, and Her Majesty is always in an awful rage afterward." She smiled at me. "He kicked up a mighty fuss when you disappeared, you know. He keeps asking what Her Majesty is doing to find you and insisting his own men are involved in the search."

She seemed so sure I would be pleased at the news that I didn't know what to say. And I wasn't displeased, exactly. It was nice, even, to know that someone had pressed the issue of my sudden disappearance. But why him? And why did he suddenly care now after sixteen years during which he hadn't so much as looked at me once?

"Oh. Well, I suppose..." I managed at last, my words trailing away when I could think of nothing else to say.

"He's staying in his old townhouse," she told me, still smiling. "You know, the large one at the top of Palace Way. It's been empty for so many years that it's rather strange to see hustle and bustle all around it again."

"I see…well, thank you, Gertie." I tried to pull myself together. "It might be best if you don't tell anyone that you saw me here. Even the other maids. For both our sakes'."

She nodded so hard I had no doubt of her agreement. And the fear lurking at the back of her eyes reminded me that she had something to lose as well.

"I'll just be going, then." I backed toward the open door behind me. "Thank you for…" I waved my hand vaguely around us. "Everything."

She dipped into a very belated curtsy. "Of course, Your Highness. And I hope we'll see you again soon." The way she peeped up at me, hope having replaced the lurking fear, told me she didn't mean in a situation like this. She would be happy to see me storm the front gates.

If only I were capable of such a thing.

My head whirled as I climbed back down the vines, my thoughts moving too fast to leave any room for fear. Before I knew it, I was on the ground and crawling back through the drain. The city wall was in much worse repair than the castle one, and I would have better luck slipping into the city from the forest than from the castle.

I had to dodge another patrol just outside the castle wall, but I found an unmanned and unlatched side gate into the city without trouble. Whatever increased security concerns gripped Alida, they were firmly centered on the castle.

I stopped to pull on my cloak, although the night was a warm one, raising the hood over my head. Keeping my face down, I slipped through the streets, making my way toward the large, central Palace Way. The broad road led from the main entrance of the city straight through to the castle gates, and the upper section was lined with mansions—town homes for the nobility when they visited court from their main estates.

Like Gertie, I found the sight of burning lanterns at the door of the duke of Lestern's mansion startlingly incongruous. It had been dark as long as I was alive.

I lurked in the shadows on the other side of the street, trying to decide on my next move. Nothing in me felt comfortable at the idea of approaching my grandfather. But I also had nowhere else to go and no one else to turn to.

Alexander's safety meant more than my feelings of past rejection or present uncertainty. And while I had no reason to suppose the duke loyal to me, he had certainly shown himself lacking in loyalty to my stepmother. Perhaps while he did not care for me personally, he still wished to see his daughter's blood on the throne. Whatever his reasoning, I felt fairly certain I could trust him with the knowledge of my presence in the capital. Of course, whether or not he would actually help me was another question.

Except now that I stood here, I realized I had a more immediate problem than his willingness to act on my behalf. How was I to approach him in the first place? I could hardly knock on his front door and announce myself as the missing princess. And in the middle of the night, no less.

I pondered the problem for some time with no brilliant ideas coming to me. Much of the night had now passed, and I still hadn't slept at all. My eyelids kept drooping, only to jerk open again at some unfamiliar city sound. Daylight might bring more of an opportunity for slipping into the house and finding the duke, but it would also bring a much higher likelihood of someone else seeing and recognizing me before I managed to accomplish it.

I shifted my weight from foot to foot, trying to ease the discomfort in my muscles as I waited and unsuccessfully tried to come up with a solution. If only Alexander were here. He would

128

know what to do. His expertise might lie in the forest, but he had never shown himself at a loss that I could remember. He had always found a way to rescue us from the childhood scrapes we had gotten ourselves into.

As I agonized, more time passed, and I noticed the darkness around me lightening. I straightened. One way or another, I couldn't stay here much longer.

But before true dawn arrived, movement across the street made me straighten and strain to see through the gloom. A figure appeared from a side door in the ducal mansion. He left it propped open behind him as he shook out a small object I couldn't discern in the darkness. But despite the lack of detail, the figure was too familiar for me to mistake. What was the castle steward doing at my grandfather's home?

But only a moment of reflection brought the obvious answer. One at least of the staff dismissed by my stepmother had found another position. The older man had been steward long before my birth, and I didn't hesitate. My feet almost flew across the cobblestones between us, my momentum nearly sending me colliding into him as he turned back to the door.

"Watch yourself, miss," he said, as he steadied me. His calm tone managed to convey disapproval without being actually rude, and I almost laughed in my relief.

"Bronson! It's me!" I didn't let go of my clutch on his arms, so I felt him stiffen.

He stooped quickly to peer up under my hood.

"Your Highness!" he breathed.

I nodded wordlessly, and before I knew what was happening I had been whisked off the street and through the door into a passageway only slightly less dim than the outside.

I nearly stumbled, and he steadied me again, taking a firm grip on my arm and almost dragging me through the quiet house. A flash of elegant furnishings and slightly faded draperies, and I found myself deposited in a small sitting room. As soon as the door closed behind us, Bronson released my arm and bowed deeply.

"Your Highness."

"It's good to see you, Bronson," I said. "I heard about what happened up at the castle, and I can't say how glad I am to see you here."

He looked up at me sharply. "At the castle, Your Highness? Don't tell me you've been up there."

"Don't worry," I said with a smile. "I climbed in a window."

"Climbed in a window?" His eyes widened, and he looked like he wanted to reprimand me. But either my new status or our situation silenced him. "Well, you made the right decision coming here, Your Highness."

Seeing his familiar face and hearing him use my title gave me a courage I hadn't expected. Despite all my fear and weakness, I had been raised royalty. I straightened my spine.

"I'm here to see my grandfather."

"Of course." He bowed again. "I will fetch him immediately."

The drawn curtains caught my attention from the corner of my eye, and I hesitated, remembering the early hour. But the thought was quickly followed by a reminder of my circumstances. Alexander's face lurked behind my eyes. Some things were important enough to be woken for.

"Thank you," I said, and with a third bow, the steward slipped from the room, closing the door firmly behind him.

I sank exhausted into a chair and put my hand over my eyes. I wasn't ready for this meeting, and I wished desperately I could take the chance to sleep first.

The sound of the doorknob turning came more quickly than I had expected, and I leaped to my feet, one hand flying uselessly to my hair before falling again. I had spent two nights sleeping in the woods and one crawling through abandoned drains. It was altogether best if I didn't think about my hair.

The tall man who entered the room was familiar, although I

had only seen him once before. He closed the door behind him before turning and meeting my eyes across the room. For a drawn out moment neither of us spoke or moved, and then he sank into a deep bow.

"Your Majesty."

The address made me suck in a breath, fighting back tears. Only Alexander had ever called me that.

I said nothing in reply, and he crossed the room, stopping several feet short of me. A brief look of uncertainty crossed his face—the expression out of place on his otherwise commanding features. Was it facing his granddaughter properly for the first time that put it there?

His hand twitched, almost unconsciously, toward one of the chairs, and I wasn't sure whether to laugh or cry. It looked as if the truth were somewhat simpler. The great duke didn't know how to conduct himself now that he was no longer the highest ranked person present. As host I could see he wished to offer me a seat, but as my subject, he was bound to follow my lead when it came to sitting or standing.

After another awkward moment I took pity on us both and sank back into the chair I had just vacated. A brief lightening—almost a smile—crossed his features, and he took a seat facing me. But still the silence stretched between us. I didn't know what to say to this stranger, who should have been nearly as dear to me as my father.

"Blanche," he said at last, and I stiffened. "I'm so glad that you…" His voice trailed off as he absorbed my expression. "I'm sorry. Your Majesty, I should have said."

I forced my limbs to relax back into the soft chair. I needed to guard myself more closely—I hadn't meant to react so obviously to the sound of my name, a sharp reminder that this man and I did not know one another. I schooled my features into calm and inclined my head.

He cleared his throat and tried again. "I'm so glad that you're safe. And that you came here to me."

"I was surprised to learn you were still in the capital."

"You were?" His brows creased as he looked across at me. "When your own safety was not assured, and with that usurper sitting on your throne?"

I shrugged, struggling to keep my voice light. "You must excuse me for not realizing my safety was of particular concern to you." I held his gaze, willing strength into mine.

"Concern?" He stood abruptly and turned, rubbing a hand down his face before turning back toward me again. "Of course I was concerned, Blanche."

I drew in a shaky breath and thrust my clasped hands into my skirts to hide their trembling. Despite the years of rejection, already I felt myself succumbing to the allure of believing I still had family who cared for me.

"Snow." My voice came out almost too faint to be heard. I swallowed and tried again. "My friends and family call me Snow."

He stilled, something passing through his eyes that I couldn't read. When he sat back down, he moved slowly as if unaware of his own movements, his eyes still glued on me.

"You look so much like her, you know," he whispered. "Except for the coloring."

I swallowed again and nodded. "So I've been told."

Silence stretched out again, and I could feel the weight of it. Far too much hung between us to be resolved simply or with a single conversation. I needed to remember why I was here, and it wasn't for a family reunion.

"I heard that you were the one to go to for information," I said, and he straightened, the new softness in his face replaced with an alert look. "I need to find out what has happened to a huntsman named Alexander."

I hadn't expected the name to mean anything to him. But I had hoped for an assurance that he would look into it, question his sources, perhaps, whoever they might be. But there was no mistaking the look on his face as soon as I spoke Alexander's name.

I sat up straight. "You know him? Alex?"

"Of course." He looked at me questioningly for a moment, and then understanding transformed his face. "He didn't tell you?"

A sick feeling filled my stomach. "Tell me what?"

"I thought you had sent him to me. I suppose he never said... But he certainly allowed me to assume." He narrowed his eyes, as if distracted by his memories, before shaking his head. "He came to me on your behalf. With notes from you for other members of the court. I was so relieved to hear you were alive, that the woman who calls herself queen hadn't managed to get to you. I only wish Alexander had been willing to tell me where to find you. It would have made things easier when..."

I leaped on his words. "When what?"

He grimaced, his expression half sad, half apologetic. "When Alida acted on her suspicions and had him arrested."

PART II
THE REBEL

"*A*rrested?" I leaped to my feet, only to wring my hands together before sinking back down again. Better arrested than dead, at least.

But how long before one became the other?

"Has he been harmed? What has she done to him?"

My grandfather's mouth twisted, and he sighed. "He's in the castle dungeons for now. A little roughed up, perhaps, but nothing he can't handle."

I glared at him, but his expression didn't change, and I was the first to look away, sighing. I might not like it, but he was right. Alexander was tough.

"So how are we going to rescue him? What have you been planning?" I tried to focus on the problem and not on images of Alexander bruised and bloodied, lying on some pile of straw in the dark of a cell. Far away from the open sky and trees he loved. All for me.

The duke's jaw tightened, and I narrowed my eyes. "You are making plans to rescue him, aren't you?"

"It's not exactly that simple. And you are my first priority. Now that you're here…"

I stood to my feet, anger spilling out of me.

"No. Rescuing Alexander is our first priority."

He made no move to stand himself, his hands reaching out in a placating gesture. "Once you are on the throne, in your rightful place, freeing him will be a simple matter."

I shook my head in disbelief. "We are not taking that chance. The queen could decide to have him killed at any moment. After all, she was willing to kill me—her own step-daughter."

At that he did stand, his face nearly as angry as mine. "She is not the queen. *You* are the queen."

I refused to back down, meeting his gaze without flinching. Fear for Alexander gave me courage where fear for myself had only leached it away.

"Then, as your queen, my orders are that rescuing Alexander is our number one priority. Starting right now. I would like to hear preliminary plans by the end of the day."

A look almost of wonder crossed his face. Slowly he dropped onto one knee.

"Yes, my queen." He looked up at me, the look of warmth from earlier returning as his voice dropped to a whisper. "You look just like her right now."

It took all of my will power and training to keep my face stern and impassive.

"In the meantime, I would like the chance to wash and sleep," I said.

He stood quickly to his feet. "Yes, of course. You are no doubt exhausted after..." He looked at me questioningly, but I didn't feel the need to enlighten him about where exactly I had been hiding.

He gave a wry smile but didn't press me further. As he led me from the room, he spoke quietly over his shoulder.

"My servants are to be trusted, but I would still prefer not to advertise your presence more than necessary. Bronson has already directed my new housekeeper to prepare a room for you herself."

I didn't need to ask to know where he had sourced a new housekeeper. Hopefully his own steward and housekeeper had been left behind in Lestern and weren't feeling threatened by the new arrivals.

"So Alexander brought my notes to you," I said as we walked.

The duke nodded once. "He believed that I would have the necessary connections and acumen to contact them safely." He glanced at me briefly. "And he was right."

I clenched my teeth, upset not that Alexander had shown the good sense to involve my grandfather, but that he hadn't spoken to me about it. Had it been his plan all along? At least it explained why he had been so reticent with information on his final visit, slipping away without giving me a proper update. Our little plan hadn't been relying on only the two of us, after all. And clearly he had been reluctant to tell me the truth of his activities.

But reluctant because he feared I would disapprove, my prejudice against my mother's father too great to allow me to see good sense? Or merely because he had feared to wound me by bringing up the grandfather who had never loved me?

I gave an internal sigh. And there was my answer. I might doubt myself, but Alexander had always acted only out of care for me.

"Your list was sound," my grandfather said, as if wishing to reassure me. Not that he understood the reason for my crestfallen state. "And happily I have been able to add some names to it. I believe your disappearance panicked Alida. She has been making hasty decisions, and we have reaped the benefits."

I looked at him questioningly.

"She has raised taxes and demanded excessive displays of loyalty from the court." He raised one sardonic eyebrow. "Expensive displays. And she has limited freedom of movement among the populace."

"Even for the nobles?" Surely she could not be so foolish.

He shook his head. "Not yet. It has mainly been her own servants, and to a more limited extent the citizens of the capital. But your court isn't foolish." He gave a harsh laugh. "Or not all of them, anyway. They can see which way the wind is blowing. How long before she extends her decrees and restrictions? It is no way to rule, and even your father would never have countenanced such actions against his own people."

I hissed in a breath at his derisive mention of my father, and the duke looked quickly away. A heavy silence fell between us as we climbed yet another flight of stairs. He stopped in front of a plain door.

"Blanche." He quickly corrected himself. "Snow, I mean. I didn't intend to suggest—"

I shook my head and brushed past him, opening the door for myself. It had been a long night, and I didn't intend to discuss my father with my grandfather. Not right now, anyway.

He put out a hand to prevent the door closing. "I apologize for the room. You should have the grandest suite, of course. But as I said..."

I sighed, staring pointedly at his hand. "It doesn't matter. None of that matters in this situation."

He hurriedly removed his hand from the door, but a sudden thought made me stop before closing it.

"These nobles—the ones you say will support my claim. I want to meet them for myself. Look them in the eye." I didn't pause for his opinion. "You'll arrange it?"

He held my gaze, a look in his eye that might have been approval, before nodding once. I started to close the door only to pause again.

"And don't forget Alexander. I want a plan by this evening."

I didn't even look for his nod before thrusting the door closed. When I turned, the housekeeper herself was waiting for me, a joyful look on her face.

"Your Highness! I'm that pleased."

I managed a weak smile. "Thank you, Mrs. Preston."

She bustled about, assisting me as if she were one of my maids or a lady-in-waiting. Now that I finally found myself in a safe place, I could barely muster the energy to lift my arms to assist her in removing my gown. And as I sank into bed, I had to admit that while I felt too many conflicted feelings about my grandfather to even name them all, there was one feeling I couldn't deny —relief at having someone to share my burden. Someone older and more experienced to carry the load and do what needed to be done.

See—weak, said my inner voice. *Weak, as always.* But I was too tired to pay much attention, sleep already reaching out to claim me.

When I woke that afternoon, it took me a second to remember where I was. And then a second more to believe it. As I had crept through the forest toward the capital, I would have more easily believed that my next sleep would be in the castle dungeons than in a guest room of my grandfather's home.

But that thought promptly reminded me of who had been spending his nights in the dungeons, and I hurried out of bed. Bearing in mind my grandfather's warning, I didn't make use of the bell pull to call for a maid. Instead I washed in the basin and pitcher left out for me and began to struggle into the simple dress I had brought with me.

When the door suddenly opened, I froze half-way through the process, caught in an awkward pose. But only Mrs. Preston came through, carrying a tray laden with food. As soon as she saw me she put it down and rushed over, tutting and protesting as she did so.

"You cannot wear that old thing, Your Majesty!"

I noted that sometime between last night and this morning her familiar old address for me had changed. Was my grandfather responsible?

She soon had the dress back off and had opened a large wardrobe. Somehow my grandfather had managed to have it stocked with elegant and expensive gowns fit for a queen. Presumably while I slept, since I couldn't imagine they usually lived there. I looked at them with some misgiving. How much was I to be indebted to him when I still didn't know what had caused his about-face toward me?

But only a moment's reflection reminded me of the task I had set him. Did the presence of these dresses mean he had already arranged a meeting for me with the other loyal nobles? Just the thought made me submit unprotesting to being dressed in an elaborate gown of deep royal purple embellished with golden embroidery. If I wished to win over my court, I needed to look the part of a queen.

Mrs. Preston hovered over me as I ate and then hurried me through the house back to the same sitting room as the night before. I wasn't in the least surprised to find my grandfather already there awaiting me. The sight of him sent a strange mix of resentment and relief coursing through me, leading my stomach to riot against the food I had just filled it with. I took a deep breath and pushed it back down into place. Now was hardly the moment to be sick.

"Grandfather." I gave a regal inclination of the head in response to his formal bow.

He surveyed me with pleasure. "I'm glad to see we had your measurements correct."

The dress wasn't a perfect fit, but it was close enough that I didn't challenge his words.

"I have been wondering how you managed such a thing."

He smiled. "As you may have noticed, I have been fortunate enough to expand my staff of late. And one of my new acquisitions is a skilled seamstress recently departed from the palace. An excellent woman, I am told, who knew your measurements by heart. She has been hard at work ever since she arrived many weeks ago." He gave me another bow. "An act of faith, you might say, that I would have the opportunity to host my queen."

I shook my head. It seemed he thought of everything. And that explained the fit. My adventures in the forest had made their presence felt in my body, bringing subtle changes to my shape. I would have to search out this seamstress and get her to adjust the gowns.

I opened my mouth to ask about Alexander, but the duke cut me off.

"I have done as you commanded."

I looked at him eagerly, but his next words deflated me somewhat.

"We are to host a small party here this evening. A select gathering of like-minded members of the court. And even a few of the city's more wealthy and influential merchants." He looked at me with a knowing look. "No dancing, you understand. Just an evening of music and conversation. By invitation only, naturally."

He worked fast, I would give him that. And his ability to arrange such a thing at this short notice said much in support of his earlier words about his own power and influence. I studied his face. My father had often spoken with me of his thoughts and observations on the members of the court—with one notable exception. A glaring omission in my understanding of the nobility of Eliam.

"So tell me, Grandfather, how you can act against the queen with such impunity, while the rest of the court cowers in fear."

He looked over at me with raised brows. "I have not gone so far as to actively oppose her, you understand. Although she no doubt suspects—or even knows—that I stand against her." He paused. "There's a reason your father married your mother. And it wasn't just because she was so beautiful and loved by everyone who met her."

A wistful expression crossed his face before it turned business-like again. "My estate is the largest in the kingdom, and the oldest. Our family is well-connected and well-respected." He smiled, showing his teeth. "And we are extremely wealthy."

He shook his head. "And I have one other advantage as well."

"Oh?" I cocked an eyebrow at him, amused by his calm summary of his strengths.

"I'm not a sixteen-year-old girl living in the queen's own home." Something like anger flashed in his eyes. "I'm old and wily, and I come with a great many servants—and, more importantly—guards. If she wishes to move against me, she could not hide her intentions. It would have to be a show of force. And she seems to retain enough sense to know that if she did such a thing, the entire court would turn against her. At the moment their fear keeps many of them in check. But if she showed herself so willing to act against the court itself, their fear would propel them in a different direction."

He shook his head. "My death at her hands would probably be the single most effective thing I could do for your cause." He gave a wry smile. "But I'm afraid I'm not quite altruistic enough to hope for such an eventuality."

"No, indeed." I shivered. Whatever I felt for my grandfather, I didn't wish for Alida to have him killed. "Thank you for organizing the meeting so promptly." The words tasted a little bitter in my mouth, but I forced them out anyway.

He smiled. "It was my pleasure."

I drew a deep breath. "And Alexander? You have plans for his escape?"

"Ah." His smile fell away. "That is not such an easy matter."

"No, I did not suppose it was." I met his gaze steadily, letting him read the resolution in my eyes. When it came to Alexander, at least, I had no doubts and no hesitation.

He sighed. "A direct assault is naturally out of the question at this point."

I inclined my head. "Naturally."

"Which means we must attempt to get both in and out of the dungeons without detection. And we must bear in mind that we don't know what state your huntsman will be in."

My heart seized at his words, and I tried to pour extra steel into my expression. I would not leave my oldest friend and most loyal subject to the queen's mercy for a moment longer than necessary. *And your love,* reminded my inner voice. *Don't forget that.* I pushed the thought away. Even if I was not in love with Alexander, he would still deserve better than to be left in captivity until we had managed to free the entire kingdom.

My grandfather sighed again. "One of the guards who takes regular shifts on one of the side gates is open to receiving a bribe. I have dispatched someone to discover when he next has night duty. I believe a team of three will be the right size for the job from there."

"Excellent." I nodded once. "There will be four of us then, since naturally I will be one of the party as well."

CHAPTER 16

 y grandfather might claim me as his queen, but that didn't mean he would allow such a pronouncement to stand without argument. A great deal of argument. In fact, we were still arguing about it when the first guests of the evening arrived at the front door of the ducal mansion.

My grandfather seemed to think I would see sense and back down if he could just get me to understand how dangerous the mission would be and how important I was to the kingdom. But I was all too aware of both those things already. I felt them in the weight of fear and responsibility that dragged me down with every step I took.

But I had spent weeks training in the forest, honing myself into someone stronger than the person I had been before. And yet still I had sent Alexander alone into danger on my behalf. And danger had found him.

I knew from my father's teachings that such was the life of a monarch. If I did succeed at gaining my rightful throne, this weight of responsibility would never completely leave me. And all too often, others would be called upon to bear the danger. But

I had not yet won my throne. And I knew in the deepest parts of me that I needed to do this. Needed to face my fear.

For this one time, I needed to prove to myself—and to those who I hoped would serve me—that they mattered to me. That I was willing to bear danger alongside them and for them. If I sheltered in this house until others had secured me my throne, I might never be able to make the decisions that would need to be made in the years to come.

And then there was the reason I would never tell my grandfather. That I still didn't entirely trust him. If his men came back and reported that they hadn't been able to access the castle, how would I know if that was true, or if the whole thing had been a ruse to pacify me?

And so I stood firm.

I could see my grandfather wished to forbid it outright, but the arriving guests served to remind him of the quandary he had put himself in. He had apparently decided to devote his considerable resources to making me queen. Which meant he couldn't order me to do anything.

I was a little ashamed of the small feeling of power it gave me. And yet, despite all the assistance he had so far given me, I was unwilling to allow him to waltz into my life from nowhere and start ordering me about as if he were a truly parental figure. He had yet to earn that right.

And, of course, as soon as the door opened and the guests began to pour in, we both assumed our court masks, putting our disagreement to the side. We received them in the duke's spacious ballroom which had been filled with large potted plants, low couches, and high tables of refreshments.

Unlike the last time I had faced the court, each of the guests on this occasion bowed or curtsied low to me and greeted me as Your Majesty. My grandfather—and perhaps to some extent my notes—had done their work well. But their eyes still conveyed a range of uncomfortable emotions, just as they had done at that previous audience. Discomfort. Shame. Fear. But also a new one. Hope.

None had the bright light of fervor or devotion in their eyes. They stood against my stepmother, or perhaps with my grandfather. I still had to win them over if I wished them to follow me for my own sake.

And so I allowed the familiar atmosphere to sweep me back to the years I had spent growing up in a castle and the countless such parties I had attended. I put on my most regal manner and attempted to charm everyone I spoke to. It was a delicate effort since I needed to strike a careful balance.

There was a great deal of sympathy to be gained by emphasizing my youth and vulnerability. I was a sixteen-year-old girl who had recently lost her only remaining parent. And my stepmother was trying to depose and murder me. Playing to their hearts would win me sympathy and possibly some loyalty.

But I also needed to reassure them that my stepmother was wrong—I wasn't too young to sit on the throne. And that was less easily done. And also more personally painful. Because it involved reminding them that my father had been a good king, and that I had done everything at his side. They could trust me because they had trusted him.

The first few times it took everything in me to keep my tone light when I mentioned him. But to my surprise it became easier as the evening wore on. The more I talked of him, the more natural it became. By the time I made my way around to the baron of Carstone—a distant cousin on my father's side—I was actually able to laugh with him over some shared reminiscences of visits he had made to the castle when he was an adolescent and I was a child.

"I thought he would never let me visit again after that," he said when our chuckles subsided. "I don't think I'd ever seen him so angry."

I shook my head. "Well, it was his favorite horse, Roger. And far too big to ride. I seem to remember I even warned you about it at the time."

The baron rolled his eyes in an undignified manner. "Yes, I'm sure you did. You were always trying to tag along or interfere with my fun in some way."

I rolled my eyes back at him. It might not be queenly, but it was too enjoyable to talk to someone at least somewhat close to my own age. Someone who had shared something of my childhood.

After my mother's death, my father had kept me close, and there had been few other children at the castle for me to form friendships with. Other than the occasional visits from Roger and a few of my other distant relations, I had spent my time with my father or on my stolen escapades with Alexander. Looking back, my father had no doubt known of all our adventures. He had encouraged my friendship with Alexander—one that kept me far closer to him than friendships with other girls of the court would have done. And I had never regretted the lack or seen my life as missing anything. Until now, when I wished I had stronger bonds among the nobles of my kingdom.

Roger's face dropped as a moment of silence fell between us. "He did let me back, of course. He was a good man."

"And a good king," I murmured.

Roger looked up at me. "Aye, that he was." He sighed. "We all grieve for him."

I nodded, my breath suddenly tight in my throat. My cousin squeezed my arm, sadness and discomfort lingering on his face. "I...I really am so sorry, Snow."

I nodded, wordless, and felt almost relieved when my grandfather swooped down and swept me away. I needed a moment to gather myself again.

But I didn't have long. The count and countess of Ellsmore wished to speak with me. The presence of the older couple had surprised me a little. It was true they had looked almost sympathetically at me when I faced the court beside my stepmother, but I hadn't included them on my list. I had always had the distinct impression they disapproved of me—ever since I was a child. I always felt too young and too pretty and too foolish in their eyes.

But the serious way in which they offered their condolences and their support for my reign made me rethink my assessment. Oh, their eyes still suggested disapproval—and no doubt they would have preferred someone older and more staid in my place —but it seemed their loyalty was solid, after all.

Several senior merchants wanted to speak to me next, all ones I recognized from consultations they had attended with my father. Their conversation focused on the queen's new taxes and the stifling effect her reign was already having on the economy. I responded with concern, voicing my dislike of such policies, and they left looking more than satisfied with our conversation. My grandfather had been looking pleased as well until he had disappeared half way through the interaction.

I looked around for him, wondering how many more people I had yet to speak to and how much longer the party might be expected to last. I wasn't tired, exactly—I had slept most of the day, after all—but I was weary in a way that had nothing to do with sleep.

I spotted him eventually near the door, deep in conversation with Bronson. And after a moment of observing them, my eyes narrowed, and I made a direct line across the ballroom floor toward them. I didn't know my grandfather well yet, but something in his posture suggested a concern I hadn't seen there earlier in the evening. And Bronson I did know. To the guests he probably looked entirely composed, but to me he looked downright worried.

I tried to keep my face equally neutral to the gaze of outsiders as I abruptly joined them.

"Trouble?"

My grandfather looked up at me, and a quickly hidden frown suggested my presence was both unexpected and unwelcome.

"Snow."

"You've had some news?" I had no reason to suppose it was news of Alexander, and yet concern for him made me too anxious to beat around the bush. "Tell me at once."

The two men exchanged a look before my grandfather reluctantly spoke.

"We have heard back about the guard roster. The guard in question is on duty tonight only."

My heart rate sped up as excitement raced through me, leaving me alert where before I had felt weary. Thank goodness I had spotted them. I suspected my grandfather would have failed to mention this piece of news until the morning otherwise, when it would already have been too late.

"So when do we leave, then?"

The duke shook his head, the movement subtle given our location. "We can't go tonight. We're not ready. We'll have to wait for the next roster."

I stared him down. "Absolutely not. That's too long to wait. And what preparation can we really make? Our wits will serve us as well tonight as any other night, and we were always relying on them to see us through."

"Snow, it's too danger—"

I cut him off with a tilt of my chin and a flash of my eyes. "I think you mean *Your Majesty*. And we no longer have time for argument. I will make my farewells and retire for the evening." I glanced down at my complicated gown. "I'll need a change of clothes before I slip out. Have your men meet me in the kitchens in an hour." I paused. "Or will they need two?"

My grandfather let out a slow, defeated breath. "One should be sufficient in the circumstances."

I nodded once and turned to leave them. As I walked away, I heard Bronson mutter to the duke.

"When did she grow up?"

A small smile slipped across my face. I would no doubt remember all my failings soon enough, but for now the anticipation of seeing Alexander again lent me a fevered sort of courage. No more waiting around. The time had come to act.

When I faced the dark walls of the castle beside three men I had never seen before, my courage slipped somewhat. But I reminded myself that I had crept in here once before already and escaped without harm. That made two escapes, in fact. We could do this.

We had left the city behind, approaching the small side gate from the trees. Somehow in the hour it had taken us to prepare, the duke had gotten word to the gate guard about our approach. I hadn't asked how, and I didn't really want to know. My head was already full of far too many things as it was.

One of my companions knocked on the wooden gate in a strange rhythm, and after an extended moment that had my heart racing, it slowly eased open. A gruff looking man put his head out and glowered at us.

"I hope you brought extra. I don't like all this last minute business."

The man who had knocked nodded. "You'll receive it plus the usual fee on our return. As always."

The guard glared even more ferociously but made no protest. I hadn't known that was the arrangement, and it relieved me somewhat. Insurance against his deciding to report us before we could escape. Still, I pulled the hood of my cloak more firmly around my face, keeping my head angled down. We were all in agreement that it would be far better if the guard didn't recognize the fourth member of our party.

I was the third one through into the castle grounds, taking note of the second guard snoring on the ground. No wonder the guard didn't like short notice arrivals if he needed to drug the other man on shift.

Thankfully the awake guard seemed to show no particular interest in me, and we had soon left the wall behind us as we moved through the scattering of trees. The men I traveled with clearly knew what they were doing, moving swiftly and silently so that I had to concentrate hard to keep up.

They had introduced themselves back in the duke's kitchen, but my nerves had been thrumming so hard I only remembered the name of the leader. Tarver. I suspected he might be the captain of the duke's guard. No doubt he had only been sent on this mission because I had insisted on coming. I hoped he didn't resent it.

For all my nerves and racing heart, this first part turned out to be the simplest portion of the rescue attempt. I had half expected my grandfather to have an equally neat arrangement for gaining access to the castle itself, but no such suggestion had been forthcoming.

"What's the plan?" I asked, slipping up beside Tarver as quietly as I could. For the first time I agreed with my grandfather's reluctance at having to execute the rescue so hurriedly. It really would have been better to have this conversation before now.

Tarver looked down at me, but I couldn't read his expression in the dark.

"Now we have to hope we get lucky, Your Highness." His tone made it clear he did not approve of such a haphazard approach.

I shook my head. "Ebony, remember?" I had come up with my own code name and was rather proud of it. I didn't want to risk someone overhearing one of them using my title. Of course, I was hoping we wouldn't approach anyone close enough to be overheard at all, but it was better safe than sorry.

He dipped his head once in acknowledgment but said nothing. Not exactly encouraging, but I pressed on.

"I have a way in, if we need one."

He actually stopped at that, wheeling to face me, his men falling in to flank us.

"*You* have a way in, Prin—uh, Ebony?"

"Yes." I tried to sound confident and sure. And not in the least offended by his doubt. "I did grow up here, remember."

He exchanged a quick look with his men, before stepping aside.

"Lead on, then."

I hoped he couldn't see me lick my lips nervously as I strode forward ahead of them. Coming in on an upper floor when we wanted to end up in the dungeon wasn't ideal, but it was better than no access at all. Hopefully there wouldn't be too many servants forced to work late into the night as Gertie had been doing last time I was here.

When we arrived at the base of the vines, the three men exchanged another look, but I didn't hesitate, and none of them protested. Together we scaled the wall, and I hoped they noticed that I didn't hold them back, moving as quickly and confidently as any of them. All my recent practice was paying off.

My neat curls, arranged and securely pinned in place by Mrs. Preston herself, made finding and releasing a hair pin easier than it had been on my last ascent. I popped open the window and swung into my dressing room, quickly moving away from the window to leave room for the men to enter.

When we all stood crammed into the small room, I thought I detected an impressed look on Tarver's face. I straightened, my head lifting. When we returned safely, I hoped he would report to my grandfather that I had not been dead weight—or worse—on this rescue.

Tarver looked around the small space. "I suppose these are your rooms?"

I nodded.

"Well, as you said, you know the palace best. Lead on."

I swallowed. This was what I had wanted—or close enough. But my clammy hands and roiling stomach apparently hadn't received the message.

I carefully eased out into my bedchamber, relieved to find it empty and lit only by moonlight. I gestured the others through, but we all paused by the door that would lead us out into the corridor. My sight glazed over as I considered our current location and our goal—the dungeon.

"I think we should be safe if we take the long route," I whispered at last.

"The long route?" asked one of the men whose names I had forgotten.

I shrugged. "It's an old building and several kings have added new sections or redesigned, so it's something of a maze. There are shorter and longer routes to most places, and all the inhabitants know the shorter ones. The servants won't be using the longer ways. We'll just need to watch out on the corridors where they intersect."

"We're in your hands," said Tarver, with a gesture toward the door.

I bit my lip. Did he sound afraid? Or was that in my head? I shook myself and eased open the door, quickly checking the corridor beyond.

"All clear. But move quickly," I whispered over my shoulder, and then I was off down the cold stone floor.

I forced myself not to run, moving as quietly as I possibly could so my straining ears would have no impediment. But my loudly beating heart had other ideas, and I was sure I wouldn't hear anyone approaching over its noise.

Lanterns burned at regular intervals in this wing, so there was no chance to disappear into the shadows. I picked up my pace, deciding speed mattered more than complete silence. My three companions kept pace without making any sound I could discern. A skill I envied. No doubt their hearts maintained a normal rhythm rather than overwhelming all their senses.

When we at last pushed through a door and then through a second opening covered by a hanging tapestry, I breathed a soft sigh of relief. There was no such thing as safe here in the heart of the castle, but this corridor was a lot safer than the ones we had just traversed, at least.

No lanterns burned here, but the way was lit by the moon, shining through several uncovered windows. Tarver looked around with a raised eyebrow.

"I see what you mean."

I shrugged. "We use all the rooms on occasion. Mainly when we have large parties of foreign royals visiting. But most of the time they sit empty." My eyes caught on a pile of dust in one corner. No doubt the overworked servants had decided the upkeep of these wings was of least importance in their list of duties. A very good thing for us.

I led them more confidently now, down a branching corridor and then another one before pushing through a door to a winding staircase.

"For the servants to use when we have guests in these rooms," I explained.

We all spiraled downward, the trip seeming to take far longer than its actual length warranted. How much of the night had now passed? How much still remained? I imagined Alexander's surprise when he saw us, and some of my earlier excitement and courage returned.

The bottom of the last flight sobered me, however. I looked up at the men on the stairs behind me.

"This comes out near the kitchen. If there are any servants still awake..."

Tarver descended to stand beside me. "How far from here to the dungeons?"

I closed my eyes and recalled my internal map of the castle. It wasn't too far, and we could go some of the way, at least, in a lesser-used corridor. I opened my eyes again.

"Far enough." I grimaced. "But I think we can do it."

He nodded once. "This part of the castle I know. But if you think you know a better way…"

I didn't bother to ask how exactly he knew the underbelly of the royal castle. Instead I shook my head.

"No, you lead." I suspected both his hearing and his instincts were keener than mine. "If you make a wrong turn, I'll let you know."

He made a brief hand gesture to the men behind us, and they pulled in close. I kept my face impassive. Tarver was doing a good job of keeping his true feelings hidden, but he couldn't appreciate having a princess tagging along. Not when he was clearly used to soldiers who followed his commands as opposed to young girls who assured him they'd correct him when necessary.

Still, we stepped out into the corridor as one solid unit and moved swiftly and quietly through the servants' level. For a few moments, I could actually pretend I was one of them.

And then a slight noise up ahead sounded, and the three men closed in around me, whisking me backward into a shadowed alcove and shielding my body with their own. I grimaced from my hidden spot, not even attempting to peek past to see what was going on. Not really one of them, after all.

Two servants passed, their slow footsteps and lack of conversation suggesting exhaustion. At least that worked to our advantage, since they apparently failed to examine the shadows around them. And there were shadows down here. When my father ruled, these corridors had been lit as brightly as the higher levels. But apparently Alida had replaced the lanterns with flickering tallow candles. A much cheaper—and less pleasant—alternative.

Only once did I have to surge forward and nudge Tarver down an alternative corridor. He moved instantly to comply, not stopping to question me. Whatever he thought privately, he had been well chosen for this job.

We finally halted just outside the entrance to the dungeons. Only a short flight of stairs and a guard room now stood between us and the cells. I tried to calm my breathing. Alexander was so close, and yet still so far.

"Please tell me you have a plan for this, at least," I whispered. I tried to surreptitiously wipe my palms on my skirts. It hit me suddenly and forcibly that someone was going to suffer for this. Obviously I hoped it wouldn't be us. But neither did I want it to be any innocent servants. The guards who had sided with my stepmother—for money and power, no doubt—on the other hand...

Tarver drew a short, solid club from his belt. "We're to avoid any killing, if we can." He gave me a stern look. "Don't you come through that door until I come back out to call you. Do you understand, Ebony?"

I flushed at his use of my code name, a subtle reminder that I wasn't in charge here, despite my royal title. I nodded quickly. If they were going to be subduing the guards with brute force, I was aware enough to know I had no place in such a scenario.

I flattened myself against the wall next to the door, and Tarver gestured his men forward. Pulling open the door, the three of them rushed through, pulling it closed behind them. A startled exclamation filtered through, followed by several crashes and a number of grunts and groans.

I trembled, straining to hear and trying to follow the action on sound alone—an impossible task. Sooner than I had thought possible, the door swung back open, and a tall figure appeared in the corridor. I pushed myself off the wall before my mind registered that it wasn't a familiar figure.

I shrank back again instantly, hoping the escaping guard

hadn't seen me. But as his gaze skittered up and down the corridor—moving frantically without locking on to anything—I saw him inhale.

I didn't have time to think. I barely had time to act. But I couldn't let him call an alarm or we would be finished.

CHAPTER 17

J launched myself off the stone behind me, jumping at his back and slinging both hands around his neck. He staggered for a moment and nearly fell before regaining his balance. Any shout had been strangled by the dead weight now clinging to his throat.

I hung on grimly, my feet dangling just short of the floor, as his hands scrabbled at mine. My dangling weight worked to my advantage, though, and in his panic, he couldn't shake me free.

His fingers fell away from mine, and he thrust us both backward, crossing half the corridor in two strides. My back hit the stone wall with a bone-jarring thud. Pain raced through me, panic close behind as I struggled unsuccessfully to pull in a breath.

Instinct rather than conscious thought kept my hands locked around the guard's neck. But as he stepped forward, clearly preparing to slam me back against the stone again, I didn't think I could hold on through another hit.

And then something ripped me away from him. I reached out blindly, trying to regain my hold while still attempting to suck in a breath. But instead of calling an alarm, the guard crumpled to the floor. My own feet found the stone again, and the hold on me released.

I instantly dropped to all fours, retching and coughing as I forced air into my lungs. I took several deep breaths before looking up. Tarver and one of his men both hovered uncertainly over me. Shakily I pushed myself back to my feet.

"I'm all right," I said, although neither of them had asked.

I thought I saw a glimmer of relief in Tarver's eyes, however. What orders and threats had my grandfather handed out about my well-being?

"Our apologies, Your—Ebony. That one got away from us."

I moved gingerly toward the open door, my back throbbing. "I couldn't let him call an alarm. But next time I'm bringing a dagger, or something. It would be easier."

Alarm flashed through Tarver's eyes, and I managed a weak smile.

"I jest, Tarver. I sincerely hope there is no next time."

"As do we all."

I glanced at him sharply. Was he hoping he would never be ordered on another mission with me? Or just that we would need to make no more jail breaks? His face gave nothing away. As we all passed into the guard room, dragging the unconscious guard with us and closing the door, he inclined his head toward me, however.

"Our thanks for dealing with our oversight. We would all have been lost if he called an alarm."

I smiled, straightening my spine and then wincing at the pain in my back. It quickly faded, however, replaced with pride and excitement. I had done it. I had saved us, and now nothing stood between me and Alexander.

The third member of our party had already begun binding and gagging the guards inside the room, and the other two moved to help him. I, on the other hand, flitted between the unconscious prisoners until I found one with a sergeant's insignia. And, more importantly, with a ring of keys hanging from his belt.

I had it removed within moments and barreled through the door on the far side of the room.

"Ebony! Wait." Tarver's low call didn't slow me. I trusted that they had already checked this long passage for guards, and I could wait no longer.

I raced past the closest cells, the doors of which all stood slightly ajar. When I encountered one that was closed, I almost couldn't stop, sliding along the dirt floor. But a second later, I had the bars gripped in both hands as I peered through. It took a moment for my eyes to adjust to the increased darkness down here, but I didn't need them to recognize the voice that cried, "Snow!" in a low whisper.

And a second later I could see him, his tall figure achingly familiar. Dark, tangled hair. Stormy, gray eyes. My gaze roamed over him, noticing a bruise on one side of his face, and a rip in his left sleeve, the edges of the material stiff with something dry and brown. My hands tightened on the bars.

"Your arm!"

He crossed over to me in a single stride, his hands closing over mine.

"It's nothing. I'm fine." His voice was low and quiet. "But what are you doing here? It isn't safe!"

He seemed alert despite the late hour—no doubt the sounds from the guardhouse had roused him. Assuming he was sleeping at all down here.

"We're here to rescue you," I mirrored his whisper, suddenly remembering there might be other prisoners down here, and we were attempting to keep my presence a secret.

"We?" He tried to peer up the passage before looking back at me. "I assume you can't mean those children?"

I shook my head, my face indicating my opinion of that suggestion, and he let out a breath.

"You went to your grandfather?"

I nodded, but I was already fumbling with the key ring, fitting one after another into the lock on his cell door. We could catch up when we were safely back in the duke's mansion.

It seemed to take forever, but at last one of them turned with a satisfying click. Alexander was out into the passage in two strides, his hands flitting up and down my arms as if to check I was truly there and in one piece.

I swayed, my body betraying me with its desire to lean into his embrace. But my mind reasserted control, remembering what had happened last time I tried to throw myself at him. I stayed upright.

I turned back toward the door to the guard room before hesitating. Swinging back around, I glanced uncertainly down the dim passage.

"Are there other...?"

I didn't want to free someone who was locked up legitimately. But the dungeons had been rarely used in my father's reign— anyone arrested by the royal guards was promptly transferred to the magistrates in the city for due process. So the chances seemed high that anyone kept here now was here for opposing Alida...

Alexander held out his hand, and I placed the keys into them without hesitation.

"Wait here," he said.

I glanced uneasily backward as the door behind us opened, but only Tarver came through.

"Ebony?" he called quietly.

I moved to join him, and his eyes, apparently adjusted to the lower lighting now, moved past me and down toward the cells.

"Was he not...?" He looked worried.

"He's out. But we thought...other prisoners..."

Tarver grimaced but made no actual protest. I bit my lip. Hopefully there weren't too many of them, or it would severely complicate our escape. And Alexander had looked mobile enough, but if any of them had been down here for longer...

I pushed away the thought. I wasn't leaving anyone here to rot if all they had done was stand against my usurping stepmother.

Alexander reappeared a moment later, an older man behind him. Only one, and he appeared to be moving under his own power. I breathed a sigh of relief.

They stopped in front of us.

"Is that all?" I looked at Alexander for confirmation, but it was his companion who answered, his voice as low as Alexander's had been.

"You don't want to go letting out Barcher—" He paused, his eyes taking in my face as his brows lifted in surprise. "Your—"

"Ebony," I said quickly, cutting him off. "And if that's the case, then we need to get moving."

Alexander quirked an amused eyebrow at me as we all passed into the guard room, and I glared at him. He seemed to have relaxed somewhat since having the chance to eye my companions —apparently he deemed them competent enough for a prison rescue.

An underlying tension still radiated from his frame, however, as we moved back out into the corridors. He kept close to me, hovering protectively despite the fact that I was the rescuer in this scenario. I rolled my eyes but didn't tell him to back off.

We were still in danger, but somehow his solid presence calmed me. It felt as if I had been unable to breathe properly ever since he disappeared but had only realized it now that he was back with me, relatively unharmed.

Thankfully exiting the castle was a great deal easier than entering it. We climbed back to the servants' ground floor level and then let ourselves out a side door, leaving it closed but unlocked behind us. It hardly mattered if they worked out how we had fled once we were gone.

The ground seemed to fly beneath us now that Alexander

was beside me and, all too soon, we had reached the side gate again. The second guard still snored, slumped in an awkward position on the ground. The other one raised his eyebrows at the sight of our increased numbers and looked uneasily between us.

Tarver held out a leather pouch, however, and the other man moved to take it.

"You'll find the extra in there."

The guard hesitated for a second, but his hand had already closed over the pouch, and he gave a reluctant nod.

As we slipped through the gate and out into the forest, I bit my lip.

"Don't worry," said Alexander's voice in my ear. "He won't talk now. He would have to admit his own role in it if he did."

I nodded, breathing a little easier. Trust Alexander to recognize my discomfort and move to reassure me. I had almost forgotten what it was like to have someone around who knew me so well.

By the time we re-entered the city, I thought I could detect a faint lightening to the darkness. We all picked up the pace in unspoken agreement, reaching the mansion well before true dawn.

The side door opened for us before Tarver could knock, Bronson ushering us inside. His eyes lingered briefly on me before taking in our two additional companions.

With the mansion door closed behind us, I slumped, tension draining from me. Alexander was there instantly, his hand under my arm, guiding me to one of the wooden chairs littering the large kitchen. I wanted to protest, but I wasn't actually sure how much longer my legs would continue to support me. It seemed a tidal wave of exhaustion had been waiting for the nervous energy to subside.

As soon as I was seated, I looked at our unexpected extra rescue. He caught my questioning look and bowed deeply.

"It is an honor, Your Highness." He grinned. "Or is it still Ebony?"

I smiled back, unable to help liking his rough manner.

"Actually, the correct address would be Your Majesty." Bronson's gaze was trained at something on the wall above the newcomer's head, his stiff posture expressing his disapproval.

I hid a smile as I remembered that Bronson himself had first addressed me as Your Highness when I had stumbled unannounced into the mansion. I couldn't blame anyone who defaulted to the title I had borne my whole life.

"My apologies, Your Majesty." The man bowed again, although the way his eyes danced made me think he found the steward amusing.

"This is Carter. One of my mentors and the best huntsman we have."

"One of the best, me lad, although I thank you for the compliment." The older man smiled affectionately at Alexander.

Carter. The name rang a vague bell. No doubt I had heard Alexander mention him before.

"I suspect he was locked up for being too close to me," said Alexander grimly.

Carter gave a rough chuckle. "Now that I won't thank you for, boy. I might be getting on in years, but I have more threat in me than that, I hope."

Alexander smiled reluctantly. "That you do, old man. That you do." He clapped him on the back.

"So what were you locked up for, then?" I asked.

"Turns out I didn't like taking orders from that Randolph fellow," said Carter with a shrug.

Just the mention of the guard's name made my heartbeat pick back up, but I tried to keep my face impassive.

"And while I was more than happy to search for you, Your High—Majesty, I took exception to the idea that you should be escorted straight to Randolph rather than back to the castle."

This time I did shiver, and Alexander stepped even closer to my seat, although he made no move to touch me.

"It seems I must thank you for your loyalty, then." I nodded at the older huntsman.

"No need to thank me, Your Majesty. I ain't the kind for treason, even if it wears a pretty crown." He frowned. "And you'll find most of your subjects feel the same way." He shook his head with a wry grin. "They just have more sense than this old man and keep it to themselves."

"Too bad the guards don't feel that way," said Alexander, the word *guard* sounding more like a curse.

"I think you'll find many of them do," said a new voice. We turned to find my grandfather had joined us. He looked comfortable despite seeming out of place in the kitchen.

"I haven't observed any great loyalty from them so far," I said bitterly. I rubbed at my forehead. I knew I didn't sound queenly, but the exhaustion was dragging at me. I could see Alexander watching me with concern out of the corner of his eyes, despite the fact that no one had yet seen to his arm.

"None of this was the work of a moment," said the duke. "Alida has no doubt been preparing for the king's death for a long time."

I drew in a breath at the mention of my father's death, and a warm hand landed on my shoulder. Despite the best of intentions, I couldn't help leaning into it. He squeezed once and then withdrew his grip, and I tried not to let the sudden empty feeling show on my face.

"No doubt," I said, glad to hear my voice didn't tremble. "And I'm sure she has put all these new taxes to good work, pouring into the purses of her newly loyal guards."

"Indeed." My grandfather inclined his head toward me. "But I am happy to report that many of your guards are not so easily bought. Many of the current number are new recruits from the last two years. While many of the older ones have found themselves seeking positions elsewhere in the kingdom. She has been weeding out their number with careful precision, moving just slowly enough not to arouse any outright questioning."

I swiveled slightly in my chair to face him directly, my brows rising. "And you know this, how?"

He gestured toward Bronson who lingered at the back of our group with Tarver, although the other two members of our rescue party had disappeared. "My most recent servants are not the only castle refugees in my employ. I started to notice an increase in guards seeking positions eighteen months ago. It took a fair amount of digging, but by the time word of your father's death reached me, I had a fairly good idea of what sort of situation I would find here. Naturally I lost no time in making my way to the capital to pay my respects."

The wry twist to the way he said *respect* made me tense, unsure if the sentiment were meant for my father or stepmother. I ran another hand across my forehead. I suspected some deeper point lurked behind his mention of the guards, but I needed more sleep before I faced off with my grandfather.

I surged to my feet.

"I'm retiring to my room for some sleep," I said. "We will speak further when I wake up."

All five men bowed to me immediately, and I swept out of the room. If they intended to make me queen, I needed to remember that from now on, they answered to me and not the other way around.

CHAPTER 18

*D*espite the exhaustion, I didn't sleep as late into the afternoon as I had the day before. My mind and heart were both too full. My mind with wondering what steps we needed to take next, and my heart with Alexander. I needed to see him again and be sure he was really well. And I wanted to know what exactly had happened.

Mrs. Preston failed to appear this time, so I abandoned my wardrobe of fancy new gowns for one of my old ones that I could slip into unaided. When I poked my head out of my room, I spotted a footman at the far end of the corridor, so I pulled back inside and waited until his footsteps had faded before venturing back out.

Of course I didn't actually know where to go, but ended up deciding on the small sitting room I had used previously. My instincts proved right when I thrust open the door and found Alexander and my grandfather in quiet conversation.

They broke off abruptly at the sound of the opening door, both springing to their feet at the sight of me. When they started to bow, I waved a hand and sighed.

"Enough of that. Please. Not when it's just us."

"Very well," said my grandfather, but they both still waited for me to be seated before resuming their own places.

"So, what have I missed?" I looked expectantly between them. Part of me resented the fact that they hadn't called for me earlier, but I pushed the feeling aside, recognizing it as a child's petulance. I had ordered them to let me sleep, I could hardly now be upset with them for respecting my wishes.

Neither of them seemed quite sure where to start, and I used the pause to drink in the sight of Alexander. He looked a little paler than usual, perhaps, and the bruise on his face looked more prominent in the bright light of day. But its yellows and greens suggested it wasn't new, and he wore a fresh shirt, this one without rips and with a bulge beneath the sleeve that suggested he now wore a bandage on his arm.

"You start." I gestured at him. "What happened?"

He grimaced. "Nothing worth reporting. I was keeping up with my usual tasks while liaising with the duke on the side and planning my return trip to you when I was woken one night by two guards standing over my bed, their swords at my throat." He shrugged uncomfortably. "There was little I could do, and I've been in the dungeons ever since."

My eyes lingered on his bruised face, and he shrugged uncomfortably. "Oh, Randolph visited and muscled me around a little, asking a few questions, but he hardly seemed dedicated to the task. I think Alida ordered me locked up because she knew I would never be loyal to her, but I don't think she really believed I knew your whereabouts. I think she's just growing increasingly nervous and desperate to act."

"Interesting that she doesn't believe you're working with Snow," said the duke, his eyes flitting between us. There was something in his eyes I couldn't read, something that made me shift uncomfortably in my seat.

Apparently Alexander shared my unease, his hand tapping

against his leg in an uncharacteristic way. He looked over toward me but dropped his eyes before I could meet his gaze.

"I think..." He cleared his throat. "That is, I believe Alida thinks that if I had been responsible for Snow's escape I would never have returned."

He glanced at me again, the slightest flush on his face. Oh. I sat back, my own cheeks heating. She thought that if I had fled with Alexander we would have simply run off together and never looked back. Were my feelings so obvious? Did the whole court know of them? Or just my stepmother?

My grandfather looked between us with a raised eyebrow, but I couldn't bring myself to hold his gaze, staring down at my clasped hands instead.

Alexander cleared his throat again. "I suspect she thinks you rescued Snow, Your Grace. She's furious about it, but not yet confident to challenge you directly."

The duke drummed his fingers thoughtfully against the arm of his chair. "Yes, I can imagine she might suspect such a thing." His eyes flitted briefly back to me. "And naturally I would have done so if I had realized the need or seen the opportunity." He looked back at Alexander. "And, of course, there is no known connection between the two of us. It seems to me the situation could have been a lot worse."

I wanted to disagree, my eyes caught on the bulge beneath Alexander's sleeve, but I had to admit my grandfather was right. I myself had imagined many worse possibilities. I forced my mind away from them, reminding myself that none of them had come to pass.

"So how did I go last night?" I asked instead, turning to the duke.

He raised both eyebrows. "Tarver gave you an excellent report. Seems to feel they would have been in trouble without you."

A small smile played around Alexander's lips and a warm look filled his eyes.

I blinked in surprise. "That's very kind of him, but I didn't mean the rescue. I meant the party."

"Oh." This time it was my grandfather who looked startled, although he quickly pivoted, clearly turning his mind to the earlier event of the night before. I doubted he was ever thrown for long, the duke of Lestern.

"Party?" Alexander looked between us.

I hurried to explain, not wanting him to think I had been socializing while he was locked away for my sake.

"My grandfather threw a last-minute social event for a select few loyal members of court. So they could all have the chance to eyeball me and make their assessment." I turned to the duke. "So, how did I do? Will they support me?"

"You did very well." My grandfather looked at me with warm approval, and I hated how much I liked it. I still hadn't decided if I wanted his good opinion.

"Of course she did," said Alexander, quick to my defense as always.

I rolled my eyes at him. "They'll support me then? Are there any we need to be concerned about?"

The duke shook his head slowly, but my heart sank anyway. There was something more, I could tell.

"So why don't you look more pleased?" I asked.

He sighed. "They support your rule. Especially since they know I stand behind it."

I nodded slowly. As much as I resented it, I could also understand it. My grandfather had shown himself to be knowledgeable in the ways of court despite his long absence. I could hardly be surprised that he would inspire more confidence than a sixteen-year-old girl on her own. It struck me suddenly that if I did succeed in gaining the throne, he would be the logical choice of regent.

I regarded him with new suspicion. Was that what this was all about? Was I supposed to exchange one false parental figure who wished to use me as a pawn in their quest for power for another?

But another moment's reflection brought calm. Sixteen years holed up in his coastal estate didn't exactly suggest a power-hungry figure eager to take control of the court. If that had been his intention, he would have done better never to leave the court at all. If he had been a present grandparent, loving from the start, I would have eagerly run to him over Alida at my father's death. No, something else motivated him.

"They want more troops," said Alexander, his grim voice reminding me of the actual topic under conversation.

The duke nodded. "They support you, but they're concerned about the guards. Alida has shown herself to be just ruthless enough that they're afraid of what she'll do if she sees the court openly turn against her. And I can't really blame them. She just might be fool enough to respond with violence and attempt to impose martial law or some such idiocy."

I slumped back into my seat. "So we need to build an army of our own?" I rubbed a hand across my eyes. "How long is that going to take?" And how many people would die if it came to civil war?

"Not as long as you might think."

I looked up quickly to catch the dangerous gleam in my grandfather's eye.

"Lestern," I said, the word more of a breath.

He shrugged, although he couldn't hide his satisfied smile. "Once I began to realize what was happening, I decided my treasury could wear a little extra burden for a while."

I sat up straight, scooting forward to the edge of my chair. "All those dismissed guards—the loyal ones?"

"Not all, of course. But a great many. Once the word got out that the duke of Lestern offered fair wages and conditions, it was astonishing how many young men decided a life by the sea was just the life for them." He grinned, and it showed all his teeth.

A slow smile spread across Alexander's face as well. "So all you need to do is call them?"

The duke turned slowly to me, although Alexander had asked the question. His drumming fingers continued to tap.

"I could, of course. But there's no denying it will take time." His brows lowered slightly. "And the longer you're here, the more likely word of your presence will get out. So I've been thinking of another alternative." He met my eyes, his own serious. "I would like it if you visited Lestern yourself."

"What?" I stared at him before looking across at Alexander. My friend looked thoughtful, his gaze traveling back and forth between me and my grandfather.

"Think about it, Snow." The duke leaned forward. "It will get you away from the capital and away from that woman. And it will give you a chance to see and meet my troops for yourself. You can travel back here with them. There isn't a safer place you could be than in their midst. They're a small army composed entirely of guards with no loyalty for Alida."

"You'll be coming too?" I let my skepticism color my voice.

He shook his head immediately. "We don't want to raise Alida's suspicions any further than they already are. And, anyway, it would be better for you if I wasn't there."

"Oh?" I raised my eyebrows at him.

"As I said, these men have reason to resent Alida. And they have reason to be loyal to me. This is your chance to show yourself among them—to give them a reason to be loyal to you."

I bit my lip, considering his words carefully. There was sense in them, from whichever angle I looked. And they backed up my earlier conclusion. Despite whatever had led him to shun me up until now, my grandfather had so far shown no sign of wishing to use me. He seemed to truly wish me to rule.

I swallowed. If I couldn't take the throne without an army,

this seemed like the best chance I was going to get. I didn't like the thought of running from the capital so soon after I'd arrived, but I would be foolish to turn down this chance.

The threat of civil war still hung over me, though, clouding any hope I might feel. What was I thrusting my kingdom into?

"What happens when we return?" I asked the duke. "How many are to die for my cause?"

"None, I hope," he said with perfect calm.

I clasped my hands together, hoping desperately he wasn't just saying what I wanted to hear.

"You think the threat will be enough?" I asked.

He nodded. "With our own army behind us, our supporters in the court will stand with you when you make your claim. And the rest of court will follow. Alida isn't exactly beloved, and yours is the rightful claim, after all. Plus she's paid off her guards, remember. They don't follow her out of love or loyalty. They won't fight when they see what stands against them—they won't be interested in risking their lives for a hopeless cause."

For the first time since I entered the room, I smiled. His words made sense. Maybe we could actually do this. Maybe I could win back my throne and free my kingdom without any bloodshed at all.

A sharp knock on the door had barely sounded before it was thrust open, and a man I didn't recognize strode in. He looked only at the duke, giving a small half-bow.

"Your Grace, I have an urgent report." His eyes slid sideways onto me, and he faltered, stepping back. "Your...Your Highness! But how...?"

His eyes slid back to my grandfather, so I stood to my feet, drawing his attention back to me.

"Yes, it is me. What is your report?"

He hesitated, gazing blankly between us all, and I narrowed my eyes.

"You may safely deliver the report to me." I looked over at my grandfather, my face requesting his endorsement of my pronouncement.

He nodded, no trace of discomfort on his face. "Certainly you may deliver your report to Her Majesty."

The man swallowed and gave a full bow. "Indeed, I did not mean...I am merely astonished. My report was concerning you, Your Majesty."

"Me?"

He shifted uncomfortably. "I am certain of my source, so your presence has caught me quite off guard."

"Deliver your report, if you please." Iron sounded in the duke's voice, and the man bobbed another half-bow.

"Of course. I have just received word that the usurper queen has discovered the location of the true queen." His amazed eyes turned to me again. "Somewhere deep in the forest. And she has sent some sort of weapon against her."

CHAPTER 19

I gasped and stumbled back, sinking into my chair, my eyes flying to Alexander.

"The children," I whispered.

My grandfather took one look at me and turned back to his agent. "What sort of weapon? Were you able to learn that much, at least?"

The man frowned. "No. But there has been talk of a newcomer. A man from Eldon. He hasn't mingled with anyone, but the queen has treated him with favor. And there are rumors around him. Rumors that he holds great power."

"Eldon?" Alexander cursed under his breath. "Sterling!"

My grandfather looked from Alexander's thunderous face to my pale one. Then back at the man.

"Thank you for your report. You may go. Naturally you must speak of this to no one. Particularly about the queen's presence here."

The man nodded and bowed, a half-bow to my grandfather and then a full one to me.

"Of course, you can be assured of my silence—as always.

Indeed, this report had filled me with some dread, so allow me to express my great relief at seeing Your Majesty safe."

I managed a weak smile and a nod, and the man bowed again before hurrying out of the room.

My grandfather looked between Alexander and me. "One of you explain."

I stood up and paced once across the room, stopping by the empty fireplace before spinning back around. "I have been sheltering in the forest for some weeks. In a secluded cottage. A group of children live there, without defense of any kind. If my stepmother has sent a weapon against them…" My knees suddenly gave way, and I sank into the closest chair.

My grandfather frowned. "Children? That is…less than desirable. I suppose we must…" His drumming fingers picked up their pace. "This talk of a weapon sounds strange to me, though. Why would she not send a contingent of guards? Or perhaps she has done so as well?"

He seemed to be talking half to himself, but Alexander answered. "I think I might have the answer to that. But it isn't one you're going to like." He sighed. "As you know, I was in Eldon myself until quite recently. I only returned when I was sent back with a message—a warning."

I vaguely remembered him mentioning this before, but his subsequent news about my stepmother's murderous orders had driven it from my mind. To my grandfather it was new, however.

"What sort of warning?" The duke leaned forward, his eagle eyes trained on Alexander. "I heard they had solved their difficulties there."

"Yes, they did. They defeated a woman who had amassed an arsenal of magical objects gifted across our lands in generations past by the godmothers. She was destroyed, but one of her henchmen escaped. A rather wily man who had spent years traveling the kingdoms collecting objects for her. He has previously caused trouble in both Marin and Palinar, apparently, assisting in prison breaks there."

"The Eldonians captured him, but he subsequently escaped, and the royals feared he had fled into Eliam. And that he might have had one or more godmother objects with him when he did so. Princess Celine believed he was just the type to have secreted some somewhere as emergency supplies. So she sent me to warn Eliam."

He grimaced. "But I'm afraid it sounds like he fled straight into Alida's arms. I strongly suspect this 'weapon' they speak of is actually some sort of magical object. Bear in mind that Alida still needs it to look like Snow's death was an accident, and one not of her doing."

The duke frowned. "This complicates matters. If only we knew what he had brought with him."

"There is no use wasting time on such wishes." I leaped back to my feet. "We must leave immediately."

"You?"

"Of course. And Alexander. We had just determined we were to leave, anyway, had we not? We will travel to Lestern, but we'll go to the cottage first. If we hurry, we still have a chance of beating the queen's messenger there—whoever he may be." I just hoped it wasn't Randolph and we didn't end up meeting him in the forest on the way.

"If there's a magical object involved, I don't like the idea of your being there at all," said my grandfather. "I can send experienced men of my own to protect the children."

I was shaking my head before he had finished speaking. "We know the way, we can move faster." I bit my lip, honesty compelling me to add, "Well, with Alexander along, anyway." I looked across at him. "I assume you're coming?"

"Of course." He gave me a look as if I were crazy. "Where you go, I go." He smiled without humor. "And I'm in almost as much danger here as you, remember. I did just break out of prison."

I laughed once, a short sound which quickly died. This latest news had driven his recent escape from my mind entirely.

My grandfather opened his mouth, but I cut him off. "We have no time to waste on argument. We have to leave immediately."

"Let me send some men with you, at least."

I frowned. "More people will just slow us down. I trust in Alexander." I bit my lip. "And I intend to convince the children to come with us to Lestern. But I'll have to tell them the truth, and I've already sent danger in their direction and upended their lives. I don't think I'll win any extra points by turning up with a collection of unknown guards."

"Let me send Tarver, if no one else. You've already had a chance to see my captain's competence."

"Carter will want to come too, I expect," said Alexander. "He won't like the idea of remaining cooped up here in this mansion for weeks on end. And his presence might be a danger to His Grace."

"If we're to go all the way to Lestern with the children in tow, we'll need a wagon," I said. "You both claim Tarver and Carter are extremely competent in their different ways. Can they follow with a wagon? Can we trust them to get it to the cottage without drawing any attention?"

"Of course," said Alexander, at the same moment as my grandfather said, "Naturally."

"Excellent." I nodded briskly. "That's decided then. Alexander and I will leave immediately. Tarver and Carter can follow behind with a wagon and supplies as quickly as they can. I'll need to pack." I turned to my friend. "Can you give Carter directions on how to get to the cottage?"

"Of course."

I wasn't sure either of them actually approved of my plan, but I didn't intend to give them any further chance to raise objections. I did hesitate in the doorway, though, looking back into the room.

"Thank you for your hospitality, Grandfather. I trust I will see you again soon enough."

He slowly shook his head, a strange light in his eyes. "I trust so also. In fact, I grow increasingly certain of it by the hour."

We left as twilight was starting to descend, the earliest we could risk slipping through the city. Bronson had already reported whispers of an escape from the dungeons, but people seemed scared to speak of it too openly. Extra guards milled around, but in the busyness of the city, we avoided them without too much trouble. In fact, the ease of it supported my grandfather's statements. These weren't experienced guards who had spent years defending this castle and our capital.

I wouldn't have dared to find a path through the forest in the darkness on my own, but the trip was immeasurably easier with Alexander to lead me. The moon gave so little light I would have been walking into trees without him, but he somehow found a path anyway. And we easily avoided the patrolling guards given the light of their lanterns.

"Fools," muttered Alexander after one such interruption. I didn't disagree.

Soon enough we had left the patrols behind and were making even better time. Inwardly I marveled at the chance that sent me once again fleeing alone through the forest at night with only Alexander for companion and guide. But how different this trip felt. Still frantic, still hurried, but we had a purpose now that our other blind flight had lacked. And I no longer started at every sound, a dead weight, slowing Alexander down.

I had barely stopped to think in the last few days, but I

allowed myself now to ponder as I let Alexander lead us. I had fled the castle alone, weak, and virtually friendless. And I had returned slightly stronger but even more alone, with no idea how to find or rescue my missing friend. But now, even though fear gripped my heart for the children who had become like family to me, I was leaving the capital with not only my rescued friend, but with information and allies and the promise of an army.

And yet even that paled against the sense of satisfaction that came from knowing that I had done it. I had said I would rescue Alexander, and I had done so. Tarver himself had said they couldn't have done it without me, hadn't he?

Take that! I said to my inner critic, now fallen silent. *There is strength in me after all.*

But my mind replied only with an image of little Poppy clinging to Daria's side as they waved me farewell, the others ranged behind them. What good was my strength if I couldn't prevent harm coming to those who had befriended me without motive, gain, or guile? Every way I turned, I brought harm to someone.

I pushed my feet faster, and Alexander, a single stride ahead of me, responded by increasing his own pace. In tune with me, as always. Had he even rested since his escape the night before? I hoped so.

We stopped briefly to rest a short time before dawn, on our way again by the time the sun was well in the sky. Weariness dragged at me now, but still I moved faster than I had ever done through the forest before. The combination of my training and Alexander's presence made the miles fly by.

I wanted to keep going, but when Alexander insisted we stop for a midday meal, my body protested the truth of his words.

"We'll move faster if we keep up our strength," he said. He didn't have to say the words for me to know that I had started to flag. I sank down onto the ground.

"A brief rest, then."

He silently handed me cold rations from a large bag he carried. I watched him, surreptitiously at first, and then increasingly openly. That he saw himself as my protector I didn't doubt. It had always been that way between us. But I had rescued him. What did he think of that? Did he still pity the poor, lonely princess as he had implied in the cottage clearing what felt like a lifetime ago?

"What is it?" he asked warily, throwing a small twig at me as if we were on one of our old jaunts through the woods, and I was merely plotting some new escapade to get us into trouble.

"What did you think when you saw me appear in front of your cell?" The words tumbled out before I had quite resolved to say them.

He looked startled, his gaze dropping to the ground.

"Alex?"

"In truth?" He looked up at me briefly before his eyes fell away again. "I thought it merely another dream."

My heart sped up, and my hand clenched around my food. Had it been rescue he dreamed of? Or me? But that I did not have the courage to ask.

"When I realized you were real, I felt joy, and then fear." He shook his head. "And then pride." He smiled across at me, his momentary embarrassment seeming to be gone. "I'll admit I didn't imagine you would manage to rescue me. Although I was terrified you would try."

I could see he meant no malice with his words, but anger shot through me, tapping into a deeper well I hadn't even known I carried. No wonder I always doubted myself, when my best—and really only—friend always doubted me.

"Why didn't you tell me the truth? About my grandfather? That you were working with him."

Alexander frowned, his face darkening and then flushing. He said nothing.

I had thought myself content with the knowledge that it must have been concern for me that drove his silence. But I realized in this moment that it wasn't enough. He called me his queen, and then he hid things from me. Important things. Because he was afraid I couldn't handle them. What sort of queen did he think I would be?

"I know you were trying to protect me, but it just left me vulnerable. I need to know you trust me."

Still he said nothing, and now he wouldn't even meet my eyes. A horrible thought washed over me, and I gasped.

Perhaps I had been wrong about his motives. "Did you think I would forbid you from contacting him? Out of anger and resentment that he ignored me all those years?"

Alexander swallowed. "Snow, I..."

I stared at him, but he didn't complete the thought. I shook my head, tears in my eyes that I battled to keep from falling.

"How can I ever rule when my closest friend in the world doesn't trust me to make the right decision? To be capable? Am I just supposed to be a puppet ruler? A pretty face to wear the crown and smile at the crowds?"

"No, of course not! Snow!" He met my eyes at last, looking horrified. "You will be an incredible ruler. I don't doubt it."

"But you do," I whispered. "It's obvious. You doubt me."

"No." He looked torn, his features twisting. "I don't know why I didn't tell you. You're brave and strong, you've proved that many times over in the last few weeks. And you have a kind heart, the sort that people are drawn to. Just look how those children welcomed you. And how easily you won over half your court with only one party."

"Sort of won them over," I muttered. "Don't forget we need an army to satisfy them."

He ignored my grumble. "But you're also a girl who just lost her father. A girl I—" He cut himself off, swiftly shaking his head. His voice dropped almost to a whisper. "I don't always see things clearly where you're concerned. It's me who makes the poor decisions, not you."

I swallowed, trying to understand his words and what was behind them. They sounded almost as muddled as my own thoughts half the time. With a deep sigh, I let my anger flow away. Just as Alexander apparently found it difficult to forget I wasn't still a lonely child, I sometimes forgot he wasn't that much older than me. If I was allowed to still be finding my way, didn't I need to extend the same courtesy to him?

"It's all right," I said, causing him to look up quickly. "But I need you to promise you'll never do it again. Never keep information from me to protect me. From now on, we make decisions together."

He nodded, regret clear on his face. "That's an easy promise to make. It should have been that way from the beginning."

I smiled at him, relieved to have peace restored between us. It had never felt right to be at odds with Alexander. But the smile didn't last long. I took my last bite and stood. Things might be well with the oldest of my friends, but I had recently acquired some new ones, and fear for them tugged me onward.

Our pace somehow quickened again after that, and we made such good time that we stumbled into the clearing as the last of the sun's light disappeared.

The clearing was deserted, although smoke rose from the chimney. But I knew from experience that meant nothing. Racing across the open space, I flung open the unlatched door.

Astonished faces turned to greet me, and I counted them rapidly. One, two, three, four, five, six.

"Where's Daria?" I gasped.

Silently they all drew back from where they had been clumped together around a familiar figure stretched out motionless in front of the fire.

"Oh Snow!" Poppy ran toward me, tears streaming down her face, and flung herself into my arms.

I swayed from the impact of her small weight just as Alexander pushed through the doorway behind me, his eyes quickly taking in the scene.

We hadn't moved fast enough. We were too late.

CHAPTER 20

*B*ut even as I had the awful thought, Daria turned her head weakly and smiled at me.

"Hello, Snow." Her gaze traveled to Alexander, and her smile grew. "And hello, Alexander."

I almost dropped Poppy at the second shock, racing forward and falling onto my knees beside Daria, Poppy tumbling from my arms and kneeling beside me.

"Oh, you're alive! Oh, thank goodness."

"Only just," said Ben. I had never heard him sound so grim.

"And here you are," said Anthony from beside him. "Right on time."

Daria glared at him from the floor. "What are you saying, Anthony? This isn't Snow's fault."

"It's mighty funny timing is all I'm saying," said Anthony, crossing his arms over his chest.

"This whole thing seems too strange to understand," said Ben. But he looked at me as if hoping for an explanation.

Two tears ran down my cheeks. "Oh, Daria, Anthony's right. It is all my fault."

"No," Alexander said quickly from where he still stood by the door. "It's *her* fault."

"What?" Anthony uncrossed his arms and turned belligerently toward Alexander. "Don't try to blame this on Daria."

"No, no," I jumped in quickly. "He doesn't mean Daria. He means…" I swallowed, nervous now that the moment for truth had come. "He means Queen Alida."

"Queen Alida?"

"The queen?"

"What?"

Multiple voices spoke at once, astonishment or skepticism visible on every face.

"Why would the *queen* want to hurt Daria?" Ben's soft voice spoke last of all.

I grimaced and rubbed at the moisture on my face. "She doesn't. Not specifically, anyway. She wants to hurt me."

"You?" Anthony scoffed.

I took a deep breath. "I'm afraid I haven't been honest with you all. My name isn't really Snow. Well, Snow is my nickname." I paused. "My name is Princess Blanche."

All six of the standing children drew back, their eyes round and bodies stiff. Daria, who still lay before me, tightened her hand spasmodically around mine.

"Princess?" asked Danni, still staring at me as if I had two heads. "Why would a princess want to live in our cottage?"

"Because her stepmother tried to kill her," said Alexander.

The children all started again, as if they had forgotten his presence. Ben looked at him searchingly, and Anthony recrossed his arms.

"So I guess you really are a royal huntsman. We should have guessed who she was when we realized she had a huntsman trailing her around."

Now it was Daria's turn to scoff, the sound weak compared to Anthony's. "Don't be ridiculous, Anthony. How could we possibly have guessed she was really the princess?" She shook her head. "I can't believe it. The princess!"

I squeezed her hand, looking down at her face. "I'm so sorry, Daria. I'm so sorry I never told you the truth. I thought I was protecting you, but really I was just afraid that you would kick me out if you knew the truth." I gestured at her. "And you would have been right to do it, too! Look at what's happened! I should never have stayed here."

Ben's heavy sigh sounded behind me. "I do wish you'd told us the truth. But I doubt we'd have sent you away." I looked up at him, and he gave me a long-suffering look. "Daria can never resist a good sob story."

"Why is your stepmother trying to *kill* you?" piped in Jack, apparently uninterested in the part where I was a princess.

"Because she wants Snow's throne," said Alexander. "Snow is the true queen."

"Of...of course." Daria struggled to push herself into a sitting position. "Your Majesty."

I shook my head and pushed her gently back down. "Don't be silly. I'm still Snow to you."

"I still don't understand," said Louis, who had been standing quietly to one side, his brow wrinkled. "What happened to Daria? And what does it have to do with you being a princess? Or queen, or whatever?"

"Well..." I rocked back onto my heels and glanced at Alexander. "To tell the truth we're not entirely sure about that. We didn't tell anyone about you all, I promise. But somehow the queen learned that I had been here. She thought I was still here, in fact. So she sent some sort of...weapon. We hurried to warn you as soon as we heard, but obviously we were too late. What happened?"

I addressed the final question at Ben.

He shrugged uncomfortably. "Well I don't know about any weapons. Maybe this had nothing to do with you, after all."

Alexander stepped forward, his eyes keen. "Tell us exactly what happened."

"Daria, Anthony, and Louis just got back from a trip into the village," said Ben.

"Just this afternoon," said Danni. She looked a little put out, and I wondered if she had resented being left behind.

"Yes, this afternoon," said Ben, unworried by the interruption. "They had bought all the necessities, and there must have been a little money left over because Daria also bought herself a new dress."

Daria flushed and indicated she wanted to sit, so I helped gently raise her, using several cushions to prop her against one of the chairs.

"I've been growing so much that I desperately needed a new one. It was a little finer than I would normally look at, but the peddler was so kind and friendly. He offered it to me at such a bargain that I couldn't resist."

Ben took back up the story. "When she got home, she sent the rest of us out of the cottage so she could try it on. All except for Poppy who begged to stay and help her tie the laces."

Poppy, who had been surprisingly silent since her first outburst, crawled up to Daria and tucked herself under her arm. Tears poured down her face.

"I didn't mean to pull them so tight. I promise. But I've just learned how to tie them myself, and I wanted to show Daria how good I've gotten."

"Of course it wasn't your fault," said Daria, squeezing her. "You don't even have the strength to tie them like that." She looked up at me. "Honestly, I don't know what happened. One moment Poppy was showing me how she could lace them properly, and the next they were just getting tighter and tighter. I tried to tell her I couldn't breathe, but I couldn't even get the words out. And then everything went black."

"It's a good thing Poppy was with her," said Ben. "When Daria collapsed and Poppy couldn't get her to wake, she ran screaming out to us." He shook his head, eyeing a pile of material next to the fire. "There's something bewitched about that dress, I swear. The knot looked simple, but we couldn't get it undone. It wouldn't budge at all. In the end, we had to cut the laces. And they were mighty hard to saw through, too. If it had taken a few seconds longer, I'm not sure we would have been able to revive her. She'd only just started breathing again when you both came bursting in."

"That's the dress?" asked Alexander, pointing at the pile of material.

Danni nodded.

With quick strides, he took the broom from beside the door and crossed over to it. Using the handle, he scooped it up and flicked the whole thing into the fire.

Several of the children gasped, and then a bang and a hiss silenced us all as the smoke turned green for a moment before returning to its usual color. Everyone looked at each other with wide eyes while silence reigned.

"Well. I think that answers that question," said Alexander at last.

I nodded, still too shocked to actually speak.

"It does?" asked Louis, at the same moment as Anthony said, "What. Was. That?"

Alexander sighed and ran a hand through his hair. "We have reason to believe that Alida may have recently gotten her hands on some twisted godmother items. Ancient ones. We were afraid one of them might have been the so-called weapon she sent against Snow. I'll confess I didn't immediately think of a dress, however. Or more specifically the laces, I suppose."

"Oh dear." Daria looked flushed again, but I was glad to see the healthy color on her face. "I suppose it's partially my fault then. I was looking at the peddler's other wares, when I noticed that dress tucked away at the back. I was a little embarrassed to ask to see something so fine—especially for myself, so…"

She paused and then finished in a rush. "So I told the peddler I was looking to buy a dress for a friend. Foolishness, of course. And he must have thought I meant Snow. He gave me such a low price for it, but I never thought…"

"No, indeed, how could you?" I patted her shoulder. "There's nothing whatsoever for you to feel bad about. If it's anyone's fault it's mine for putting a target on you all."

"The fault—as I said earlier—lies with Alida," said Alexander, and I gave a small smile, able to relax at last now that the immediate danger was past.

"Yes, fair enough. On that we can agree, I suppose. I'm more than happy to share the blame with her."

He shook his head at me, a smile lurking around his eyes, and Anthony snorted in the background.

"Sounds to me like there's plenty of blame for everyone."

"Oh, shut it, Anthony," said Danni.

"Well, if Daria's all right and the dress is burned, I suppose that means we should be thinking about dinner," said Louis. He eyed the now perfectly ordinary looking fire uncertainly. "Do you think it's safe to cook on that? Should we douse it and shovel out the wood and ash and start again?"

"It's probably not necessary," said Alexander. "But then it can't hurt, either. Given we don't really understand whatever that enchantment was, or how it might have been twisted. I can help."

Jack also raced to assist them, Ben a slower but steadier help in his wake. Danni bustled Poppy away to help prepare the food, and I took the opportunity to whisper to Daria.

"I really am so very sorry that I didn't tell you the truth."

She shook her head, already looking much stronger than when we walked in.

"I was the one who said you didn't have to tell us anything." Her eyes strayed across to Alexander. "So I suppose that means

192

you're not star-crossed lovers on the run." She looked a little wistful.

I pulled a face. "No, I'm afraid it's rather more complicated than that."

She dropped her voice even lower. "But you do love him."

I pulled back, startled, and eyed her warily.

"Don't worry," she said. "I won't tell anyone." Her face turned sad. "I suppose a queen and a huntsman might be a bit too wide a bridge to cross."

I swallowed, my own eyes caught on Alexander's strong form as he carefully shoveled ash into a large bucket.

"He certainly seems to think so."

"Oh, Snow." Daria gripped my hand, and I managed a tremulous smile for her.

"But that is the least of my worries, I can assure you. A murderous stepmother and a stolen throne have a way of driving other thoughts from your mind."

She shook her head, her eyes wide, clearly still growing accustomed to the truth of my story. I pasted on a brighter smile and stood to help Danni and Poppy with the food. I only wished my words had been true. That I was not so selfish as to find thoughts of my heart constantly creeping in despite everything else I—and my kingdom—faced.

We told the children a little more of our situation over the meal —leaving out the details, of course, but focusing on our planned destination. I had expected a great deal of opposition to the idea of their accompanying us to Lestern, but the incident with the dress seemed to have scared them, although none of them admitted it outright.

"It's not as if we haven't been to Lestern before," said Daria, meeting Ben's eyes across the table. "Why not make another trip?

We should be safe enough in the duke's castle until things settle down. And then we can return."

I winced slightly at her words but didn't actually contradict her. In truth, if I succeeded in gaining the throne, I intended to bring the children to the castle where they wouldn't have to break their backs chipping slivers of gemstone from an abandoned mine all day. And if I didn't succeed...well, it likely wouldn't be safe for them to return here. Not now that it seemed the queen knew of this cottage. Who knew what vengeance she might wreak in such circumstances?

I had destroyed it for them, their haven. And it made me want to cry. But I also knew that if I told them they could likely never return to their life here, it might make it harder for them to leave now. And their safety was the most important thing. We all needed to leave—and soon.

Unsurprisingly, Anthony proved the most reluctant to agree to our proposed plan, but in the end, we won everyone's agreement. It took them a full day to decide what to pack and what to leave, as well as shutting things up for a long absence. The chickens they released to run wild with a promise that I would gift them more from the duke's own stock. The goat, of course, had to come with us, but I figured we could tie him to the back of the wagon easily enough.

The younger children inevitably squabbled over what they would have room to bring, and Ben and Daria were hard-pressed to both get the cottage in the necessary order and intercede between the younger ones. Daria eventually lost her calm—the first time I had ever seen it happen—and chased them around with a wooden spoon, threatening to paddle them all.

They just ran from her, shrieking with laughter and pretend fear, and she eventually collapsed into a chair and massaged her temples. After a prolonged moment of silence, she looked down at the spoon in her hands and then up at me.

"I've never tried to do that before. I don't know what came over me."

"Don't worry, you were never going to catch them," I said with a grin. But when I saw she looked truly guilty, I rushed to add, "No doubt it's a lingering effect of the enchantment."

She gratefully latched on to that excuse, although I could see in her eyes that she knew as well as I did the true cause of her overflowing stress. Leaving her home—perhaps forever, because she wasn't a fool—was huge. And leaving for the unknown, with the responsibility of five younger children weighing her down, was even bigger.

We busied ourselves with packing and sorting, but after a while, I looked over at her. "I won't abandon you all, I promise you that. As long as I'm able, I'll do everything to make sure those children are cared for. And my grandfather will too. I'll make sure of it."

She smiled at me, gratitude in her eyes, even if she didn't voice it.

Tarver and Carter arrived with the wagon that evening. They appeared to have reached some sort of happy rhythm that allowed them to work together efficiently. Albeit with very few words. I hoped that the addition of seven new members to the party—all thirteen or below—wouldn't cause them too great a shock.

We spent the night at the cottage, since traveling in the dark was less than ideal with a wagon and animals in tow, and left the following morning. No doubt my grandfather would have preferred to send more guards with us, but we were already a large party, and a larger one would only attract more attention. Instead we were relying on the skills of Carter and Alexander— both to find us a path and to hide our tracks.

Our intention was to remain in the forest and away from any main roads all the way to Lestern. With so many extra guards in his employ, Tarver assured me that the duke's lands had never been so free from crime.

"We even have them patrolling our section of the forest," he explained with a small, wry smile. "Since we needed something for them all to do."

I had made three journeys through the forest at this stage, but none of them had been anything like this. The younger children all rode in the wagon, while the older ones and I alternated between walking and riding. Alexander and Carter were rarely in sight—either ahead scouting our path, or behind covering our tracks. Which left poor Tarver to bear the brunt of our company.

To my surprise he took it easily in stride, however, and Alexander soon had fierce competition for Jack's hero worship. Even Louis and Danni seemed to fall under his spell, and he was the only one who could coax non-surly conversation out of Anthony.

"I have a lot of nieces and nephews," the captain told me with a grin when he caught me looking at him with astonishment. "And they all live in Lestern. I've been well trained." He winked at me, and I shook my head. My grandfather had clearly chosen his captain of the guard well—and for more than his fighting skills. I found my curiosity over Lestern growing with each day of our trip. What would the small city be like? And what would I learn of my grandfather there?

CHAPTER 21

*T*wo days into the trip I was watching Anthony with concern, when Daria sidled up to me. I transferred my concerned gaze to her, but her dark skin carried the healthy flush of exertion, and her black braids—pinned to her head as always—looked as glossy as ever.

She rolled her eyes at me.

"I'm fine. No lasting ill-effects, I promise. And that's not going to change however many times you look at me with concern."

I gave her an apologetic grin. "Sorry, I can't help myself."

Daria nodded subtly over toward Anthony. "And he's going to be fine, too." She bit her lip. "At least, I hope so."

"I know he never really warmed to me," I said. "But I've never seen him so consistently dour. I think he hates me for upending all of your lives."

Daria shook her head quickly. "It's not you. It's Lestern."

"Lestern? You mean the city?"

She sighed. "I told you that we've only been to Lestern once before, didn't I? But I don't think I told you when. It was four years ago. And that was the trip where we found Poppy…and Anthony."

"Anthony is from Lestern?" I looked over at him, my brow wrinkling. As I watched him, my heart sank. "I'm guessing he doesn't exactly have fond memories of it?"

Daria bit her lip. "It's one of the reasons we've never returned. That and the distance. It got harder once we had smaller children with us."

"So Poppy was only...what? One? When you found her?"

Daria nodded. "She doesn't remember anything of Lestern. Or any home other than our cottage. But Anthony was nearly eight. He remembers all too well."

Her gaze lost focus, her eyes turning glassy as memory took her. "He was so scrawny back then." She gave a little laugh. "Not that Ben and I were much better. Thinking ourselves so old because we were soon to turn ten. Well, Ben was, anyway, but I wasn't too far behind." She shook her head. "Thinking we could care for a baby."

"And clearly you could," I said softly, still amazed at what they had achieved. "Just look at Poppy. She's adorable."

Daria's eyes softened. "Yes, that she is. And infuriating." She laughed again. "But thank goodness Jack was older when we found him. I'm not sure we could have survived it twice."

"Don't underestimate yourself," I said.

Daria's eyes remained fixed on the younger girl in the wagon. "Her mother had just died when we found her. A woman in the market was looking after her—they had been neighbors apparently. But we heard her complaining to the woman in the next stall that she didn't have the time or energy or coin to be caring for someone else's little one." Daria shook her head. "She sounded like she meant to abandon her to the streets. So I offered to take her in exchange for a deduction on the cost of our purchases."

She looked disgusted. "She didn't even ask how we meant to care for her. She couldn't have been more pleased to hand her over to someone else. I suppose it was a guilt free way for her to be rid of an extra burden."

I noticed Daria's hands curling into fists and felt the same anger sweeping through me. And grief that any baby could be in such a situation.

"What about her father?" I asked softly.

"He had abandoned them before the mother died, apparently," said Daria.

I took a steadying breath. How different my life would have been after my mother's death if I hadn't had my father to love and care for me. For all my grief, how much I had to be grateful for.

"And Anthony?" I asked, keeping my voice low so as not to be overheard.

A look of concern flitted across Daria's face.

"Anthony wasn't so simple." Her face twisted. "We sort of stole Anthony. On our way out of the city."

"Stole him?" I blinked. "But we don't have slaves in Eliam."

"No, not slaves. But we do have apprentices. And Anthony's parents sold him to a mean master. One who beat him. And who wouldn't release him from his apprenticeship until he had earned back what the man had paid. Only somehow with food and board, the original amount never went down."

"But that's terrible! We have laws against that sort of thing. Why didn't he go to the duke?"

Daria shook her head at me. "No doubt an apprentice with family or friends to advocate for them would do so. But a seven-year-old with no one? I don't think he even knew such a thing was possible. We had seen him in the market and talked to him on several of the days. But we were strangers and didn't know what to do for him either. And then, on the last day, when we had loaded up our little cart to leave, he appeared from nowhere and begged us to take him with us."

Her face twisted. "How could we say no? We figured his master could never find us far away in the middle of the forest.

And we were right. So far. But we've also never returned to Lestern."

Her concerned eyes returned to Anthony. "He looks very different now, of course. I'm sure no one would recognize him."

"That doesn't matter," I said firmly. "We're going to Lestern under the duke's protection. All of us. If anyone tries to give Anthony—or any of you—any trouble, you direct them to me." My eyes fell on Tarver, leading the wagon forward. "Or better yet, Tarver. He's the captain of the duke's guard, you know. No one will give you trouble once they learn you're friends with him."

"But his master might have a legal claim…"

I shook my head again. "Not from what you've described. And I'd be more than happy to tell him so myself." I glowered into the surrounding trees, wishing I could indeed have the chance to talk to the man. "But I don't think there's any chance he'd try to press any so-called claim when he realizes what sort of connections Anthony has now. If he even recognizes him in the first place."

Daria's face immediately brightened. "I'm going to tell Anthony. And Ben. They'll be so relieved!"

She hurried off, and a fresh wave of guilt rocked me. How much stress had they all been laboring under since our decision to leave for Lestern? All those weeks that I lived with them, and I had never found out their stories. Too busy hiding my own, I supposed.

I resolved instantly to change. If I wanted to be a good queen, I needed to care about my people—truly care. And that meant individuals as well as the kingdom as a whole.

That evening I approached Tarver after we made camp for the night. The quieter pace of travel had given me some time to think, and I didn't want to put off my conclusions any longer.

"I'd like a weapon," I told him, not wasting time on preliminaries.

His brow creased. "A weapon, Your Majesty? I don't understand."

"I've been thinking about the rescue. I didn't take a weapon with me because it seemed pointless when I didn't know how to use it. But it would have made things a lot easier against that guard. I might not have needed you to save me if I'd been armed. So I'd like a weapon."

There was a moment's silence.

"And I suppose some training in how to use it, too," I added.

His mouth twisted, and I felt a pang of sympathy.

"If you're thinking that my grandfather would disapprove, just remember I'm your queen. I outrank him." I fixed him with a mock stern look that made him smile reluctantly.

"I suppose you do, Your Majesty." He ran a hand along his jaw, and his gaze turned assessing.

"You'd need to build up more arm strength before a sword would do you much good. And some specialized skills as well. We don't have time for that. But I suppose there's some sense in your carrying a dagger. And I can probably give you at least enough training to ensure you're not a danger to yourself carrying one on your person."

He sighed. "Doesn't mean you'll be competent to fight with one, though."

I nodded, eagerly. "I understand, and I'm not expecting miracles. Or to get into any knife fights. I just want to know it's there if I need it."

It didn't take long after that for Tarver to produce an elegant dagger and sheath. And we started my first lesson at the next opportunity: how to hold it and how to draw and sheath it safely.

I didn't mind him keeping it simple because the idea of ever actually stabbing someone made me feel queasy. But then I was currently the target for a murderous royal campaign. And if it ever came down to my life or an attacker's, I didn't want to hesitate.

Later, around the campfire, when most of the children had fallen asleep, I sat down next to Alexander. He smiled a greeting, passing me a hot cup of tea which I took gratefully.

But eventually he sighed. "What is it, Snow? I can see you looking at me out of the corner of your eyes, you know."

I looked away, a little embarrassed. "I just wanted to check that you aren't, well, mad at me."

"Mad at you?" He looked genuinely surprised. "Why would I be mad at you?"

I looked across the fire in Tarver's direction. "Because I asked Tarver to give me a weapon and some training."

Alexander turned fully to face me, regarding me in silence for a moment.

"Am I supposed to be angry because you want a weapon, or because you asked Tarver instead of me?"

A flush rose up my neck. He was far too astute.

"I don't know. Both? Neither? Don't listen to me." I started to push myself to my feet, but his hand shot out and grabbed my arm, pulling me back down.

"No, don't go."

I sank back onto the ground, and he let me go instantly. I tried not to look at the spot on my arm that he had touched.

"Snow, I meant what I said the other day. I've made some bad decisions where you're concerned, but all I've ever wanted was for you to be safe. And happy."

He sighed and looked into the fire. "So I think it's a great idea for you to be armed." He shot me a stern look. "As a last resort measure only, of course."

I nearly giggled.

"And I think you should get what training you can from the best. And that's not me."

I opened my mouth, but he chuckled and shook his head. "If

you're about to try to reassure my manly pride, there's no need. I can fight well enough, I suppose, but I'm not a trained guard. When you wanted training on forest craft and basic self-defense techniques, I was happy to help out. But I'd rather you learn to use a knife from an expert."

I looked at him, the firelight soft against his strong features, and my heart melted a little more than it already had. I should have known better than to think he would be angry. He cared far too much to put his own pride ahead of my well-being.

I felt myself unconsciously leaning toward him in the flickering glow, my eyes focusing on his lips. Abruptly I pulled myself back and scrambled to my feet.

"Well, uh, thank you, Alex. For understanding. Good night."

I turned and fled toward my bedroll. Stupid darkness. Stupid firelight. Making everything feel romantic. Stupid feelings. Would they ever go away and let me love someone who might actually love me back?

I sighed as I slid into bed. Not as long as he kept acting like my best friend and everything I'd ever wanted all rolled into one.

Three days later we arrived in Lestern. Tarver had me in the wagon with the younger children, the hood of my cloak pulled up over my face.

"I can vouch for my guards," he had said. "They all have reason to hate Alida. And the servants at the castle come from loyal families who have served the duke for generations. They know to be discreet. But I can't speak for everyone in the city. It would be far better if no one outside of the castle encounters you during your visit."

Which meant this was my only real chance to see the city. So while I kept my hood low, I did try to peek under it, just to see what Lestern looked like. My first impression was of a military outpost. Guards seemed to patrol not only along the simple wall that surrounded the small city but also everywhere I looked.

But bearing in mind the recent increase in guard numbers, I tried to look past that. My second impression was of a neat city, with busy, industrious-looking inhabitants. The buildings, the streets, the people—even the bright flower boxes—looked ordered and well kept.

I couldn't see the water, but the smell of the sea pervaded everything, and the call of gulls sounded above the usual hustle and bustle of any city. Lestern certainly didn't compare with the capital in size, but it was still bigger than I had been expecting, and we passed more than one market square.

This was the place where my mother had spent her childhood. If she had lived, would I have come here every year for summer visits? A highlight of my year, perhaps, and my grandfather a dearly loved presence. But I pushed the thought away. If my mother had lived, everything about my life—past and present—would have been different, so it didn't bear thinking on.

All too soon the wide cobbled street led us into the courtyard of the castle. Only when the gate closed behind us did Tarver relax, gesturing for me to climb down and come forward. The castle was small compared to the one I had grown up in, but neat and ordered like the city around it. I found myself drawn to it. Relaxing in a way I hadn't expected to.

A steward and housekeeper waited inside the entry hall to greet me, along with a number of other senior staff. Each bowed or curtsied low and addressed me as Your Majesty. Clearly a fast messenger had been sent ahead of us to prepare for our arrival. I had expected Tarver to enter with me, but he seemed to have disappeared—to the guard headquarters I supposed. The steward and housekeeper looked at me as if I were in charge rather than a guest, and I felt a brief moment of panic. But then Alexander, Carter, and the children all entered, and I responded on instinct, making the necessary introductions and giving orders for rooms to be prepared and our belongings to be appropriately disposed of.

And then I was receiving a tour along with a stream of information about the castle and city. And yet I had no difficulty taking it all in and storing it in the proper compartments of my brain. In a cottage in the forest I had been hopelessly out of place, my skills meaningless, but in charge of a castle, I was at home. I had done much of the day-to-day organization in my own castle for more than a year. Ever since my father's health had deteriorated to the point where he had become bound to his rooms.

It was strange now that I thought of it—although it hadn't struck me as odd at the time. While my father still lived, Alida had been rightful queen and should have taken on such roles. In fact, she should probably always have been doing them—or had a hand in them, at least. Had I stepped up because she was unwilling? Or had the servants always brought everything to my father or me? Now that I thought about it, I couldn't be sure. Perhaps they hadn't liked the answers they might get from my stepmother.

Whatever the reason, I slipped into life at the Lestern castle with remarkable ease. I soon discovered that my grandfather had indeed commanded that I have full authority in his absence, and I thanked him mentally for the thought. With each day that passed, I felt confidence returning to me. Our haphazard adventures so far had almost made me forget the skills and abilities I did have to offer.

Each morning I trained first thing in the small castle courtyard with Tarver. I noticed he had a different group of guards training beside us each day, and I suspected he was giving as many as possible a chance to see me for themselves. I worried that my obvious ineptitude would be to my disadvantage, but he assured me one morning that it was quite the opposite.

"They see you training like one of them, taking instruction when needed, and they respect that far more than pretty jewels and fine gowns. Could you imagine your stepmother out here every morning with the youngest recruits? They're impressed. Take my word for it."

He had been busy since our arrival, recalling guards out on more distant patrols, drawing up plans, and preparing supplies for a march through the forest. Some guards would have to be left, of course—enough to maintain order in Lestern. But the bulk would travel with us to the capital.

A surprising amount of work was involved, and Tarver ran everything past me and Alexander, who had become my shadow. I suspected he felt uncomfortable that we found ourselves in an unfamiliar location and had assigned himself as my personal guard. When I challenged him on it, however, he assured me that he was merely attempting to learn more about castle life.

"You wanted to learn about forest craft," he told me with a grin. "Aren't I allowed to be interested in what it means to command a castle?"

I shook my head, giving him a friendly shove, but I liked his solid presence at my elbow too much to consider sending him away. And particularly when it came to Tarver's reports, I valued his input. He had more to offer on getting a large number of people safely and quickly through the forest than I did.

I didn't trust his excuse, though, and still thought he was protecting me. He had been such a favorite of my father's that he had often been included in our conversations, and even in meetings where he really had no place as a huntsman's son and then huntsman himself. It was the reason he had been sent to Eldon, after all.

With my reassurances about Anthony, the children had taken to exploring the city with great interest—an enormous relief to the castle staff since they had begun by thoroughly exploring the castle itself. They brought back regular reports of the city to me, so that I almost felt as if I had the chance to get to know it myself.

Nothing they said contradicted my initial impression. Or the idea that my grandfather was a fair lord, beloved—or at least respected—by his people. The castle staff spoke of him even more highly, although they gave me the impression of a sad man. And with portraits of my mother everywhere around the castle, I hardly had to question why.

At first I had found them confronting, but I had secretly grown fond of them. They helped me to imagine her as she had been in the various phases of her childhood and youth. As she had been when this castle had been her home. She seemed to infuse every part of it, and I had never felt so close to her. It was a stark contrast to my own castle where only her official portrait in the royal gallery and a small one in my father's desk remained. Alida hadn't liked reminders of her predecessor—more beautiful and more beloved than herself.

Every sign confirmed that my grandfather was an excellent choice of ally. But nothing answered the true questions that still lingered in my heart. Questions borne from a lifetime of his absence. Questions that I suspected only a conversation with my grandfather himself could ever truly answer.

And perhaps I would have the chance to ask him those questions soon. Because as comfortable as I felt in Lestern, we were needed back in the capital. We had come here to collect an army, and it was nearly ready.

I was alone in my grandfather's study, reviewing yet another report from Tarver, when Daria wandered in.

"You'll never guess who showed up at the castle today," she said.

"Hmmm?" I tried to pull my mind away from guard numbers and rationing provisions.

"You'll never guess who just turned up," she repeated. "Poppy's father."

"What?" That shocked me enough to get my attention. "Her father? But I thought he abandoned her as a baby."

Daria nodded, and I could see the conflicting emotions in her face. "But we ran across that woman at the market. The one who cared for her after her mother died. She recognized Ben and me and seemed pleased to see Poppy again." She frowned. "I guess word got around, and her father wanted to see her for himself."

I raised an eyebrow. "Or he wanted to see how his daughter ended up staying at the castle. And how it could benefit him." I hated to be so cynical, but I still felt sad every time I looked at Poppy and wondered how anyone could have abandoned her.

"Yes." Daria dropped into a chair, her eyes worried. "I have to admit I thought the same thing. But what if he truly wishes to reconnect? I couldn't deny her that chance."

"Is he here now?" I sat up straighter when she nodded.

"Don't worry," she said. "None of us have said anything about you. Even the little ones. We've been watching them like hawks."

"And who's watching Poppy now?"

I had no sooner asked the question than the door burst open and Danni ran screaming into the room. Daria leaped to her feet and seized the younger girl by her shoulders.

"You're supposed to be with Poppy. Where is she?"

"Dead!" wailed Danni. "I think she's dead." And then she burst into floods of tears.

CHAPTER 22

 either Daria nor I had ever run so fast as we sped down the corridors toward where Danni had left Poppy. Alexander appeared at some point during our sprint—drawn by his sixth-sense for me being in trouble, no doubt.

When we burst into the small receiving room, Louis was kneeling on the floor beside Poppy's still body, looking terrified. He scrambled to his feet when he saw us and rushed over. We ignored him, racing to take his place at Poppy's side.

She wasn't breathing, just as Danni had said, her face pale and her limbs limp. I shook her but got no response.

"What happened?" asked Daria, looking at the other two over her shoulder.

"I don't know," said Louis, looking desperate. "He seemed friendly enough. Gave her some presents. And then said goodbye. She seemed happy, and then next thing we knew she collapsed."

"Wait, get back." Alexander thrust me aside. He knelt beside Poppy and began to examine her carefully, patting her pockets and even checking her small shoes. When he reached her hair, he stopped.

"I don't recognize either of those." He pointed at a knot of brightly colored ribbons and, tucked behind them, a small pearl comb.

"Me neither." Daria leaned closer.

He gestured her back, whipping a handkerchief from his pocket and using it to cover his hand as he pulled both free from her hair. In two steps he was up and at the small fire in the grate.

This time there was no bang or hiss, but the green smoke that emerged hung in the air looking more like oil than smoke before it finally dissipated. As it did, Poppy gasped and sat bolt upright, her wide eyes flying between each of our faces.

"What happened? Where am I?" And then with a confused lilt. "Did I fall over?"

"Oh Poppy!" Daria folded her into her arms and began to cry all over her, much to the younger girl's disgust.

She had soon wriggled free and scrambled up to her feet.

"Where's my new comb?" She looked around the floor and then fixed her eyes on Danni who had sunk into a nearby chair, her face still white. "Did you steal it?"

"I'm afraid that wasn't just a comb, Poppy," said Daria in a serious voice. "It was magic, like my dress. And it nearly killed you. Thankfully Alexander has destroyed it."

Poppy immediately burst into noisy tears, her wails making her accompanying words indecipherable. Alexander and I looked helplessly at each other, but Daria once again took her in her arms and patted her curls while murmuring soothing nothings and making faces at us over her head.

Alexander sidled up to me. "Is she upset that she nearly died? Or that I destroyed her comb?"

Danni snorted, her normal color returned. "Good luck working it out. She probably doesn't know herself."

"Maybe we should…" Alexander gestured at the door.

Danni snorted. "Coward." But she also grinned at him.

I, on the other hand, didn't fault him in the least. I couldn't since I was hard on his heels as he slipped away. Now that I knew Poppy was going to be all right, my mind was moving too furiously to stay and attempt to make sense of a five-year-old's emotions.

"Why would she try to kill Poppy?" I burst out as soon as we were alone in the corridor. "Why would her own father be part of such a scheme?"

Alexander didn't bother to ask who *she* was. "How did she know we were here?"

We stared at each other for a silent moment as we both processed the consequences of this question. There could be no doubt that the so-called present had come from my stepmother. Or that she had somehow gained access to a collection of ancient godmother objects—through this Sterling person, no doubt. Which meant that despite all our efforts, news of my presence in Lester had reached her.

"We need to leave," I said. "I'm only endangering everybody again with my presence."

"We're already preparing as fast as we can," said Alexander, running his hand through his hair in frustration. "And it doesn't make any sense. What does she gain by killing Poppy? Is she just trying to get revenge on you for surviving this long?"

"And how could a father do that to his own child? I know he abandoned her—but trying to kill her?" My mind kept circling back to this question.

"That's assuming he was her father," said Daria, emerging into the corridor and closing the door firmly behind her.

"Poppy's fine," she said in response to my questioning look. "She's calmed down completely because Danni gave her the ribbons out of her own hair."

"Oh, that's kind of her," I said. Danni had bought them in the market with the pocket money I had given her, and naturally Poppy had been badgering her to be allowed a turn with them ever since.

"I think she feels guilty because she was supposed to be watching her when it happened."

"She couldn't have guessed the items would be magical," I said, instantly determining to find Danni some new ribbons as soon as I could.

"No, and I never should have left them. I had a bad feeling about that man, but I thought it was just because of his abandoning her..." Daria sighed. "I should have stayed with them."

"And what could you have done?" asked Alexander. "None of us saw this coming."

"You don't think he was her father?" I asked Daria, returning to her first comment.

"Well, if this was an attack from your stepmother, then probably not, right? I'm sure word has gotten out about her situation from that woman in the market. It was probably just a way for someone to gain access to the castle. No doubt whatever agent your stepmother sent wasn't expecting things to be quite so locked down here. The servants are all incredibly loyal."

I nodded slowly. It made sense. Except for one thing.

"But why would the agent want to kill Poppy? Surely that wasn't what he was sent here for."

"Yes, about that." Daria sighed. "Once she calmed down, I managed to get the story out of her. And I think the ribbons were perfectly ordinary ribbons. It was most likely the comb that was enchanted. It turns out the ribbons were for her, but the comb was supposed to be a present for you. To thank you for taking care of her. Poppy told me you already had a comb, so she didn't see how it could hurt if she just played with it a little first."

"That agent, whoever he was, clearly doesn't have much experience with children," I said. "Not if he thought leaving that comb with a five-year-old was a safe way to ensure it made it to his intended destination."

Daria snorted. "And that's the truth. Although it was wrapped apparently. He probably thought that would make it less likely she would touch it herself, but I'm sure it just made it more appealing to her."

"We need to leave," I told Daria, ignoring Alexander's sharp look at my words. "First thing in the morning. Before this agent finds out he was unsuccessful and tries again."

"That's assuming he has another object," said Alexander.

I put my hands on my hips. "Do any of us want to take that risk?" I looked at them both with raised eyebrows, and neither spoke. "You're all to stay here. That was always the plan for now. The duke's staff will take good care of you, I'm sure of it. And I'll leave orders that no further strangers are to be admitted. For any reason."

"I wish I could come with you," said Daria. But when I tried to speak, she added hurriedly, "But I know I would only be in the way."

"I'll miss you." I embraced her. And it was the truth. She might be several years younger, but life had made Daria just as capable as me in different ways. And she had shown herself a true friend.

"Will you come to court when I win my throne?" I hadn't dared to ask her before now, afraid she would say no.

A smile burst across her face. "I always wanted to see the capital."

"Then see it you shall," I said. "I'll personally give you a tour."

"When you're queen, you might have more important things to do."

"Never," I assured her.

"Oooh, is this the bit where we get to start making requests?" asked Danni, appearing suddenly in the doorway.

"Danni!" Daria glared at her.

"What?" Danni asked defensively. "You're always saying we're not allowed to ask for things, but we're friends with a *queen*. Surely we could ask for a few things." She looked at me. "Just little things," she added hopefully.

"She did eat all our food all those weeks back in the cottage," said Louis. "And she was no help at all with chores."

"I was a little bit of help, surely," I protested weakly.

Alexander gave a cough that I was fairly certain hid a laugh, so I shoved him, although I kept my attention on Louis and Danni.

"When I win my throne, you can ask me for anything you like."

Both children whooped, and Daria looked horrified.

"I'm not promising I'll give it to you," I hastily clarified. "But you can ask."

"Good enough for me." Danni grinned and turned to Louis. "Just wait until we tell the others." Both of them took off down the corridor, and Daria sighed.

"Now you've done it." She shook her head at me. "And I suppose I'd better get back in there since they've left Poppy on her own." She disappeared before I could say anything else, leaving me and Alexander alone in the corridor again.

"The guards aren't ready to go," he said, looking at me with concern. "What's in your head?"

"We need to leave now," I said. "Ahead of the guards. Even with the utmost discretion, Alida is going to hear about a large troop of guards marching on the capital. We want her to hear about it. But so far she seems to know our movements all too well."

I spoke quickly, knowing he wasn't likely to approve of my plan. "She'll be expecting us to be among the guards. But we need to get to the capital first. And in secret. Because the only answer to all of this is that she must have a spy among us. One who even managed to work out where we had been in the forest."

"But that's impossible," Alexander protested. "Neither of us told anyone."

"No," I said. "But there was a fair bit of travel back and forth. And remember the queen's agent didn't turn up at the cottage itself, he came to the town. As a peddler, too. Maybe they'd only worked out the general area. And it doesn't make sense that word of my presence here came from Lestern itself. There wasn't time for the information to filter out into the city—if it even has— then get all the way back to Alida, only for her to send her agent with that object, and for him to then figure out a way to infiltrate the castle. She had to have sent him not long after we left the capital ourselves."

Alexander shifted uneasily. "I did hear from Tarver that His Grace informed the rest of the loyal courtiers of the basics of our plan. He wanted them to know troops were coming, and they just needed to be patient."

"See!" I stared into his eyes, willing him to see the logic of my argument. I didn't want to have to order him to accompany me back, protesting all the way.

"Yes, it does make the most sense," he admitted at last. "But I'm still not sure why you want us to sneak back immediately."

"We're going to arrive unexpectedly and discover who the spy is. And then we're going to use them to our advantage."

Alexander raised an eyebrow. "Feed them misinformation?"

I nodded, and he actually grinned at me.

"That's one sneaky mind you have, Your Majesty."

I gave him a deep curtsy and a grin. "Why thank you, Old Friend." When I straightened up, we both turned serious. "Now we just have to convince Tarver."

CHAPTER 23

C W e were back in the forest more quickly than I had anticipated. The captain had made little attempt to dissuade us from our plan—whether it was from a lifetime of following orders, or because Tarver hadn't grown up with me and held a greater respect for my rank, I couldn't be sure. He had attempted to get us to take a squad of guards with us, but Alexander had talked him out of it, claiming he could more easily hide our passage with just the two of us. When Carter volunteered to join us, Tarver capitulated.

"Don't have much desire to be left back here when the action is all happening in the capital," Carter had told us when we left Tarver's office. "And you can't very well claim I'll be a hindrance to you in the forest, young one."

Alexander took the teasing with calm good will. "I'm glad to have you along."

I had smiled, the best response I could muster. In truth, I had been disappointed. If our plans succeeded—and with my stepmother seeming always one step ahead of us, I no longer felt so confident in that—then this would likely be my last opportunity to be alone with Alexander. There would be no more headlong flights through the forest. Not unless the worst happened, I supposed, and I couldn't wish for that.

And so it was the three of us making our way through the trees. Well, three of us plus the horse. It had been Carter's suggestion, but when Alexander supported it, I hadn't wanted to demur. Clearly despite all my training, I would slow them down on foot. Tarver had offered us three horses, but both Alexander and Carter refused.

"Can't keep in touch with the forest from the back of a great beast like that," Carter had said.

There was no question we moved faster with me astride. And my poor abused muscles were more familiar with the back of a horse. Still, it was the longest such trip we had made, direct all the way from the coast to the capital. I would have liked to see the cottage again, maybe stop for a night there, but it wasn't on the most direct route, and we didn't want to risk the chance it was being watched.

With just the three of us, and moving at the fastest pace we safely could, we reached the capital after dark on our fifth day. Even at night, the city felt large and noisy after Lestern. But also familiar. Lestern had been my mother's home, but this was mine.

We arrived unannounced at the side door of the ducal mansion, and I was half afraid everyone would have gone to bed, and no one would hear our quiet knocks. But the door swung open soon enough, a suspicious looking Bronson falling back to let us inside.

"Your Majesty!"

"Do you ever sleep, Bronson?" I asked affectionately.

"I was just on my way in that direction, Your Majesty," he said with a bow. "I can only be glad I was not more prompt on this night. But what are you doing here? We aren't looking for the guards to arrive for days yet."

"Excellent." Alexander clapped his hands together and smiled. "That's the idea."

Bronson looked between us all wearily. "I suppose I'd better be calling His Grace back out of bed."

"Thank you, Bronson," I smiled at him. "With our apologies, of course."

"Of course, Your Majesty." He bowed himself backward out of the room.

"Well, it looks as if we did it." I turned the smile on both of my companions. "They're not expecting us. So we can only hope the spy isn't expecting us either."

Any astonishment the duke felt had been quashed by the time he met us in our preferred sitting room. And it was he who came up with the plan once we had explained our suspicions to him.

And thus, the very next night, I found myself once again dressed in a fine gown and greeting guests at a last-minute social event. Every one of them greeted me with astonishment, still thinking me in Lestern, so it seemed we had managed to keep my presence secret for a day, at least.

Carter had declared himself happily settled in the kitchen and determined to remain there until he was free to return to hunting, but I had dragged Alexander along with me. He greeted guests beside me, dressed as a courtier rather than in his usual leather. I was still secretly determined to go through with my plan to make him my Chief Adviser, as we had joked about in the forest weeks ago—although it felt more like years.

No one showed shock or surprise at seeing him, any more than they showed confusion as to his identity. They were too used to seeing him at my father's side. I suspected if Alexander had wanted a more exalted position than huntsman, my father would happily have given it to him. No doubt my friend would try to refuse such a thing when I ruled as well, but I intended to be extremely persistent.

Tonight as we circulated, we had a plan. Carefully we spread the information that our troops had moved faster than planned. They had already arrived with me at their head and were camped just outside the capital, ready for our command to move in. We asked everyone to be ready. When the court was called to the castle, we needed them all there.

It was only an exaggeration of the truth, not an entire fabrication, and all the more believable for it, we hoped. But still an important enough piece of information to send the spy hurrying to inform the queen. The duke had his people ready to follow every guest from the moment they left the party. If anyone made contact with the queen, we would know about it.

I kept my court mask in place, smiling and accepting congratulations from the courtiers, while I weighed each one with my eyes, wishing I could see into their hearts. Had I been right about the count and countess of Ellsmore after all? Did their disapproval of me stretch more deeply than they let on? Or was it one of the merchants perhaps? Lured to the side of my stepmother with promises of wealth and favor—perhaps even a title.

I hated the suspicion in my heart for these people I hoped to rule. In truth I didn't want it to be any of them, and I kept trying to think of a way around it.

I certainly didn't expect Alexander to tap me on the shoulder and signal for me to accompany him from the ballroom before the night was even over. One look at his face and any thought that it might be on a personal matter evaporated.

"Come," he said. "Down in the kitchens."

My mind immediately flew to Carter. He had been planning to spend the evening in the kitchens. A dreadful sensation washed over me. He had been so friendly and pledged his loyalty so freely. He had been locked away for defying Alida. And Alexander trusted him.

I tried to shake the thought from my head, but it had lodged there now. What if his imprisonment had been a ploy to gain our trust? Who else had the skills to have tracked us through the forest? And he had certainly known our plans ever since the rescue. In fact, he had been determined since then to stick by my side.

I glanced sideways at Alexander. I didn't want to believe it for his sake. How much it would hurt him to be betrayed by his old mentor. Perhaps I was merely letting my imagination run away with me. But it would explain the hard look on his face now, the mask that I suspected hid some sort of pain.

I followed as fast as my party slippers would allow, unable to question Alexander further given the servants we kept passing. When we burst into the kitchen, several kitchen hands looked over at us in astonishment. But the cook merely gestured toward a large storage room that opened off one wall.

Alexander hurried ahead of me and yanked open the door, disappearing inside. I paused for a moment to gather myself and then followed him.

But no moment of calm could have prepared me for the sight of the elegantly dressed courtier inside. He sat in a single wooden chair, held down by Carter's firm hand on his shoulder, and his expression as he looked up at me was anguished.

"Oh!" I gasped, nearly staggering backward. "You!"

CHAPTER 24

"*I*t's always the ones you don't expect, I'm afraid, Your Majesty," said Carter gruffly. "Wouldn't be good spies otherwise."

I looked between them, my heart racing and my thoughts swirling in confusion. So Carter wasn't the spy, he had just caught them? Or was this all part of some ploy to cast suspicion away from himself?

I forced myself to focus on the courtier in the chair.

"But Roger—we're family!" I said. "Tell me it isn't true."

My cousin's face twisted at my words, and he looked as if he wanted to speak, but Alexander cut in instead.

"What happened, Carter?"

The older huntsman ran his free hand across his chin. "Well, as you know, I was settling in for a quiet evening in the kitchens."

Alexander snorted, and Carter grinned. Clearly my old friend still believed in his mentor.

"Well, quieter than you lot were having at any rate. I know the duke has his people set to watch all these fancy ladies and gents once they depart for the eve, but I thought there was no harm in an extra pair of eyes."

"No indeed," Alexander murmured.

"And it occurred to me as how the immediate arrival of a small army might be news Her False Majesty up there at the castle would be wanting sooner rather than later. And, sure enough, down comes this gentleman, looking to flirt a little with the kitchen maids and slip out the side door when no one was watching."

Carter barked a laugh. "But old hands like me are always watching."

Roger groaned, and I examined his face, trying to read it. "I suppose this is the part where you protest your innocence."

"Yes!" He sighed. "Well, no, not exactly."

"And what's that supposed to mean?" Alexander leaned over him in a threatening manner, but Roger didn't draw back. Instead he straightened his shoulders, focused his gaze on me, and a took a deep breath.

"I did try to sneak out to go up to the castle. But not because I was so anxious to take her your news. And you have to let me go. Now."

Alexander leaned back, crossing his arms across his chest and laughing without humor. "Good try."

Roger continued to look only at me. "You know me, Snow. You've known me your whole life—nearly my whole life. I have no loyalty to Alida, and I wouldn't betray you. Not willingly."

I frowned. "What do you mean?" I wanted to hold onto the hope that my own cousin couldn't be the one betraying me. But then neither did I want to accept the idea that it might be someone who would bring Alexander such pain.

"It's my family. You heard..." He paused for a moment, visibly shaken. "You remember that my wife had twin boys, only a year ago."

I nodded.

"Well, Alida has guards stationed at our house. We live in constant fear. If I don't assist her..."

"What?" I balled up my fists—the only physical move I could make in the confined space. It did little to release my pent-up energy. At least the anger chased away the tears that had been threatening to surface.

He had admitted to it—even if he claimed to be doing it under threat. I gave Carter a quick glance. I supposed that absolved the old huntsman, at least. My whirling thoughts circled back to my stepmother, and I couldn't help a protest.

"But that's despicable! Threatening babies!" But even as I said the words, I remembered who I was speaking of.

Roger's face looked sad, lined where it hadn't been before. How had I not seen it when we laughed together at the earlier party?

"Are you really surprised?" He asked me. "This is Alida we're talking about. You were little more than a baby when she married your father, but she never warmed to you, did she?"

I flinched, but he held my gaze while I considered his words. He had spent enough time at the castle to see her constant subtle efforts to deride and undermine me. Even as a small child.

"We can have someone confirm it." Alexander's anger had been replaced with a thoughtful expression. "If there really are royal guards stationed at his house, I mean."

I glanced over at him and nodded, and he disappeared from the storage room. The rest of us remained behind in silence. I wanted to believe Roger. Desperately. To believe that neither Alexander nor I had suffered betrayal from someone close to us.

And that was what scared me most. I couldn't let myself be blinded by my own wishes and desires. If I did, it could prove a fatal misstep.

Should I call my grandfather down here? Get his opinion? But something in me resisted. I appreciated his assistance and valued his counsel, even. But I needed to stand on my own two feet.

I stared at my cousin, weighing his words in my mind with the person I knew. Alexander reappeared.

"Someone has been dispatched," he said.

"The presence of the guards isn't my only proof," said Roger suddenly.

I turned back to him eagerly.

"I knew you were in the capital earlier—we talked at the duke's previous event. But Alida didn't come for you, did she? And she hasn't come for the duke, either. Or any of the courtiers he's conspiring with. I haven't given her anyone's name."

I bit my lip. It was true enough. And I should have thought of it. A spy in our midst could have done a lot more damage than they had so far.

"So why not? What have you told her?"

"It's not so much what I've told her. Which is nothing about our plans, by the way. It's what I can *see* for her."

"Ohhhh…" I rocked backward as realization dawned. "Oh, I see." No wonder it was my own cousin, then.

"Snow?" Alexander sounded unimpressed with being left in the dark.

"The mirror," I said. "She needs you for the mirror. It still won't answer to her?"

Roger nodded, and Alexander looked as if he were finally catching on.

Carter cleared his throat. "Apologies for being a bit dense, Your Majesty. But what does a mirror have to do with this?"

Roger answered for me. "The royal mirror of Eliam. Surely you've heard of it? The set of royal mirrors are ancient godmother gifts given to the monarchs of each of the kingdoms —passed down from generation to generation."

"Oh, aye." Carter frowned. "I think I've heard something of it. But what does it have to do with your betrayal?" He looked suspicious, as if he feared Roger was fooling me with a pretty story. But my cousin's words made far too much sense.

"It only works for members of the royal family," I said, "but it allows them to observe over long distances. We can watch over our own people, or we can even use it to communicate with the royal families of the other kingdoms."

"But it only works for members of the royal family," Roger repeated, his face giving the words added emphasis.

"It should work for Alida herself, of course," I said. "It should have worked as soon as she married my father. Possibly even as soon as they were officially betrothed. But it never has. He always just said that magic is funny like that, and it follows its own rules. Or rather, it follows the High King's rules, I suppose, since it originally comes from him."

"Ha!" Roger shook his head. "I'm sure Alida loved that. You were too young to remember, but my family was visiting the castle for the wedding, and I remember when she found out it wouldn't answer to her. She was in such an almighty rage! I wasn't very old myself and hid for nearly a full day."

"Apparently it always answered to my mother," I said quietly.

Roger looked at me sadly. "Yes, it did. That's what my parents said, anyway. But then she was a very different woman from Alida." He paused. "I think that's partially what made Alida so angry. She could never measure up to your mother. Not in any way. Not to the court. And here was evidence the godmothers themselves—or at least the High King they serve—felt the same way."

"So what does all this have to do with you?" Carter gave Roger a shake, his hand still firmly keeping him in place.

"Roger is my cousin," I explained. I looked at him. "Does it work for you then?"

He nodded unhappily. "I only wish it didn't. I was never sure if it would or not. I'd only ever seen it once, when I snuck into your father's rooms to take a peek at the age of ten. But a guard found me before I could actually try it out."

"So Alida has been threatening your family to make you use the mirror for her." I shook my head. "I never dreamed of such a thing."

Roger sighed. "I wish I'd lied to her at the beginning and said it didn't work for me. Because it turns out she can't see what I do when I use it, even if she's standing right behind me. But unfortunately I didn't know that the first time, and I reacted visibly to the first image I saw. So then she knew."

He ran a tired hand over his face. "I've been telling her as little as I can get away with, but I had to give her something. When she asked for your location specifically, I knew that if I lied, my family would pay the price." He hung his head. "So I told her about the cottage, although it was hard to pinpoint its exact location from the mirror. I hoped that might save you. And I told her about Lestern, too."

He looked up at me. "It was such a relief to see you that first night, and to know you were safe, after all. I'd been feeling sick for days. It wasn't as bad with Lestern. I thought you would be safe enough there, at least."

I wanted to yell at him, to tell him that my friends hadn't been safe in either location. That he had nearly killed children with his information. But I restrained myself. I might not be a parent, but I thought I understood something of how they must feel. Could I blame him for exchanging the mere chance that someone else might be hurt for the life of his own babies?

Silence fell, and Roger looked between Alexander and me.

"You do believe me, Snow, don't you?"

Slowly I nodded my head. "I do. Your story makes sense, especially given the patchy information Alida seems to possess." A great weight had lifted off me at the knowledge that he hadn't willingly betrayed me.

"Well then," said Alexander slowly. "I guess the only thing left to do in that case is to decide how to proceed."

"You need to let me go," said Roger urgently. "The only reason I was trying to sneak out is because Alida had already summoned me up to the castle tonight. I thought I could fit in both things…" He looked over at me. "I wasn't going to tell her about you, of course! But she'll no doubt have me look in the mirror and ask what I see of you. I can lie for a while. Say you're still in Lestern. But it won't work forever."

"No, and I don't want your family at risk if she has an agent who can confirm I'm no longer there." I sighed. "I left the castle in a state of lock down, so I hope that would take a little while at least."

I turned to Alexander. "How far away are our troops? When can we face the full court?"

Alexander looked uncomfortably at Roger, but I just shrugged. "If he decides to turn against us, we're already lost anyway."

Alexander sighed. "Once we decided to leave, Tarver resolved to march his guards here as fast as he could. They'll still move more slowly than us, though. So I'm expecting them three days behind."

"That puts them only two days away." I thought it through. "And there will be no hiding them once they've arrived, so we'll have to move quickly after that."

I looked back at Roger. "Can you tell my stepmother that you see me still alive and well? She did make an attempt against my life in Lestern, but her agent might have reported that unsuccessful, so we can't risk your lying about it."

Roger's face twisted, but I hurried on before he could attempt an apology.

"But you can tell her that you see me in the midst of a great host of guards. Just marching out of Lestern. No doubt her agent has already reported about the massing troops, so I don't think we're giving anything away there, but we'll let her think she has more time than she really does. When we call for the court, I want it to take her by surprise."

"Of course, Your Majesty," Roger said, giving as much of a bow as he could given his constrained circumstances.

"You can let him go now, Carter," I said.

The huntsman looked unhappy with the order, but he removed his hand, and Roger quickly stood.

"I must leave immediately."

I gave him a sudden embrace, nearly knocking him off balance. "Thank you, Roger. And I'll talk to the duke. See if we can't send some of our own guards into your house disguised as servants or something. That way if the queen ever does decide to act, at least your family will have a chance."

A light kindled in Roger's eyes. "Would you, Snow?"

"Of course." I stepped back and gestured for the door. "Now get going!"

PART III
THE QUEEN

CHAPTER 25

The duke wasn't exactly pleased to know we had found and dealt with the spy without his input, but he didn't actually have any fault to find with our final decisions. I filled him in on everything that had happened as we sat alone over breakfast.

"I've known the baron since he was a little boy," he said. "The Capstone lands border on Lestern. There's no way he would side with Alida by choice." He shook his head. "I never even considered him as our leak. But I should have thought of that mirror!"

"I didn't think of it, either," I said. "None of us did. I didn't even know it would work for Roger. But there's no point dwelling on the past. We need to focus on our plans moving forward."

My grandfather regarded me with an approving smile.

"You're going to make an excellent queen, Snow."

A warmth rose up inside me. He seemed so much more confident in me than I was in myself. "Do you really think so?"

"Of course. You are your mother's daughter."

Ah. There it was. My mother. Did he really see and approve of me? Or was he blinded by his love for her? I put down my spoon.

"Yes, I am my mother's daughter, though I never knew her. And my father's, too. And your granddaughter. So tell me, Grandfather, why I never saw you before my father's death."

I looked across the table straight into his eyes. He shifted in his seat, more uncomfortable than I had ever seen him, but I didn't back down. The moment of confronting my stepmother was fast approaching, and if we succeeded, I suspected the court would appoint him as my regent. This was a conversation he and I needed to have.

"That was…a mistake. I can see that now."

He paused, but I said nothing, waiting for him to continue.

"My own dear girl also lost her mother far too young. And with my wife gone, she was all I had. I doted on her, I admit. And why not? She was not only beautiful but kind and intelligent and strong." He shook his head, and I saw moisture in his eyes. "I wish you could have known her."

Searing pain pierced through me. How desperately I wished it too. But I forced my face to remain immobile, impassive as he told his story.

"We often visited court, and it seemed only natural that the young king himself would fall in love with her. I was so proud on the day of their wedding. So proud to see a crown on her head, as she deserved. All the kingdom rejoiced on that day."

Pain lanced across his face. "But then a year passed. And another. And another. And my girl became so sad. Your father—to his credit—assured her that he loved her even without an heir, but she knew her duty." He looked across at me and quickly shook his head. "No, it wasn't about duty. It was always about love. How much she wanted a baby of her own to love." He lowered his voice. "She always loved babies."

My breath hitched, and it took all my strength not to break down in front of him.

"And so she made her fateful wish," I said. "A daughter. Skin as white as snow. Lips as red as blood. Hair as black as ebony. And so she unknowingly wished her own death. If only she could have known she was killing herself."

I had thought he would flinch away at that, turn from me, the blame finally clear on his face. But instead he looked across at me in surprise.

"Killing herself?" His keen eyes narrowed as he examined my face. "Or killed by you?"

I sucked in a gasp to hear the words put so baldly.

Concern filled his eyes. "Is that how you have thought of it all these years? My poor Snow! You are not responsible for her death."

This time I couldn't control the tremors that ran through me.

"I didn't mean to, of course," I said. "I was only a baby. But I did kill her. Do you really mean to claim that's not what you've thought all these years?"

"No." He shook his head vehemently. "No one knew my daughter like I did. She was already weakening—although with what I don't know. Your coming may have hastened the end, but it was coming just the same. I had seen it for months before she fell pregnant, and it was eating away at me, although the doctors claimed they could find nothing wrong. Your arrival allowed her to leave this world on so much joy. She loved your father—strange as it sometimes seems to me—and she was so happy to have a part of herself to leave for him. So happy to hold you in her arms before the end."

Tears ran down my face, and I made no effort to wipe them away. "Then how come you never came to court again after her death? How come you didn't want to know me?"

His hand tightened around the handle of his butter knife, his eyes staring down at it unseeingly.

"I wanted to see you, Snow. I wanted desperately to see you." He swallowed. "But I was afraid. Deathly afraid." He looked up at me, and his haunted expression was nothing like the confident one he usually wore. "I have never told anyone this, but I was afraid that seeing you after her death would break me in a way I could not mend. I had already lost my wife and my only child. I thought I could not risk opening up my heart to you. And I could not bear to see her face looking back at me from yours. Not when I knew I would never truly see her again."

He paused, and silence filled the breakfast room, a heavy weight upon us both.

"And then the months passed and became a year," he said. "And I began to wonder if perhaps I was wrong. I thought of what my girl would have wanted, and I knew she would want us to be part of each other's lives—to know one another. I began to prepare for a long overdue visit to court. And then I got the invitation."

Rage transformed his face, and he threw the knife from him. It landed with a loud clang against an unused plate, and we both froze in shock at the jarring noise. Slowly his face calmed, the tension in the room receding.

"Gracious," he said, "I thought such strong emotions had long faded. But it seems they are still there to be recalled." He shook his head. "I have spent long years learning to master my emotions. You must forgive me if sometimes they still slip."

I swallowed and licked my lips, but no words emerged. Even if I could have made my throat work, I didn't know what to say.

My grandfather drew a deep, steadying breath. "I received the invitation to the wedding of King George and Alida. Perhaps I should even have seen it coming despite my absence from court. She came from a new branch of the nobility, poor and without power in court. But she was beautiful enough, I suppose, although nothing to your mother. And Alida had never made a secret of the fact that she believed she had been born to be queen. She pursued your father relentlessly, though he showed no great interest. When he married your mother, she left court, poisoned, no doubt by disappointment and hate."

"But she returned," I said, the words little more than a breath.

"Yes." My grandfather seemed to deflate before my eyes, looking his age for the first time since I had met him. "She must have returned as soon as she heard of your mother's death. No doubt she hounded your father unceasingly. But still, I thought…"

His eyes grew distant before he sighed and refocused on me. "I had thought your father's love for my daughter sincere. And I could not forgive him for marrying again so soon. For replacing her. And all my new resolve washed away. I vowed never to set foot in a court where someone else ruled at your father's side instead of my daughter."

His eyes seemed to bore into me. "At the last she gave him you. He had a piece of her. An heir. He did not need another wife. Especially not one he did not love, and who did not love his child. One who cared only for herself."

He sighed. "I am an old man, and when I look back on my life, I can see my mistakes. I let my anger at him rule me, even though it meant being separated from you. I could not have one of you without the other, since he never liked being separated from you. And I could not forgive him for his weakness. But it is you and I who suffered the consequences of my unforgiveness. In hindsight, I cannot say whose mistake was greater—the king's or mine—or how different things would be now if I had let love dictate my actions instead of bitterness. With me standing strong beside you, Alida could not have acted as she did."

He stood up and crossed around the table to kneel in front of me. When he took my hand, his grip felt strong and warm.

"I should have put you first. Will you forgive me, Granddaughter? Will you put the past behind us and start afresh?"

I licked my lips and looked away from him. I wanted to say yes so badly. To accept his apology and his love. To bask in the knowledge that he had never blamed me for my mother's death—that I might not have been indirectly responsible for it at all. But others of his words pricked at me.

I pulled my hand away.

"My father was a good man. A good father. A good king."

My grandfather froze and then heaved himself into the seat beside me with a weary sigh. He opened his mouth to speak, and then closed it again, regarding me thoughtfully instead. Several long breaths hung between us. I watched him out of the corner of my eye as he considered my words.

"I'm sure he loved you," he said at last. "Although I wasn't around to witness it for myself. He certainly seems to have trained you well for the role you will have to bear, so I cannot fault him there." He hesitated. "And who am I to rule on who is or is not a good man?"

I stood to my feet, pushing my chair back so quickly it nearly toppled. "He was a good man. And a good king."

"In many ways he was a good king. He was fair to his people and just in his dealings. His policies were—by and large—good ones, and he made no unnecessary taxation demands."

"But…" I spoke the word for him since it hung so loudly in the air between us.

"But he was also weak, and that is not a good quality in a king."

I opened my mouth to protest, but he held up his hand to stop me.

"Think for a moment. I know you loved him—as you should. But you are no longer a child, Snow, and you are about to ascend to a throne. It is time for you to see things as they truly are. Can you really deny it? He allowed that woman to badger him into marriage, although he had no love for her, of that I am sure. And worse, he showed no care for his kingdom in doing so. All these years our kingdom has stayed on course because he retained the good sense to prevent her interfering in his rule. But while he may have overruled her, he also failed to truly check her. Even you were not protected from her, were you? How she must have poisoned your childhood." His last sentence was uttered in a whisper, and it carried self-blame as well as grief.

I tried to push his words away from me, but I felt them well up and crash over me, like a wave I wasn't fast enough to escape. I struggled to breathe, and still he went on.

"He fostered no relationships between you and other young nobles. Relationships that might have served you when he was gone. Instead he chose to keep you close with him. And then as he grew sick, you must have seen how things began to deteriorate. He closed his eyes to what that woman was doing in his final years, choosing the comfort of his sick bed, unable to act through his pain. You yourself, in your person, are his shining legacy, reflecting all his strengths. But your situation..." He shook his head. "That is the legacy of his weakness. And but for your most loyal friend, it might have meant your death."

He had been looking at the ground as he spoke, but he looked up now and pierced me with his gaze. I gasped and collapsed back into my chair, the tears streaming down my face unchecked. How much it hurt to admit that he was right. To see my father as he truly was—a loving man, but a flawed one—and not as the hero of my childhood. But the deepest part of my heart whispered that it was true. And that I had already known it.

"I do not mean to wound you, Snow," my grandfather said, taking my hand again. "I wish only to see you come through your crucible of fire and emerge the stronger for it. A granddaughter I can bow to with pleasure—a queen who will lead our kingdom out of trouble and into prosperity."

I looked into his face, and I could read the sincerity there. And I knew with blinding clarity that it was only due to his support that I had any chance of ever taking my father's place and sitting on his throne. Inside I felt as if I were breaking, but I could not withhold from him what he wanted.

"I...I understand, Grandfather. And I forgive you. Perhaps...

perhaps when this is all over, you can tell me more about what my mother was like as a girl. I should like to know more of her."

Light broke across his face, and he squeezed my hand. Leaning across the short distance between us, he placed a kiss on my forehead.

"I should like that more than anything, Granddaughter."

Somehow I forced my legs to lift me to my feet. "I find I am no longer hungry. I shall leave you now."

He made no demur, his eyes all too full of gentle understanding.

"Today and tomorrow, you should rest," he said. "And then, as long as our troops have arrived as planned, I will call the court together the morning after that. By the time Alida realizes what is happening, it will be too late for her to prevent it. She cannot close the castle gates against the court. And then you will stand up, and everyone will see the worthy young woman that I see before me. Your court will bow to you, Snow. I promise it."

I halted with my hand on the door, but I was too afraid of what he would see if I turned around. So I merely nodded before fleeing from the room.

CHAPTER 26

I spent a large part of the next two days shut in my room. It was what I was supposed to do, anyway, since we didn't want word of my presence leaking out and proving Roger a liar before the right moment, but Alexander at least could tell that something was wrong. I pushed him away, though, because this was something I had to work through for myself.

When I thought of my mother, I felt buoyed up. She had held me and loved me. I hadn't caused her death. But thoughts of her came weighted with a heavy grief. And more powerful still were the thoughts of my father.

All the grief that I had pushed away during the dangerous and fear-filled weeks since his death crashed over me now, and I spent hour upon hour crying. Only this time, I couldn't always be sure what I was crying over. Was it over his absence, my heart crying out to feel his dearly-loved presence again? Or was it grief for his failings? For the knowledge that despite all his love, he had left behind in me a fatal weakness.

Because my grandfather saw me as the best of my father, but I knew the truth. My insidious voice of self-doubt had returned with a vengeance.

You didn't want it to be true, but you have to admit he was right. Your father was weak. So is it any surprise you are too?

I tried to fight against the thoughts, reminding myself of how hard I had trained. How I had made myself strong. How I had helped rescue Alexander. But then I would remember how many people had shielded me, suffered for me. How many times I had fled, afraid.

I had always defined myself by my father, and I felt unanchored now, tossed around far too easily by every wave of my own fear and failing. I wanted to believe in the version of me that my grandfather saw. That Alexander saw. But was that just another form of weakness? Another closing of my eyes to the truth?

Could I stand up and be queen when I knew how deeply I was flawed?

The final evening came while I still wrestled with this question. Alexander brought me news of the arrival of our guards, and I could see the worry reflected in his eyes. So I forced a smile and emerged for the evening meal, at least. He hovered close to me, and I felt calmed by his presence. Surely I must have some strength and worth in me to have inspired a friendship such as his.

But he had been called away to consult on a matter of guard placement in the forest when Bronson announced my cousin's arrival, so I went to meet Roger alone, without Alexander's steadying company.

Roger, who had been sitting on one of the elegant sofas in the sitting room I had come to think of as mine, leaped to his feet when he saw me. When I had heard his name announced, I feared something had gone wrong, but he wore a smile. In fact his face looked lighter than it had done since before my father's death. The difference made me realize I should have seen something was wrong at that first party.

He hurried forward to bow and clasp my hand.

"I didn't expect to see you tonight, Roger. I hope all is well." I sat down and gestured for him to do so as well.

"No, no, nothing is wrong," he hastened to assure me. "I delivered your message as we agreed, and Alida showed no hesitation in believing it." He winced briefly. "I probably shouldn't have come, but I had to thank you in person."

"Thank me?" I raised an eyebrow.

"In the past two days, two of our footmen got into a nasty fight with each other, one of our maids broke a valuable vase, and our nursery maid was discovered drunk, if you can believe it." His twinkling eyes suggested he couldn't, and neither should I. "I'm afraid we've had to dismiss them all."

My lips twitched. "A quite incredible run of ill fortune, it would seem."

"Yes, indeed. But my wife has been busy interviewing replacements, and we are *most* pleased with our new hires. Most pleased."

"And the dismissed servants?"

He waved a hand. "Loyal, all of them. They know it is only temporary and have been given wages enough to cover the gap. But last night my wife slept well for the first time in weeks. And so I had to come and thank you."

His face turned grave. "Of course we are all hoping that tomorrow goes smoothly and without bloodshed. But none of us can guarantee such a thing. And it has tormented me to know that my family have been so vulnerable."

"Yes, indeed, I can only imagine." His words only sparked my own fears, and I thought of all the servants who still remained at the castle. If tomorrow went badly, there were far too many on hand to suffer the consequences of any outbreak of fighting.

"I hope the servants catch wind of the arrival of our guards and get themselves out of the castle in the morning," I said. "The fewer around to end up hurt or in the way, the better."

Roger's brow lowered, and he glanced quickly at me, then away.

I sat up straight. "What is it?"

"I don't think they'll be able to do that, Your Majesty."

"Why not?"

"Your stepmother is becoming paranoid." He grimaced. "She won't let any of the servants leave the castle anymore. All errands to the city are carried out by her guards. Apparently she's convinced some of them are spying on her and carrying information to rebels in the city."

I winced. Was it paranoia if it was true? At least that she had a rebellion going on under her nose, and that not all the servants were loyal to her. The image of Gertie, feather duster in hand, keeping my room in order in the middle of the night flashed through my mind.

After Roger had given me a quick goodbye to rush home to his family, I remained alone in the sitting room.

I hope we'll see you again soon. Gertie's words ran over and over again in my mind. Despite everything, some at least of the servants had pinned their hopes on me. And tomorrow I would walk into their home without warning, an army on my heels, potentially to unleash war in their midst.

The longer I thought of it, the more I felt certain of the path I must take. Neither my grandfather nor Alexander would agree. They would say it was too risky, especially for me. They would place their trust in our coup being successful. In the legitimacy of my claim. They would say that it was the job of others to take risks for their queen.

But neither of them had grown up under my stepmother's thumb. They didn't understand how vicious she could be when she lashed out, how little she cared for others. No, I could not leave the servants unwarned.

I had always understood that a ruler must sometimes let

others take on danger in their stead. It was the price of ruling, of preventing chaos. My father had taught me that. But now I knew my father had been weak, had allowed himself to be lulled into inaction when action had been needed. If I asked Alexander, if I pleaded, if I ordered, he would no doubt go in my place.

But I couldn't bear the thought of once again sending him into danger in my stead. I could no more sacrifice him than I could the servants. I refused to be a weak ruler, like my father. I would be a strong one. I would not start my reign by sacrificing those around me. I would save them—and I would do it myself. Who better to contact and convince the servants than me, anyway?

Tonight I would sneak into the castle and warn the servants. I would make a plan for them to flee and be safe, no matter what happened.

I had to wait until well after dark before I could slip from the house unseen. I wore my sturdy boots and my new dagger sheathed at my waist.

I encountered no guards on patrol as I sped through the trees toward my drain. Had the queen recalled them, or had my own troops taken them prisoner? Whatever the reason, it made my path easier. All too soon, I was back within the castle grounds, weaving through the trees toward my familiar window.

I barely had to think about it now as I scaled the vines on the wall. The ease of my ascent buoyed me. I had been right to tell no one of my plan. Alexander would have insisted on coming in my stead, but he could never have gained access so easily.

When I stepped into my dark dressing room, a strange feeling washed over me. Such a familiar place, and yet so much had changed in me that I no longer belonged here. These had been the rooms of the old Snow. A person both weaker in some ways, and more confident in others. Confident in how she saw the world, at any rate, and the people around her.

I shook off the thought. I still needed to find Gertie and get safely back out of here. I didn't have time for distractions. And yet the thought brought another, and more disconcerting, one. How exactly was I to find Gertie? It was the same problem I had encountered previously, only this time I couldn't wait here for an unknown length of time.

I hadn't pondered the issue long, however, when I heard the door in my adjoining bedchamber open. I forced myself to be cautious rather than rushing through and eased the dressing room door open slowly. But only a quick survey of the room told me the good news.

Hurrying in, I whispered a greeting to Gertie. She jumped and turned a pale, frightened face toward me.

"Oh! You scared me!" She then started and curtsied belatedly. "Your Majesty."

I waved the title away. "Never mind that right now. We need to talk."

"We...we do, Your Majesty?" She looked dubious and uncertain, and I wondered if she thought I was going to ask her to take part in some act of rebellion.

"I heard you've all been confined to the palace," I said, my words tumbling over each other. "So the rumors may not have reached you. But there's a confrontation coming tomorrow. And there will be guards involved, lots of them."

Her wide eyes reflected fear and nervous energy.

"That's why I came," I said. "To warn you all. You need to get out of here at dawn. If I succeed, you'll be welcomed back, of course. If I don't, there will be bloodshed, for sure, and I don't want you all in the midst of it."

"But...but the gates are closed and double-guarded. All of them." Her voice trembled.

"Then you need to band together," I said firmly. "Choose one of the smaller side gates. When the court begins to arrive, you all leave. Head out and hide among the trees. At the first sign of any fighting, overwhelm the guards and get out into the true forest. I'm sure if the footmen and huntsmen work together, you can take out the guards at one of the gates. You'll have numbers on your side."

Gertie swallowed. "Maybe…maybe there's an easier way?"

I raised my eyebrows inquiringly, and she almost trembled from nerves.

"The guards get a meal during the night shift. Perhaps the kitchen staff who prepare it could ensure it puts them to sleep. The guards at one of the gates, anyway, like you say."

"Yes, so you don't attract any attention. That's an excellent idea, Gertie. Can they do it?" I knew Alexander and then the bribable guard had both managed to source some sort of sleeping potion to get us past the gates previously, so I wasn't surprised to learn some was to be found in the castle, if you knew where to look.

"I think they can, Your Majesty. But…"

"What is it?" I asked as encouragingly as I could.

"It's a big thing to do. Rallying all the servants like that. I don't know if they'll take my word for it. You might…you might need to speak to them yourself."

"Of course." I stepped forward. "But we'll need to move quickly."

"All…all right." She put down her duster. "We should go to the kitchens. Come with me."

Together we ghosted through the corridors. My heart rate ratcheted up at moving so openly, but we encountered no one. When we arrived in the kitchen, the banked fires cast only the dimmest light on the deserted room. Gertie hurried to light some candles before moving back toward the doorway.

"Wait here," she whispered. "I'll find the kitchen maids who'll be taking the guards their meal. They'll be here soon enough anyway to prepare it. And I'll rouse some of the more senior servants as well."

I nodded, but she had already gone. Surveying the large room, I shivered. It seemed spooky in such a deserted state, silent and full of flickering shadows. But I reminded myself that so far everything had progressed smoothly. With any luck, I would be on my way back to the ducal mansion soon enough.

The thoughts did little to reassure me, however, and when a figure appeared in the doorway, I jumped. I immediately saw it was a kitchen maid, but it still took several deep breaths, my hands braced against the long wooden table in the center of the room, to calm myself.

"Sorry, Your Highness," the girl said, her eyes wide. "Only Gertie sent me, and she said…"

"Yes, yes." I took another deep breath. "I was expecting you. Only this place…" I waved a hand around me and managed a weak smile. "Did she explain the situation?"

"I think so. But the others will be here soon, and they're the ones to be making any decisions. I'm just to prepare the food."

She began moving as she spoke, pulling out bread and wedges of cheese and shiny apples. My eyes lingered on the food, surprised to find I was hungry. But then I'd eaten little in the last two days, my stomach roiling too unpleasantly to have much interest in food.

The girl saw the direction of my gaze and picked up a firm, bright apple, half red, half gold. With a firm slice, she cut it in half and took a bite out of one piece, offering the other to me.

"Would you like some?" she asked around her mouthful.

I hesitated for a moment before accepting the glossy red morsel. As I took the first bite, I looked up and saw Gertie standing in the doorway. She looked tormented, so I hurried to swallow, wanting to free my mouth to ask what was wrong.

Except the apple stuck in the back of my throat, a sudden burning sensation rushing down from it into my gut and up into my head. I coughed, but nothing happened. And then the burning overwhelmed me, and I collapsed to the ground.

CHAPTER 27

I hit my head as I fell, and it took a moment for my vision to clear. The burning had passed, but I could still feel the apple lodged in my throat. I tried to cough again, and panic seized me.

I couldn't move.

Desperately I tried to cough, directing my arms and legs to push me up from the floor, but nothing happened. No new breath entered my throat. And yet slowly the panic subsided. I was still alive. Or it seemed so, at any rate. And though I couldn't feel breath rushing in and out of my chest, or move so much as an eyelash, I could still hear and see.

I had fallen so that my head lay sideways, my face turned toward the door. I could see Gertie frozen there, a look of horror on her face, and then she turned and fled with an audible sob. A moment later someone new moved into my vision, and everything became clear.

My stepmother bent down over me and prodded at my shoulder. When I didn't move, she straightened again and laughed. She wore the same clothes as the kitchen maid had done a moment ago, but there was no mistaking her. Enchantment. Some sort of enchantment held me in thrall. And some sort of enchantment had disguised her earlier.

I berated myself for my foolishness. Had I been reassuring myself just a moment ago about how smoothly everything was going? It had been too smooth. Too easy. I should have seen that. And, more importantly, I never should have come here alone without even informing anyone of my plans. There was no one to rescue me now, and it was no one's fault but my own. What did my stepmother plan to do with me?

The thought of her original orders to Randolph flashed through my mind, and if I could have moved, I would have retched. Surely she would not do such a thing now. No one would believe it.

But even as my thoughts were racing, she knelt again and placed a hand on my chest. It remained perfectly still beneath her touch. She leaned in, and I thought she meant to whisper something to me, although we were alone, and there was no need for whispers. But instead her ear hovered over my mouth. After remaining motionless that way for an endless moment, she pulled back.

Her triumphant smile sickened me more than her touch.

"Dead," she breathed. "Dead at last." Then she stood to her feet and strode from the room.

For several long moments I couldn't make sense of it. And then understanding crashed through me. Her poison hadn't been meant to paralyze me, it had been meant to kill me. She thought I was held motionless by death. A new fear gripped me. Did she mean to have me buried? And what would it mean if she did? Despite her intentions, the enchantment seemed to be holding me alive without even the need for breath. Would I live forever, frozen beneath the ground?

If I could have produced tears I would have at such a horrifying thought.

Foolish, foolish girl! Why did you rush so heedlessly into danger?

But I knew the reasons I had done it. I could just see them now for what they were—foolishness. I had let my new understanding of my father make me doubt everything he had taught me. But he had been right that a ruler should never act alone. I had thought I was being strong, but instead I had been reckless. We had been on the cusp of victory, despite my previous moments of weakness. And that had been because of the support of those around me—those who had proved themselves both wise and loyal.

I had wanted to be strong—to prove myself untainted by the weakness of my father. But I could see now that in some things, my father had been right. Without me, no bloodless rebellion could hope to succeed. And with my future gone, my kingdom's hope disappeared with it.

If only someone would help me.

Please, please! I pleaded within the prison of my mind. *Someone help me!*

Before I could even bemoan the uselessness of my silent plea, a figure strode into my vision from the back of the kitchen where no one had previously been. If I hadn't already been on the ground, immobilized, I no doubt would have fallen from the shock. Because the woman before me had gray hair, no-nonsense eyes, and wings. Actual wings.

"It's about time! I thought you'd never call me."

A...a godmother!

"But of course, my dear. Who were you expecting?" She regarded the food still strewn across the table and selected a small portion of cheese, popping it into her mouth.

Poison! I screamed in my mind, but she continued chewing placidly.

She smiled down at me before seating herself neatly on the floor where I could see her.

"Only that one apple. Well, only that one half of that apple. The rest is perfectly safe. I'd offer you some, but..."

You can understand me. My thoughts, I mean.

"Certainly, my dear. I am a godmother, after all, as we have already established. And I'm afraid to say that was an enchanted potion of mine that your stepmother got her hands on. It didn't do what she thought it did, of course, so we may all be thankful for that."

You're here to free me? Hope surged in place of my earlier fear.

But the strange woman made an apologetic face. "There's only one thing that can do that, I'm afraid. So you're just going to have to be patient."

What? What can free me?

"You have to ask?" She blinked at me. "I suppose I must make allowances. We have been absent from your lands for a long time. Well, not entirely absent, of course."

What do you mean, not entirely?

She gave me a stern look. "These lands may have chosen to reject the High King and his ancient laws, cutting yourselves off from him, but that doesn't mean *he* was cut off from you. Us godmothers haven't been completely free to act—not as we would have liked—but we've been watching all the same."

Then how come you haven't helped us?

"Not helped you?" She shook her head. "How's that for gratitude," she muttered before sighing. "We opened up the seas, didn't we? Sent you emissaries from the Four Kingdoms to help. Well, admittedly they've helped Marin, Palinar, and Eldon. But that got the ball rolling well enough."

I tried to suppress a surge of resentment. *Eliam could have done with a savior as well.*

"Oh, they weren't saviors, exactly. At least, they didn't do it on their own. They needed help from the locals along the way. And besides—" She fixed me with a disapproving look. "We did send Eliam the deliverer they needed. And we sent her long before the seas opened up."

I don't...

251

"You, you silly girl! We sent you. We might not have been able to come ourselves, but we were watching closely enough to hear the desperate wish of a dying woman. And to see in her the seed that could grow into Eliam's deliverance. And so we sent you. We even did the whole white and ebony and red thing. Ridiculous, really, but since we couldn't save her, it seemed like the least we could do. A message to anyone who was listening that her pleas had been heard." She frowned. "Not that it seems anyone *was* listening."

My head reeled under this revelation.

But...but...it can't be me. I'm too weak. Just look at how I've ruined everything.

The godmother raised her eyebrows and ran them down my motionless body, sprawled rather awkwardly on the floor.

"I'm not going to deny you've made something of a mess of things. But then I've seen worse muddles come good. There's hope still. And as for this worthiness rubbish, you should put that out of your head. It's not being perfect and never making mistakes that makes you worthy to rule."

She rolled her eyes. "Believe me, if that were the requirement, no kingdom would have leadership of any kind, and the entire lot of you would be in anarchy. None of you humans are perfect. You're worthy because you were chosen for the task—appointed, sent especially—and when the moment came, you chose to answer the call." She fixed me with a piercing stare.

"You did, didn't you? You've had the chance to run—to seize your own happiness and not look back? And yet here you are, still making a muddle of things. You are the daughter of the king, and when it counted—when it cost you—you said yes. They're the only requirements that matter."

She gave me a sudden blinding smile, full of compassion. "The rest you can work on."

But—

"Humans," she muttered over the top of me. "There's always a but."

A sound in the passage outside the kitchen door sounded through the otherwise still night, and the godmother was gone. I didn't blink—I know I didn't since I physically couldn't do so. She was simply right in front of me one moment and gone the next.

My stepmother entered the room a moment later, Randolph close on her heels, and another man I didn't recognize behind him. I wanted to kick myself. I had lost my moment. I hadn't found out from the godmother what would free me. Not that I was free to act on it if I knew, anyway. The hope that her presence had brought faded. But a kernel of it still remained.

Her words had taken root in my heart. I had been chosen. Sent to rule Eliam. And I already knew how to do that—I'd worked it out just before my godmother arrived. I would rule with the help of those around me. I didn't have to do it alone. They would balance out my weaknesses.

Of course none of it mattered if I was going to be thrown down a deep hole, never to be seen again. But still, that kernel of hope remained.

"As you can see," said Alida, gesturing toward my frozen body, "it worked. You have at last been of some use to me, Sterling."

Sterling. I stared at the third man. So this was the mysterious stranger from Eldon.

"I still don't know why you didn't just send me in to deal with her," said Randolph.

Alida narrowed her eyes at him. "She has escaped me far too many times. This time I needed to do it myself. And besides, this is much neater. Even that blasted grandfather of hers can see that there is not so much as a scratch on her body."

"I'm glad you have been so successful, Your Majesty," said Sterling with a smooth bow. His blank face gave away nothing of his true feelings.

Alida smiled, but it came across more like a frown. "Both of these objects worked well, at least."

He stiffened at her implied criticism of the previous objects that she had wasted, but he didn't actually speak.

She handed him what looked like a small gold coin. "I don't know why it had to go in your mouth—most uncomfortable. But it worked just as you said it would. She saw only what I wished her to see. It's a pity it can only be used such a limited number of times, or I'm sure it would be worth a fortune. It seems to me that using it for prison breaks is most uninspired."

"I was happy to give you one of its uses, Your Majesty. I hope you will remember our arrangement."

"Oh certainly," she said with a dismissive gesture. "There is always room in my kingdom for someone with as much good sense and initiative as you. It seems it was a fortunate day for us that saw you prowling around the prisons of Marin all those many months ago."

Randolph grunted behind her, and I wondered again how she had arranged to have him released from the Marinese prison. *Prison.* Suddenly I understood something that had confused me before—the reason Sterling had fled straight to Alida. Alexander had mentioned that Sterling had assisted in some sort of prison break in Marin. It sounded like he must have met Randolph while there. No doubt they had been drawn to one another—a mutual recognition of ruthlessness perhaps. I wished I could back away from the whole group of them, but the enchantment continued to hold me in place.

"The duke's army has already arrived," said Randolph. "We've had word that they've taken up positions in the forest all around the castle. Only one of our patrols managed to make it back."

Alida glared down at me. "None of that matters now that she is gone. They have no one to rally behind. No one with a more legitimate claim to the throne than mine. I'm sure we shall have the court descend on us in the morning, however. We need to be ready for them."

She laughed, but it sounded fiendish to my ears. "I don't want anyone to question her death." She looked over at Randolph. "You know the plan. Give the necessary orders. I need some sleep before my big day."

And she swept out of the room.

CHAPTER 28

I had been afraid that Randolph, or Sterling, or both of them meant to pick me up and carry me somewhere. I hated the thought of either of them touching me. But to my surprise, they both simply walked from the room in my step-mother's wake.

A long time seemed to pass while I lay there alone, although I had no actual way to measure the time. When footsteps sounded again, Gertie was the last person I expected to reappear. The sight of her brought back the sting of betrayal, but the tear tracks still visible on her cheeks made me think immediately of my cousin. What threats had Alida used to force Gertie to work with her?

Two footmen accompanied the maid, and they both made hastily suppressed sounds of shock at the sight of me. But they soon recovered and between them gently lifted me before looking to Gertie for direction.

"To her rooms," she said, her voice soft and trembling.

I remembered her earlier trembles and the fear in her eyes when I had spoken to her in my room. I should have been more wary. More suspicious of her emotions. My mind snagged on another detail. She had called me Your Majesty as well, when before she had always said Your Highness. In my eagerness I hadn't even noticed. But perhaps she had been subtly trying to warn me that something had changed since my last visit.

The footmen soon deposited me on my own bed, after which they promptly left the room. Gertie began to work, her hands soft despite her continued tremors. I realized she was preparing my body for a funeral—or display of some sort, at least—and felt immediately grateful she had been chosen for the task.

She gently washed my hands, face, and hair, combing out my curls. I needed the service, too, still damp and dirty from my latest crawl through the drain. She seemed to have calmed somewhat by the time she dressed me in an elegant gown of deep red, a perfect match for my lips.

The sound of her voice startled me, although I could give no physical sign of it, of course.

"I'm so sorry, Your Highness. She worked it out somehow. That you'd been back at the castle. And that we were still cleaning your room." Her methodical hands fastened the many buttons on the dress, a billowing creation that I had always liked. Not that it seemed entirely appropriate for a funeral given it left my shoulders and neck bare. But no doubt my stepmother wanted everyone to see they were unmarked.

"She threatened us all," Gertie continued. "Made us take turns visiting the room regularly, day and night, to check for your return. And of course we were under orders to bring you to her under some ruse or other." Another tear slipped down her cheek. "I wouldn't have done it, but I have a family and…"

She let out a sob. "Oh, Your Highness, I wish you could hear how sorry I am. I wish I could take it back."

"It's not too late, my child," said another voice.

Gertie screamed and jumped back from the bed. I heard her

gasp, and then she reappeared. On the other side of the bed, just inside my peripheral vision, stood a new arrival. One I had only just met that night.

My godmother—if she was mine—wore an entirely different expression from any of the ones she had shown me. Her face almost glowed with serenity and wisdom, her hands crossed elegantly in front of her. And was she floating slightly off the ground? It was hard to tell when I couldn't turn my head and look at her properly.

"Not...not too late?" Gertie whispered the words, looking between the godmother and my apparent corpse. "But she's dead."

"Is she?"

I wanted to yell at my godmother and tell her to stop being so cryptic, but I could do nothing but watch the scene unfold.

"But what can save her then?" asked Gertie, her eyes so wide they seemed to have consumed her face. "If she's not truly dead?"

"Surely you already know the answer to that, my child. It is always the answer to every tale, is it not?" And with that the godmother disappeared.

I wanted to grind my teeth in frustration. It was the same non-answer she had given me. Except Gertie looked far less perplexed. Still a little shocked, perhaps, but almost excited. Had she actually understood the godmother? But even if she had, what could one maid do about it? If only she were not trapped here. If only she knew how to contact Alexander and my grandfather.

I could well imagine how frantic they would be when they found my room empty. What would they think? It seemed unbelievable to me now that I had ever thought my plan to infiltrate the castle alone and warn the servants a good one. I wished I could apologize to them.

Gertie finished her task, despite her new glow of excitement, but I could feel the difference now when she handled me. And when she had finished, she paused for a moment before turning to rummage through my abandoned clothes. When she retrieved my dagger from among the garments, I couldn't imagine what she meant to do with it. But she strapped the sheath to my leg, beneath the many folds of my skirts.

It was a kind thought, although useless to me given I couldn't move. She surveyed me with satisfaction after that, before starting and placing gentle fingertips against my eyelids. To my great relief she didn't actually close my eyes all the way, leaving me enough of a slit to see through, before stepping back and calling for the footmen to return.

Once again I was carried limply through the castle, this time taking the familiar route from my chambers to the throne room. My bearers obscured my vision as we entered the room, and it wasn't until they stopped on the dais and lowered me down that I realized what was happening. My stepmother hadn't been jesting about wanting everyone to see my dead body.

She had obviously come up with this plan some time ago, although she must have despaired of it succeeding when I failed to return. She would still be despairing if I hadn't made such a fateful last-minute decision. But silently yelling at myself would do no good. I'd already tried that.

Gertie, who still hovered nearby, moved forward to arrange my dress and limbs elegantly inside the glass coffin. And I supposed I should be grateful that it wasn't made of wood. It meant that the edges of my vision could take in some of the throne room, at least.

Just before she stepped back, Gertie leaned down close enough to whisper in my ear. "Don't worry, Princess Blanche. I have a plan."

I was fairly certain her words were supposed to fill me with relief, but a queasy feeling still roiled inside me. Despite her forced betrayal, I didn't want to see Gertie do something that might get her killed. Because I was afraid her plan didn't involve searching out my grandfather as soon as he appeared.

But I could do nothing but wait and hope. The final hours of the night disappeared, and the room began to lighten, dawn peeking in from the long windows that lined one wall. A bustle surrounded me soon after that as servants appeared to clean the room and fill it with large bowls of white flowers. A strange hush accompanied them, and it took me a while to realize it was the presence of my apparent corpse that cast such a pall over the room.

I had never been so frustrated in my life as at my inability to stand up and take action.

But all too soon, new sounds filled the room. Courtiers had begun to arrive, their curious voices changing to notes of horror when they advanced far enough to see what lay at the front of the room. A brief hush would fall, only for new voices to sound. I couldn't see all the way down the room from where I lay, but I could tell from the noise that the room must be nearly full when a sudden heart-rending cry sounded over everything else.

My heart seized. Even without words, I recognized that voice. Alexander had arrived.

I heard a commotion as if he were pushing through the crowds toward the front, and then a scuffle. He had approached close enough that I could see the guards restraining him, although I couldn't see his face. He continued to struggle against them, and it took three to hold him in place.

Alida stepped forward, taking a seat on the throne behind where my coffin lay on the dais. She gestured toward the guards.

"Allow him to approach."

As soon as they released him, he sprang forward, falling to his knees beside the coffin. His eyes traveled over me, fastening on my face and breathless lips. An agonized groan sounded, and he dropped his face into his hands.

His pain made my own heart split in two, and tears welled uselessly behind my eyes where they could not escape.

"Thank you all for gathering on this tragic occasion," said Alida loudly, her eyes roaming over the crowd. "You see us torn by grief that my stepdaughter has returned only to be struck down by a mysterious illness."

Did she really intend to act as if it was she who had called the court here today? As if there was no question of rebellion, no threat made against me? But apparently so. She continued on, thanking them for their loyalty and support at such a heart-rending time, coming so soon after her dear husband's death. I shut out her words, unwilling to listen to them.

Alexander's despairing form still knelt beside me, and I thought I would burst at being unable to leap up and comfort him. But just as I was wishing I could at least twitch a finger to show him I was still alive, a subtle movement in the corner of my vision caught my attention.

A short, familiar figure had appeared on the edge of the gathered courtiers. Gertie moved with careful grace, skilled from a lifetime of moving without being seen. No one seemed to question her presence or even notice her. And then she was kneeling beside Alexander.

He hadn't seen her approach, but he started as she whispered something in his ear. Her visible position at the front of the room caught Randolph's eye at last, and he moved threateningly forward. But whatever her message was, it had already been delivered.

My heart sank all the way into my toes. Because I had caught only two words. True love. Of course that was what all the tales spoke of. The true key to every enchantment. The answer to every problem. And Gertie had been my maid for years. She obviously knew how I felt about Alexander.

But she didn't know how he felt about me. Which meant we were all doomed.

As Randolph's hand closed around Gertie's arm and she let out a small squeak, Alexander stood to his feet. With one mighty push, he sent the glass lid of the coffin crashing to the ground, a loud crack and the sound of splintering glass filling the throne room.

And then he was back down, on a single knee this time, the court watching in shocked silence as he pressed his lips to mine.

CHAPTER 29

F ire raced through me again, this time starting at my lips and spreading down through my body. When it hit the piece of apple lodged in my throat, the obstruction disappeared. And as the heat traveled, I felt sensation and movement returning.

The warmth of Alexander's nearness, the sensation of his lips —dreamed of for so long—and the fire and freedom burning through me overwhelmed my senses. For a moment it held me locked in place as effectively as the enchantment had done.

And then Alexander pulled away, his eyes once again searching my face, and I drew in a deep, gasping breath. Randolph had released Gertie and leaped instead to seize Alexander's arm, but at the sound of my coughing gasp, he faltered.

Alexander seemed not to have even noticed him, his eyes still glued to mine. A spark jumped between us, relief and love so obvious in his eyes that my mind spun off track, forgetting everyone and everything around us. Was it possible? Could it be true? Did Alexander love me after all?

I pushed myself up slightly, meaning to reach for him, but a collective gasp distracted me. Free at last to move my head, I turned and took in the court. The entire crowd appeared to have surged forward, leaning to see what was happening up on the dais. But as I sat up further, their curiosity turned into shock and even fear. Gasps and a couple of screams filled the room as chaos broke out.

"Impossible!" screamed Alida over the noise. "Somebody do something!"

I had no idea who she was speaking to, or what she hoped for them to do. And apparently her guards shared my confusion. At least none of them moved toward me. From the expressions on their faces, they were immobilized by the same shock sweeping through the courtiers. Even Alexander remained frozen, only his eyes moving as he took in each tiny motion of mine.

But while everyone else might be held captive by shock at the apparent sight of a reanimated corpse, I had been locked in stillness for hours, stewing over exactly what I wanted to say and do if only I could move. I pushed myself into a full sitting position and scrambled out of the coffin. The soft skirts of my red dress billowed around me, and I knew with my coloring I must make a dramatic picture.

Good.

"Court of Eliam," I said in a loud, ringing voice. "I am Blanche, only child of King George and Queen Viridienne. With the death of my father, and by our laws of succession, I am your rightful queen."

Complete silence fell over the crowd.

"I have been under an enchantment and not dead." I wheeled around and pointed an accusing finger at my stepmother still seated behind me. "Although she would have had me so."

A murmur swept through the court, and Alida surged to her feet.

"Lies!"

I cut her off, my own voice sounding louder. "Are they lies, *stepmother*? Did you not drive me from my home for fear of my life and then pursue me across the kingdom? You who should have loved me and stepped willingly in as my regent. Tell me, what right do you have to the crown?"

"I...I am the queen!" Alida's usual poise had deserted her.

"You could have been the Queen Regent," I said, still speaking loudly enough for all in the room to hear me. "If you had claimed the title, I would not have denied you. But you did not. You have attempted to usurp my throne." My voice turned dark. "And the name for that is treason."

Noise swept through the court again, only this time cheers mingled with the shocked gasps.

"Long live Queen Blanche!" came a cry from the back of the room, and it was taken up by all of my supporters. Slowly the chant gained momentum as more of the court joined in.

Alida's face twisted with hatred. "This is my throne. This is my kingdom. I will not hand it over to you, a mere child. The guards stand with me. The kingdom is mine."

She turned to survey the men who lined the room. "Guards! Arrest her and all who support her."

They drew their swords and began to move forward. Shocked yells and screams rang through the crowd as the courtiers drew away from them, huddling into the center of the room. Several guards moved toward me, but Alexander threw off Randolph's restraining hand and leaped to stand between me and them.

Although he faced away from me, I could feel the way his body moved in tune with mine, every part of him focused on me. Without conscious thought I swayed toward him, wishing for a brief second that we were alone. But he didn't turn or speak to me. Instead he called out in the loudest shout I had yet heard.

"True guards of Eliam! To your queen!"

As if it was some pre-arranged signal, the doors of the throne room burst open, and a new stream of guards poured into the room, their swords already drawn. When last I had seen them, they had worn the colors of Lestern, but now they had been reattired in royal livery. It might have made them indistinguishable from their opponents, except that each of them wore three entwined scarves tied around either their arms or their heads. One white, one red, one black.

Skin as white as snow. Lips as red as blood. Hair as black as ebony. Tears sprung to my eyes. Whatever Alida had tried to do, my kingdom stood with me.

The new guards quickly broke past those of Alida's guards just inside the door and raced to place themselves in a second ring between the packed courtiers and the encircling guards. A second stream hurried to the front of the room and positioned themselves all around the base of the dais.

Muffled sobs and angry mutters still sounded from the courtiers, but each group of guards stood silently poised, just short of actual combat. For the space of a breath, I could feel the throne room teetering on the brink of chaos and death.

Behind me I heard Alida suck in a deep breath, as if preparing to shout something, but instead a new voice sounded.

My grandfather, the duke of Lestern, strode through the crowd, pushing past the guards to approach the dais.

"People of Eliam. We are a kingdom of peace, ruled over by law. We stand with the true queen—daughter of King George. And we have no wish for bloodshed." He ignored Alida, directing his attention at her hostile guards.

Many of them shifted uncomfortably, their swords wavering as they regarded the determined new arrivals.

I stepped forward to stand beside my grandfather.

"My esteemed grandfather speaks the truth. We are a kingdom of law. And it is time also that we returned to the ways of the ancient laws—as Marin, Palinar, and Eldon have done before us. We stand with the law as we stand with them."

The meaning of my words might have been lost on most of the guards, but I saw them find their home among the courtiers.

The other kingdoms would not look kindly on a usurper queen. Especially now they had returned to the old ways.

Alexander, who had moved in time with me, his attention still on the guards around us, turned to focus out on the crowd.

"She speaks truth," he said loudly. "Our true queen bears the favor of the godmothers. One has aided her today."

That got a response even from the guards, and more of them dropped their sword points, looking between each other with questioning eyes.

Someone in the crowd of courtiers shouted loudly, "Long live Queen Blanche!"

Once again the shout gained volume as more and more voices joined. Soon it seemed as if the whole room resounded to the sound of my title yelled from a multitude of throats. Tears welled in my eyes again, but I straightened my back and looked out over the crowd, hoping I displayed both strength and gratitude.

In the face of such overwhelming support, the remainder of Alida's guards put down their swords, looking lost and confused as my own guards began to round them up. My grandfather smiled proudly down at me, offering me his arm and leading me around the empty glass coffin. We approached the throne.

"It's over, Alida," he said quietly.

"Never!" She hissed. "I will never see her—Viridienne's daughter—sitting on the throne that should always have been mine. Randolph!" She turned to the one remaining loyal guard who had moved to stand by her side. "You wanted your chance. Here it is. Kill her!"

CHAPTER 30

*R*andolph surged forward, striking my grandfather with enough force that he fell away from me, landing hard against the ground. Chaos still reigned on the dais, with several of Alida's surrendered guards still milling around on the raised platform, blocking us from view of the rest of the room. Even Alexander had stepped briefly away when I took my grandfather's arm, calling for more guards to join us.

But the precious seconds Randolph spent pushing my grandfather away had given me a chance. Because faithful Gertie had done me one other service after the visit from my godmother. One I had almost forgotten.

I didn't have to think. Just as Alexander had said so many weeks ago in the forest, my muscles moved while my mind was still reeling. Stooping down, I thrust aside the foaming red material. My hand curled around the now familiar hilt of my dagger.

Drawing it free, I straightened in one fluid movement. Randolph turned toward me, his own hand drawing his sword. I lunged forward and plunged my short blade into his sword arm. He cried out, his arm jerking back, and his hand releasing his hilt. The weapon slipped back into its sheath.

Alida gave a wordless cry of fury, and Randolph steadied, blood now dripping down his arm and onto the floor. His left hand reached for my neck, and I stepped back, my skirts hampering my movement as I tried to remember how far I stood from the edge of the dais.

But the tips of his fingers had barely brushed against me when a third figure leaped from the side and tackled him to the ground. For a moment all I could see was a tangle of flying limbs as the man I had loved for years fought the man I had always hated and feared.

I stepped forward again, a small cry falling uselessly from my lips. But I could see no way to aid Alexander.

And then the movement stilled, and I saw him kneeling with one knee pressed on Randolph's back, both of his hands holding Randolph's arms twisted behind his back. The captain of Alida's guard lay, face pressed into the ground, my dagger lost in the scuffle but his rent sleeve red with spreading blood. I had done my bit to help Alexander before their fight had even begun.

"Guards!" Alexander's grim call brought several of the men marked with my colors running to his aid. The remaining members of Alida's guard had been cleared from the dais, and order was slowly descending on the rest of the throne room as well.

Only when my guards had Randolph firmly in hand did Alexander step back. But I hadn't waited to run to my grandfather's side.

He leaned on my arm heavily as he pulled himself back to his feet, but he assured me he wasn't badly hurt.

"I'm old and tough, my dear." He managed a smile. "I'm not so easily damaged, I assure you."

I still watched him with worried eyes, aware of his age. But it seemed he spoke truthfully, his movements a little stiff but otherwise unhampered. I surveyed the room. A guard gripped Randolph firmly on either side, and groups of Alida's guards sat in small huddles around the room, their hands on their heads, and my own guards standing over them.

Several others stood nearby, their eyes on my stepmother, but they hung back, clearly reluctant to place their hands on a queen —even a deposed, usurping one—without direct orders.

"Arrest her," I said, glad to hear my voice didn't waver. She drew herself up to her full height, her eyes holding mine as the guards moved in on her. But she had no moves left, and we both knew it. As I looked into her eyes, I felt a release somewhere deep inside me. For so many years she had been able to subdue me with little more than a look, my fear holding me bound. But I feared her no longer. I was free.

I turned away to show her she had no further hold on me. As I did so, however, my eyes fell on a man several steps from the dais. He lurked near a small side door, attempting to edge around a group of my guards without drawing any attention. Sterling.

"Guards!" I called loudly, startling several of the groups around me. "Arrest that man!" I pointed toward him.

He started as well at the sound of my call and lunged for the door, but my guards moved more quickly. Within seconds, they had him by the arms, dragging him up to the dais beside the restrained Randolph and Alida.

"This one, Your Majesty?" asked one of the guards. "We weren't sure if he was one of the courtiers, or…"

"His name is Sterling," I said, "and he's from Eldon. He is an associate of my stepmother, and a dangerous enemy."

The man's smooth mask had slipped, and I saw fear lurking in his eyes. I stepped toward him and dropped my voice.

"We will be making sure that ours is one prison you do not manage to break out of, Sterling."

I stepped quickly away again, not wanting to be near him a moment longer than necessary.

"You!" shrieked Alida, from beside him. "This is all your fault! You said it would kill her!"

Sterling shrugged, despite the guards' firm hold on him. "I thought it would."

The guards who had arrested Alida were distracted by the unexpected commotion around Sterling, and she managed to wrench her arms free. Before anyone could realize her intention, she drew a small dagger from her boot and plunged it into him.

She had been aiming for his heart, but somehow he had seen her coming and managed to twist away, the blade sliding instead into his shoulder. The guards holding him cursed, and one of them jumped back, freeing one of Sterling's arms.

Without hesitation, he thrust his hand into a pocket and withdrew something that I couldn't see. With it wrapped in his fist, he punched Alida in the side of the head, and she fell instantly.

One of the guards dropped to a knee beside her. But after a brief examination, he looked up in bewilderment, his eyes finding me.

"She's dead."

Before I could even process the words, a howl ripped through the air.

Randolph, grown strong in his rage and grief, flung his arms to the side, sending both the guards restraining him staggering back. He surged forward and wrapped his hands around Sterling's neck. The many guards on the dais all raced to intervene, tripping over each other in the small space.

I saw Sterling aim another punch at Randolph's side, and the giant man screamed in pain, his body swaying, but he didn't let go. By the time the guards could pry him off, Sterling had slumped unresisting to the ground, his neck crushed.

I drew in a shuddering breath, still trying to process what had just occurred. It had all happened far too fast.

Randolph dropped to his knees beside Alida's body and made no attempt to resist as my guards restrained him again, this time hurrying to bind him properly.

Alexander stepped forward to examine both bodies.

I watched in shock. "Are they truly both…"

He looked up and nodded, his face grim.

"But how did Sterling…?"

Alexander pointed at the dead man's hand which was somehow still clasped in a tight fist, concealing whatever was inside.

"I suspect he had another object stashed away. Perhaps it gave his blow extra strength?"

"We can soon find out," said one of the guards, reaching toward Sterling's clasped hand, as if he meant to pry it open.

"No!" Alexander pushed him away. "Don't touch it. Or him." He looked at two of the guards. "No one is to touch him, his clothes, or any of his belongings without gloves. And I want his body and all his possessions burned. Immediately."

He looked up at me, as if suddenly remembering I should be the one giving orders, but I signaled my agreement, and he stood.

"He made it out of Eldon with far too many of these objects for my liking," he said to me quietly. "I'd rather not take any chances."

I nodded fervently. "I couldn't agree more."

With reluctance my eyes moved to my stepmother's fallen body. "But for her we should have a funeral."

"A small one," I added quickly at Alexander's expression. "She was my stepmother, and queen for many years. She let her jealousy and hunger for power twist her, but it cannot have been easy to be married to a man in love with a ghost, presiding over a court who saw her always as inferior to her predecessor. She was the queen of Eliam once, and she shall have her grave beside my father and mother."

"Grace becomes you, Queen Blanche," said my grandfather, approaching our small huddle.

"Please," I said, reaching out to him, "you at least must continue to call me Snow."

"Very well, if you desire it."

"And you must be my regent, of course."

He hesitated. "Are you sure that is what you want? I haven't always been here for you."

"No," I said, acknowledging the truth of his words, "but you have been here for me when it mattered most. I would not have my throne without you, and I would prefer to rule with your wisdom and guidance beside me."

As we spoke, my guards had cleared the dais of prisoners and the deceased. Most of the enemy guards from the main room had already been led away, the last few still trickling from the room. The court, however, remained, some looking elated and others shocked and subdued.

"It is time for you to take your throne, my queen," said my grandfather, gesturing toward my father's grand chair.

I licked my lips and stepped slowly forward, my eyes trained upon it. How many times had I seen my father sit there? How many times had I heard him dispense his wisdom, guidance, and judgment from it?

I glanced back at my grandfather. My father had been weak in some ways—it was true. But he had been strong in others. I had determined already how I would rule—with those I trusted beside me to balance out my own weaknesses and bring wisdom where I had a lack. And my father had a place among them, although he no longer lived to guide me in person.

But he had spent a lifetime teaching me about what it meant to rule, a lifetime showing me love and kindness. I would not forget his strengths, or throw away the many valuable lessons he had taught me, just because he hadn't been perfect. None of us were perfect, after all.

Drawing in calm and peace with each breath, I turned to face the court and sat at last in my father's throne.

"Long live the queen! Long live the queen!" The cries rang on and on, servants appearing at the back and sides of the room to join in the cheer.

When I held up my hands for quiet, it took a long time to come. When at last silence fell, I took a moment to gaze out over my people.

"Thank you," I said finally. "Thank you for trusting me to rule you. I swear I will always do so to the best of my abilities. But I know I am still young. Both law and wisdom tell me I must have a regent to stand beside me—for a few more years, at least. I name the duke of Lestern, my maternal grandfather, as my regent. Does anyone here wish to refute his right to the position?"

This time the silence was complete, not so much as a rustle or a cough breaking the stillness.

"Very well, then." I gestured for him to take the smaller seat to my side. "Take your place, Prince Regent."

"I am humbled by your trust, Your Majesty," he said loudly, with a deep bow. "And I look forward to the day when you will rule alone."

The crowd burst into further cheering as he sat, order breaking down as people moved to embrace each other, laughter on many lips.

I turned to my grandfather.

"I hope I shall never truly be alone in my rule."

"No, I hope not as well." A small smile curved his mouth, and his eyes traveled past me to someone lurking on the edge of the dais.

As courtiers began to leave the room—rushing no doubt to spread the news to their families and the capital at large—I turned and looked into Alexander's face.

CHAPTER 31

houghts of the heart had been pushed aside amid the action and unexpected violence of the past minutes. But one look at Alexander's face brought it rushing back. My lips tingled from the memory of his pressed against them.

"Go," said my grandfather, "some things shouldn't wait."

I jumped to my feet, but then my steps moved slowly as I crossed over to look up at Alexander.

"Snow—" he started, but I shook my head.

"Not here."

I slipped over to the small door that led into the royal reception room to one side of the thrones. He hesitated for only the briefest second before following me.

When we stood alone at last, quiet surrounding us, I felt my muscles relax. I wanted to throw myself into his arms but, despite our kiss, there were words that needed to be spoken first.

"Your Majesty." He bowed to me, lower than he ever had before. When he straightened, a broad smile had transformed his face. "You did it. The kingdom is yours."

I shook my head, closing the small distance between us.

"No. We did it. We have been in it together since the beginning. This is both of our triumph."

"I will happily share anything with you, Snow," he whispered, a look on his face that made me shiver.

"You saved me," I whispered back.

"I told you on that first night that I would never let Randolph hurt you."

I gave a quick shake of my head. "I wasn't thinking of Randolph. I was thinking of the enchantment. Of what Gertie said…" I could feel the flush on my face. Her words echoed in my mind. True love.

A shadow of horror and pain filled his face, and he reached out to grip my arms, although I wasn't sure he was even aware of having done so.

"I was frantic when we couldn't find you this morning. We raced to court, hoping you'd come ahead of us, although Tarver stayed back to look…And then I saw you." He drew a deep, shuddering breath. "When I saw you lying there…"

"Don't think of that," I said hurriedly, leaning into his arms but keeping my eyes on his. "I'm alive. Alive and well."

"Thank goodness." His hands tightened. "Or I don't know what I would have done."

"You have always looked after me, Alex. And now…now I need to know why."

"I don't know what you mean," he said, his eyes sliding away from mine.

I just leaned in closer. "Yes, you do. You know how I feel. And I thought I knew how you felt. But then that kiss." I shook my head. "It freed me, Alex. So I need to know. Do you love me?"

"Love you?" He pulled away, stepping back from me. "You ever doubted it? Of course I love you. I can't remember a time— even as a young boy—when I didn't love you."

I stared at him, my eyes wide and my heart hammering. "But in the forest, you…And you said…"

"Snow, you are my queen. That is how I must love you. Not... not as a woman." He swallowed. "Whatever my heart might tell me."

"Alex." I stepped forward, closing the gap between us again. "You're my oldest and dearest friend. You must know that you're more than just a huntsman. Even my father regarded you more like a son. I think...I think that secretly he always hoped for this."

"And what is this?" he asked, his voice tormented. His eyes dropped to my lips.

"True love, of course," I whispered.

I swayed forward, but I didn't need to. Alexander was already closing the distance between us, pulling me into his arms as his lips came down over mine.

A different sort of fire raced through me, and my head spun. I clung to him, and he held me tighter. When he at last pulled away, we stared at each other, both of our breathing ragged.

"Snow, I—"

"Don't you dare apologize!" I cut him off. "Don't you dare apologize for the best thing that ever happened to me."

"Snow." I could feel his chest vibrating with his chuckle. "Snow, you just won a throne."

I shook my head. "I don't care. This was better. *You're* better than any throne."

"But Snow..." He shook his head helplessly. "I'm just a huntsman."

"No." I glared at him. "You're strong and loyal and smart. You're the best friend anyone could ever ask for. You have always been there for me—to get me into trouble and back out again." I grinned up at him. "And I don't want this throne if I can't have you sitting in the one beside me. I know I said I wanted you as my Chief Adviser, but it isn't true. I want you as my king."

He tried to ease away from me. "But surely you should have someone more fitting. An alliance, perhaps..."

I held on more tightly, gripping him close. "My grandfather

has connections enough. And he can handle any alliances—political ones only. I'm marrying for something far more important. Love." I lifted an eyebrow at him. "And I'm sure my godmother would agree."

"Well…" He chuckled again and relaxed against me. "If you're going to bring the godmothers into it…"

"I meant what I said earlier. We're returning to the old laws. And I seem to remember they said something about a kingdom prospering as long as it was ruled by true love."

"In that case," he said, his eyes devouring my face, "Eliam will be the most prosperous kingdom anyone has ever seen." And he pressed his lips against mine once more.

"So you really love me?" I asked when we came up for air. "I can hardly believe it. I thought you still saw me as a child. One to be protected and pitied. I thought that was why you kept things from me. And why you pulled away."

He looked at me in astonishment. "Believe me Snow, my issue was not that I saw you as a child. My issue was that I love you too well. I couldn't bear the thought of causing you pain or seeing you in danger. As for pulling away, I thought your feelings for me came from loneliness and fear. I couldn't let myself believe they could be true." He paused. "Are you sure they are?"

I laughed. "You just want me to start praising you again, don't you? I can if you like. I could go on about your excellence all day."

He grinned wryly. "Please don't. You might make me blush."

"Very well then. You can praise me instead." I smiled at him cheekily. "And tell me again how much you love me. I think it will be a while before it truly sinks in."

He shook his head. "No one else will be bemused by it, I assure you. How could anyone help loving you, Snow? Your kind heart, your hidden strength. Your faithfulness. You've borne a burden no one should have to bear for all these years as your father wasted away. And now you bear another one just as big. And yet still you stand tall."

"Only because I have you beside me," I whispered.

He placed his forehead against mine. "I will never leave you, Snow. All the days of my life."

"Excellent," said a hearty voice behind us. "I assume that's all settled then?"

We pulled guiltily apart, turning together to face my grandfather. But Alexander's hand snuck out and twined into mine, and I gave him a small sideways smile.

"Yes, yes, it's all very touching, no need to convince me," my grandfather said, but the twinkle in his eyes belied his wry tone.

"As regent, I'll have to insist on a long betrothal, I'm afraid. You are still only sixteen, Snow. But I doubt we'll get any real objections from the court to the marriage." He smiled a knowing smile. "I doubt we'll even get much surprise."

I flushed and looked down at the ground.

Alexander squeezed my hand. "You know I would wait forever for you, Snow."

I looked up to meet his eyes, my flush disappearing, replaced by contentment.

"I'm sure the time will pass quickly enough," said my grandfather. "You have a great many laws and decrees to consider and pass, Granddaughter."

I grimaced. "Yes, most of them repeals of anything my stepmother put in place, I imagine. There will be a fair amount of cleaning up to do. But some things we should get to sooner rather than later. Like the plight of the poor servants here. And those outrageous taxes."

My grandfather nodded. "Yes, I don't think you'll have any protests on your choice of a king. Not when you mean to start your reign like that."

I smiled at another thought. "And a longer betrothal will give the children time to adjust to court before they're asked to stand up as my attendants."

"All of them?" Alexander looked a little dismayed, but I just grinned at him.

"Of course! It *is* going to be a large wedding, you know. And I couldn't leave any of them out."

"Even Anthony?" He raised an eyebrow at me, and I giggled.

"Perhaps Ben and Anthony can be your attendants."

"I'm sure he'll like that so much better," he muttered.

"And Gertie!" I exclaimed.

My grandfather regarded me with a skeptical look. "You want your maid to be your attendant too?"

"What? Oh, no. I'm sure she would hate it. She'll want to help me get dressed, though." I smiled at the thought of my wedding dress. What would it look like?

"Snow?" My grandfather's long-suffering voice pulled me back into the moment.

"I just meant that we must find some way to reward her. She saved me twice over, you know."

"Yes, indeed." He nodded. "Perhaps we can find some way to express our gratitude to all the servants. This wouldn't have gone so smoothly without them."

"Oh?" I stared at him, but it was Alexander who answered.

"We thought our guards would have to fight their way into the castle grounds, at least to gain initial entry. But, lo and behold, just before the court began to arrive, a side gate popped open and servants began streaming out." He gave me a knowing look. "Apparently someone suggested they might want to get out before the excitement started. And that a side gate would be a good way to do it. Only a good number of them seemed more interested in letting us in than getting themselves out."

"Talking about that warning..." My grandfather narrowed his eyes at me.

I quickly shook my head. "I know it was unutterably foolish of me, but I refuse to talk about it today. Not when everything has worked out so well, and I'm so very happy." I flicked a sideways glance at Alexander, his hand still strong and warm in mine, before focusing back on my grandfather. "You can both berate me about it all day tomorrow, if you like."

When my grandfather opened his mouth, I cut in.

"You can consider that a royal order."

He grinned reluctantly and shook his head. "Very well, my queen. All remonstrances will be left for the morrow. What about advice, though? Are you open to hearing that?"

"Of course. Always."

"I've received reports about those children of yours. And they seem to be extremely happy in Lestern."

I nodded. "They did seem to love it there. Especially being on the coast."

"Well, I'm not sure they'd love it so much here at court."

"But—"

"He does have a point, Snow," said Alexander quietly. "Of course I would love to have them here, but they would be neither servants nor nobles. Can you really see them enjoying being stuck here as something in between, with no real purpose or place?"

I sighed. "No, of course not. But I've destroyed their refuge. I can't leave them without a home, and this is the only one I have to offer."

"Well, I admit to having a thought on that," said my grandfather. "The most detailed report I have received on their well-being came from a rather unlikely place—the captain of my guards."

I smiled. "Tarver surprised me with his skill in dealing with small children, I'll admit. He told me he has a great many nieces and nephews."

My grandfather nodded. "That he does. But the true tragedy is that he and his wife have been unable to have children of their own. As captain, they have a spacious home within the grounds of my small castle, and I know she has mourned deeply at their inability to fill it. In truth, their situation has always pained me with memories of your mother..."

For a moment his voice trailed away, and then he cleared his throat. "But it seems to me that an obvious answer lies before us. And I can assure you that while they reside in my lands, those children will never be left in want. I owe you that much and more. And I cannot imagine better parents than Tarver and his wife. Although no doubt the older two will protest any need for parents at this point."

A slow smile spread across my face. "No doubt they would, but neither would they want to be separated from the younger ones. They would gladly accept any option that let them stay together, I'm sure. And perhaps in time, they would come to see the value to themselves of such an arrangement."

I nodded. "We will need to consult with Tarver and his wife, of course. And with the children themselves. But if they are all open to the arrangement, I think it an excellent one. Of course they must still visit court for our wedding. And before then just to see the capital. And I'll want to visit them, as often as I can, and..."

My grandfather held up his hands with a smile. "I am to be your regent, remember? I'm sure there will be constant traffic between Lestern and the capital. You will have the chance to see them often enough."

"Excellent." I grinned at him. "Now, if you don't mind, I have a few more things I'd like to say to my betrothed." I turned and pulled my hand free from Alexander's so I could wind both of them around his neck.

He smiled down at me, but I saw him cast a nervous glance sideways at my grandfather. The old man chuckled.

"Don't worry, son. I was young once, too." He crossed to the door but paused with his hand on it. "But I'm leaving this door open behind me." He gave us both a stern look.

"Yes sir, of course, sir." Alexander was almost stammering.

When my grandfather had departed, I laughed up at him.

"I believe the proper address would be Your Grace. But then, you are going to be his king, you know. You're the one who should be giving orders."

Alexander just shook his head. "He's your grandfather, Snow. Rank doesn't have anything to do with it."

"Never mind that. I want to hear again how much you love me."

He leaned down until his lips were only a breath away from mine. "I love you, Snow."

"I love you too, Alex," was all I managed to get out before he closed the distance between us with the lightest and gentlest kiss I could have imagined. And I knew in that moment that together we could face any obstacle that confronted us. Even a crown would not be too heavy a burden with love like this in our hearts.

NOTE FROM THE AUTHOR

To find out what happened to Dominic's missing sister, read A Captive of Wing and Feather: A Retelling of Swan Lake. Turn the page for a sneak peek!

Or for more romance, adventure, and intrigue in a new world, try my Spoken Mage series. In Elena's world words have power over life and death—but none more so than hers. As a commonborn, Elena has always been forbidden to read and write, until a startling new ability thrusts her into the Royal Academy where she finds herself among the mageborn, including the enigmatic Prince Lucas.

To be kept informed of my new releases, please sign up to my mailing list at www.melaniecellier.com. At my website, you'll also find an array of free extra content.

Thank you for taking the time to read my book. I hope you enjoyed it. If you did, please spread the word! You could start by leaving a review on Amazon or Goodreads or Facebook or any other social media site. Your review would be very much appreciated and would make a big difference!

PROLOGUE

I stumbled, my feet tripping over dead branches and leaf litter. My heart pounded harder than my steps, although no one was chasing me.

A sweet, clear taste lingered in my mouth, but it elicited only dread. The lake had been beautiful, and the swans floating on it even more so, but I never wanted to see any of it again. I never wanted to see that man again or hear him spout such madness. I refused to believe his talk of enchantments.

I should never have followed the sound of my name. I should have listened to the townsfolk and stayed away from the forest. It had been foolishness to try to prove I wasn't afraid of it—even while nameless dread circled in my stomach.

I burst out of the trees and onto the edge of town. Just as my feet touched the road, I faltered, a burning, stinging sensation washing over my body. My hands pressed against my exposed skin, but it was gone almost as quickly as it had come.

A flash of white overhead made me flinch. Had that been a swan? I shook my head and kept my eyes resolutely down. It didn't matter what it had been. I was returning to the haven, and I would never enter the forest again.

CHAPTER 1

TWO YEARS LATER

*A*n air of excitement hung over the town. A newcomer might not have noticed it, but I could feel it like a palpable presence around me. I'd spent enough time in Brylee over the past five years to recognize its moods. I glanced longingly at the various small knots of townsfolk talking on street corners and scattered around the market square, but there was no point stopping and trying to talk to any of them.

Instead I moved faster, hurrying for the sprawling lodge house on the edge of town. My path took me past the bakery where I would usually receive a greeting or at least a wave. But on this occasion the young baker, Ash, seemed just as distracted as everyone else. He was deep in conversation with two older women who showed no inclination to leave, despite the fresh loaves already poking from their baskets.

As I passed by, I caught a snatch of their conversation.

"But what purpose could he have?" The woman sounded worried.

"Perhaps we're suspected of some sort of wrongdoing—treason even!" The second woman sounded even more concerned.

Ash—who was usually fairly sensible—made no effort to gainsay this outrageous statement.

"If you ask me, the best thing we can do is nothing," he said. "If he wishes to pretend that his visit is nothing out of the ordinary, then we must do the same. Perhaps he'll…"

He trailed off, as if even he didn't know what he hoped would happen, but both women nodded their agreement. I realized my steps had almost completely stilled and, shaking my head, I picked up my pace. If I wanted answers, my best hope was Cora. I wouldn't get anything from this group.

The dilapidated building—once an inn but now known to most of us as the haven—came into view, and my speed increased again. A brisk spring breeze nearly blew back my hood, and I grabbed at it just in time. I had an odd reputation around town, and with everyone so stirred up, I didn't want to invite trouble.

I pushed open the main door without knocking and looked around for Cora, the haven's keeper. Instead a four-year-old girl came barreling into view, an excited grin on her face.

"Lady!" She raced toward me. "Lady, Lady, Lady!"

I hoisted her up onto my hip and paused for a moment to give her a cuddle. Unlike the townsfolk, Juniper didn't care that I had no voice. I wanted to savor these moments while I still could—she would be too big for it soon. Already she seemed less and less of a baby, all long legs and waving arms.

"I made muffins. All by myself. And you can have one. And I got a new tooth. Right at the back. See."

She opened her jaws wide and tipped her head back to an angle that completely obscured her mouth. I suppressed a smile and adopted an astonished and impressed expression.

She paused for only a moment before snapping her teeth closed and continuing to prattle on, unbothered by my silence. When she began to squirm, I let her slip back down to the ground. She took my hand and tugged me down the long hallway into the large kitchen at the back of the lodge.

Clearly Juniper didn't know about whatever had the towns-folk so worked up—she would have blurted it out to me first thing if she did. I felt a surge of unease. The people of Brylee had a tendency to get worried about every tiny thing, but Cora and Wren were usually a little more sensible. If they felt the need to shield Juniper from what was happening, then perhaps it truly was a cause for concern.

"Junie, there you are!" A young woman hurried into the room, her eyes fixed on her daughter. "I thought I told you to stay in the —" Her eyes fell on me. "Oh, Lady, you've arrived. That would explain it, then."

The disapproving look she had fixed on her daughter didn't relent, but the girl let go of my hand and ran happily to her mother anyway. She rushed through an almost unintelligible sentence from which I caught the word muffin.

Wren's expression dissolved into a reluctant smile, and she nodded. Juniper ran off toward the far bench where I could see a cooling rack filled with muffins. Wren gave me an apologetic look.

"I hope you're hungry. She won't relax until you've had one, I'm afraid. I needed an excuse to be out of the classroom this morning, and Juniper has been begging me to do some baking with her."

I gave her an inquiring look.

"Frank and Selena are nearly old enough for apprenticeships now, and they're both outdoing each other trying to prove how reliable they are, so I've been wanting to give them a chance to take charge of the younger ones." She chuckled. "Juniper was a little too eager to escape her schooling, but she's still young. I wouldn't even have started her at it yet if I wasn't responsible for the older children as well."

I smiled to indicate my willingness to become a muffin taster and slipped onto one of the stools surrounding the enormous, worn wooden table that filled the middle of the kitchen. Wren and Juniper had been at the haven for more than three years now, and I knew that she took her role of teacher to the haven's children seriously. Her attention for them hadn't wavered, despite their numbers being low this year—Cora having found adoptive families for three of the younger ones only a few months ago, and two of the older ones having left for apprenticeships that she had secured.

Normally at least some new children would have arrived to replace them, but we'd been seeing fewer and fewer people making their way to the haven from distant towns. Travel all across the kingdom had been dropping from all reports.

I was glad Wren was getting a small break. And perhaps she could answer my question. Glancing toward Juniper, I confirmed she was still busy selecting the perfect muffin. When I looked back at Wren, it was with a raised eyebrow and an inquiring tilt of my head.

When she didn't immediately seem to understand, I jerked my head toward the front door and the rest of town. Adopting an exaggerated expression of concern, I mimed my best impression of the townsfolk I had passed.

A woman several decades our senior, her hair in no-nonsense braids against her scalp, entered the room just in time to witness my performance. She snorted a laugh.

"Are you sure you're not a long-lost member of my family? You look exactly like my old Aunt Florinda. She wore an expression just like that every day of her life."

Wren chuckled. Only my brown hair, thick and wavy, looked anything like Cora's—and since she always wore hers in braids, even that wasn't much of a similarity. Certainly my pale skin and blue eyes looked nothing like the warm brown of hers.

I smiled as well, but inside I hid a sigh. I knew every branch of my family tree, tracing back multiple generations—my father had insisted on it. There was no chance I had any relatives half as down-to-earth and kind as Cora. I would have to content myself with being adopted into the haven's strange family in heart, if not in actuality.

When Wren's humor subsided, I made a series of hand gestures that produced a sigh from Cora, her face falling into more serious lines. Juniper trotted back toward us before she could reply, however, proudly bearing a muffin on a little plate which she placed before me.

"What are you talking about?" She looked between us all.

"Nothing that concerns you," said Wren. "Lady has her muffin now, so why don't you get back to your letters?" She sent a stern eye toward the abandoned slate on a small, child-sized table tucked into the corner of the room. I could just make out a single, misshaped S scratched across its surface.

"But—" Juniper began to protest, only to cut herself off when she saw her mother's unyielding expression.

With a large, dramatic sigh, she hung her head and shuffled off toward the small table and chair. I bit my lip, trying to hold in a laugh.

Wren rolled her eyes. "Anyone would think I was the cruelest of mothers."

Cora raised an eyebrow. "I can't imagine where she gets the dramatics from."

Wren laughed, her eyes lingering on her daughter, but gradually the humor dropped from her face. "She does seem like Audrey, doesn't she?"

I abandoned my muffin to put a reassuring hand on her arm, despite the stab of pain in my midriff at the mention of Wren's sister.

"She'll be back, when she's ready," Cora said in a calm tone.

Audrey was sixteen—two years younger than me and seven years younger than Wren who often treated her like another daughter. She had told me once that older siblings couldn't help taking on that role when they lost their parents too young.

I had refrained from observing that not all older siblings

reacted in such a manner. For five years I had refused to mention my home, my family, or even my kingdom—it was habit now as much as intention.

Wren's mothering had irritated Audrey at times, but I knew that underneath she loved it. And you only had to look at Juniper to see what a wonderful mother Wren made. But I knew she blamed herself for Audrey's departure. They had fought the night before she left, and it ate her up inside that Audrey hadn't been back even once for a visit in the six months since she went to work up at the local castle.

I was the only one who knew there was more to the story, but I didn't dare tell Wren.

Cora met my eyes silently, and my hand dropped from Wren's arm. I returned to my muffin, keeping my face hidden from my friend. Cora didn't know the whole story either, but I knew she had at least some suspicions about the castle, and we had a tacit agreement not to mention anything about them to Wren. Wren thought Cora's antipathy toward Lord Leander was solely because he didn't send supplies to assist the residents of the haven as his father always used to do. Better that she believe her sister still angry with her than that she worry herself about something worse. Not when there was nothing she could do about it—except get into trouble herself.

Once I had finished Junie's treat, I flapped my hands to capture both of the other women's attention and re-signed my question to Cora. Wren looked between us with a raised eyebrow. She had learned some of my more common hand signals, but only Cora fully understood the makeshift communication system she and I had cobbled together.

"So you noticed the townsfolk are getting themselves all tied up in knots, I take it?" Cora's voice held enough exasperation to allay the worst of my fears.

"It is concerning, though." Wren kept her voice low, casting a warning glance toward Juniper who had abandoned her slate and was crouched down on the floor of the kitchen, closely examining a small bug. "Why is he here, of all places? And why is he trying to hide who he is?"

I gave them both a look of exasperation. They were as bad as Ash and his customers. I made an impatient gesture with my arms, and Wren gave me an apologetic look.

"Oh, sorry, Lady. It seems we have a newcomer in town. He checked into one of the inns, instead of going up to the Keep, but of course the innkeeper's wife recognized him. Apparently the innkeeper questioned him about it but was entrusted to keep the secret."

"Which naturally means the entire town now knows," said Cora with a roll of her eyes.

I gave them both a look of frustrated confusion. The loss of my voice was most infuriating at times like this. *Who* had arrived in Brylee? And what was he trying to keep hidden?

"It turns out," Wren said, realizing my exasperation, "that Brylee's newest visitor is none other than—"

A loud rapping on the door made her break off. Startled, we all exchanged glances. No one ever bothered to knock at the haven's door. It was well known to be a refuge, open to all.

"That can't be..." Wren stared toward the hallway open-mouthed. "Surely that can't be..."

"Well, there's only one way to find out." Cora marched toward the kitchen door.

Juniper, usually boisterously friendly, seemed to have taken exception to the loud knock and had squeezed herself under her tiny table. Wren sighed and hurried over to extract her while I followed behind Cora.

"Greetings," a young, male voice called from the entryway. "Is anyone here?"

I faltered slightly, and a crease appeared between Cora's brows. What was a young man—a stranger, apparently—doing at the haven? This was a safe place, a refuge for women, children, and the elderly—people who had nowhere else to go. The only young or middle-aged men who came here were townsfolk bringing supplies for the inhabitants. Ash, the baker, was a regular, bringing any unsold wares at the end of the day.

Cora stepped into the entryway, a commanding presence.

"I am the proprietress of this establishment. May I help you?"

"I hope so," he said. "I'm looking for someone, and I hear that many people find their way here." The voice sounded friendly… and vaguely familiar.

I stepped to the side to get a clearer view around Cora. A tall young man stood just inside the door, his stance confident but relaxed. He wore the simple but sturdy clothes of a woodsman, and he had a quiver and bow strapped to his back.

I stared at his olive-toned skin, tracing the contours of his face with my eyes. His brown hair looked windswept, ruffled into small curls around his ears and the nape of his neck, and his brown eyes contained flecks of gold. Everything about him was brown and green—he looked like he belonged in the forest. If this was the newcomer, I could see how the townsfolk had immediately recognized him as out of place in the town.

I didn't know why it had caused such mass concern, however.

He turned to look at me, his brow creasing slightly even as he gave me an easy smile. His eyes flicked up, just above my face, and I realized that I was once again wearing the hood of my cloak, pulled forward to shield my face. I must have pulled it up without conscious thought as I followed Cora.

"Sometimes the people who find their way here don't want to be found," Cora said, her voice cold. "We don't take too kindly to strangers asking questions."

He didn't seem in the least flustered by her response.

"But surely some who are lost want to be found?" he asked.

Cora narrowed her eyes. "I suppose that depends on who's doing the finding…" She let her voice trail off, the question implied.

If he made a reply, I didn't hear it. Instead I stumbled back half a step, my eyes widening. His voice had triggered my memory.

He had been a gangly youth when I last saw him, although still charming. There had been a whole crowd of us, gathered for some function, and he had been intent on involving the other princes in some sort of mischief. Now that I had caught the familiar note of his voice, I could see the traces of the boy showing through in the man he had become. And suddenly I understood what had thrown the townsfolk into such confusion.

This man belonged no more to the forest than he did to this remote town. He belonged in a palace, on a throne. We were talking to Crown Prince Gabriel of Talinos.

ACKNOWLEDGMENTS

Snow is a very different heroine to Celine, and I enjoyed writing her story straight after the Snow Queen. It was written across a busy time, though, including a major house move, so I am—as always—incredibly grateful to my marvelous support system.

In particular, my husband Marc, and my parents and parents-in-law, who keep my life ticking along when I'm lost deep in my writing. And to my daughter, Adeline, who is far more patient than a pre-schooler should have to be.

My beta readers, Rachel, Greg, Priya, and Ber deserve extra praise for keeping up with me during my recent hectic schedule, and helping me refine my story as they always do. And since this book is dedicated to her, I want to give a special acknowledgement to Katie who is not only a steadfast beta reader but also an incredible friend—loyal, kind, giving, hilarious, strong, intelligent, and supportive.

Alongside my old friends, I also need to thank my new ones. I'm getting to the point where I can't remember what it was like to be an author without author friends across the country and the oceans. It makes an otherwise solitary occupation both more enjoyable and more sustainable. So thank you, Kitty, Kenley, Shari, Aya, Brittany, Diana, and Marina. Stay awesome, guys!

My editing team have done an amazing job of keeping up with me, and still producing the same excellent results as always. So thank you Mary, Dad, and Deborah for working to my crazy schedules.

And to my cover designer, Karri, who comes up with incredible designs and then adds the extra touches to take them above and beyond. I love the apple on this one!

I also want to acknowledge all my readers—without you I'm sure I wouldn't be able to keep writing the way I do. I hope that, like Snow, you all have at least one loyal friend who's ready to follow you into whatever adventures life throws in your path.

And a final thank you to God, who is the best and most loyal friend that could ever be imagined.

ABOUT THE AUTHOR

 Melanie Cellier grew up on a staple diet of books, books and more books. And although she got older, she never stopped loving children's and young adult novels.

She always wanted to write one herself, but it took three careers and three different continents before she actually managed it.

She now feels incredibly fortunate to spend her time writing from her home in Adelaide, Australia where she keeps an eye out for koalas in her backyard. Her staple diet hasn't changed much, although she's added choc mint Rooibos tea and Chicken Crimpies to the list.

She writes young adult fantasy including books in her *Spoken Mage* world, her *Mage's Influence* world, and her various *Four Kingdoms* and *Kingdoms of Legacy* series that are made up of linked stand-alone stories that retell classic fairy tales.